WHEN TWO WORLDS MEET

By
ROBERT MOORE WILLIAMS

I0616783

ARMCHAIR FICTION
PO Box 4369, Medford, Oregon   97501-0168

THEY LIVED IN FEAR
OF THE "GOD" WEAPON

Kirkham came to Mars to work as an electrician for the Borrodrone Empire. He worked on simple things—broken radio sets, telescreens, etc. But when he started working on the inner electrical workings of a Martian helmet, he knew he was tampering with things better left alone. In fact, he knew that if he was caught it would probably cost him his life.

Life was cheap on Mars and its value had continued to plummet ever since the Borrodrones had taken over. They had stamped out all resistance after coming into possession of a weapon so horrible that no other power could stop it. It was the Elsar beam—the weapon of the Gods. And in their possession, this mighty force of destruction might someday threaten the Earth itself.

FOR A COMPLETE SECOND NOVEL, TURN TO PAGE 77

CAST OF CHARACTERS

WADE KIRKHAM
He had come to Mars to work on minor electronics problems for the Borrodrones—but what was his real purpose?

PAULA WILSON
When you come to Mars, you don't wander into a Martian Fortress without permission, unless you want to become a slave.

JEVNAR
A seemingly simple-minded little green Martian who professed a friendship for Kirkham. But could he really be trusted?

THE CAPTAIN OF THE GUARD
This Borrodrone was in charge of local security matters and would blow you to kingdom come at the blink of an eye.

ELFRONE
He was the exalted ruler of all Mars, and the secret to his power was a weapon of unimaginable potency!

TALL HELMET
He was the head of a Borrodrone patrol searching for a few rebel green men. Quite routine, nothing to worry about…or was there?

CHAPTER ONE

HIDDEN among the litter of electrical equipment on the work bench, a tiny bell chimed, a soft musical note that came so quietly through the thin air that it seemed to apologize for disturbing the air molecules that transmitted it.

The reaction of the big man sitting on the rough stool in front of the workbench was out of keeping with the soft chime of the bell. He moved—*fast*.

Spread on the workbench under a small but powerful lamp was an odd-looking helmet, which he had partly disassembled and which he was studying through a strong magnifying glass. Screws, tiny condensers, and a network of wiring as fine as a spider web had been revealed. Several screws had been removed from the helmet and were lying on the bench in front of it.

Lying to the right of the helmet, where the hand could grab it instantly, was a spring gun of the type that hurled a tiny needle of torguline, coated steel. Almost noiseless in operation, three seconds after one of these needles hit a human, he was unconscious. On a green man the torguline acted faster, on a Borrodrone an average of four seconds was needed to produce unconsciousness. One needle from this gun put a human out for about an hour, two needles meant about six hours of sleep, three needles and the green slaves buried him in the eternally restless sands of Mars.

When the tiny bell rang, the big man's hand literally flew to the helmet. The parts he had taken from it went back into the cup formed by the overlapping metal scales. Bending down with the helmet in one hand, he jerked open the lid of a heavy wooden box sitting under the bench. The box was filled with a miscellaneous maze of electrical equipment, radio sets, motors, testing meters, copper wire on spools. From the top of a commercial receiver, he snatched a small motor and a coil of solder. Long, supple fingers found a hidden catch on the cabinet. The top of the receiver lifted up, revealing that the equipment which belonged in this receiving set had been removed.

The helmet went in there.

The top of the receiver went back into place, the motor and the coil of solder were put back on top of it, the lid of the heavy chest was closed.

The gun went into the pocket of the mechanic's apron he was wearing.

ON THE WALL the tiny bell rang again. Reaching under the workbench, Wade Kirkham closed a switch that disconnected the bell.

Then he pulled an ordinary walkie-talkie radio set into position under the light on top of the bench and began to examine it.

Looking at him, you would have thought he was an ordinary electrician hard at work. Frowning, he bent down low to stare at the innards of the radio set. He picked up the tipped ends of wires leading to a testing meter, began to probe the leads of the set. If he knew there another person within a mile of him, the expression on his lean, sun-browned face did not reveal it.

Around the turn in the corridor, moving on feet as silent as any cat, came—a green man. His bald head, his puffy cheeks, his slender talon-tipped fingers were a light aquamarine in color. His coat, caught in a circlet of metal at his throat, was also green, but a darker hue than his skin. The rings dangling from his pointed ears reflected a shade of green.

He was a little more than four feet tall. Midgets would

have thought him tall but any human would have looked down at him.

Like a small green shadow against the wall, he moved behind the human and stood there, watching. His alert bird-like eyes went over the workbench, seeming not to miss an item on it. They probed under the bench, at the heavy box there. They moved to the right, looked thoughtfully at the single opening to the rooms beyond, then went incuriously past the grill in the wall through which thin sunlight was streaming, then came back to the human.

An odd, pensive expression then appeared in the Martian's eyes in which was mingled sympathy, and fear, and—strangest of all—yearning. It was as if the green man wanted very much to be as big as a human, but knew that he would never be. Humans were giants able to step across the space between Earth and Mars. Green men were—unable even to walk erect on the sands of their native planet.

"The damned condenser is blown," Wade Kirkham muttered.

"What means *blown?*" a thin voice spoke behind him.

Kirkham spun on the stool. His right hand moved, fast, toward the pocket in his jacket that held the gun, then moved slower when he saw who stood behind him, then stopped entirely. In his mind was the thought "—If only I dared trust him." He put the thought out of his mind. In this place, you wouldn't trust your own brother, if you had a brother here. Aloud he said, "Damn it, Jevnar, I've told you not to slip up behind me."

The green man grinned apologetically. "Hallo, Kirky," his voice piped. "I speak the human talk how good?"

"Fair," Kirkham grunted. "You wouldn't fool anybody who had ever heard any of it, but you can make yourself understood."

The green man's face registered mingled delight and

distress. He had tried so hard to learn the human tongue. "I get better do?" he said, hopefully.

"You get better *don't,*" Kirkham answered. "You will never speak like a man, Jevnar. Your vocal chords aren't right, for one thing, your mouth structure, lips, teeth, and tongue, are wrong to shape the words properly. On top of everything else, you don't *think* like a man. Your mind is different, you belong to a different race, you've got a different heredity behind you, and you have grown up in a different culture. All of these things make it hard for you to talk like a man."

On the green man's face the distress became acute. "But—I *want* like a man to talk."

"I know you do, Jevnar," Kirkham answered. Kindness crept into his voice. "But to talk like a man is a hard thing. To—" He caught himself. Behind his lips, the unspoken words pressed for utterance. "To be a man is an even harder thing." A shadow crossed his face, then was gone. "Never mind, Jevnar. You talk very well. I think you have done an excellent job in learning to talk at all."

At the compliment, the green man was as delighted as a child. Kirkham turned back to the walkie-talkie set.

UNDER THE edge of the set, unnoticed until now, was a tiny screw that had never been made in any human workshop, a screw that had come from the helmet now safely hidden in the box under the bench. When he had gathered up the parts of the helmet, he had missed this screw.

It caught his eyes, held them. A cold grayness appeared in his mind. His right hand trembled as it tried unconsciously to move toward the pocket where the spring gun was hidden. He stopped the movement of the hand. There was a chance that Jevnar had not seen the screw. Did the keen eyes of the little green man ever miss anything? Kirkham did not know and did not want to find out. Jevnar was leaning over the bench, interested in the radio set as he was interested in everything that had come from the planet across space. Kirkham felt sweat appear on the palms of his hands. There was a second chance—that if Jevnar had seen the screw, the green man would not betray him.

Kirkham knew he did not dare take this chance. The little green man had pretended to be a friend, he had made pathetic efforts to please the big human, but what was more important to any green man was pleasing someone else. If he saw the screw there and understood that it had come from the helmet, the odds were he would run straight to the nearest Borrodrone with the news.

In that case, Wade Kirkham would be swiftly gathered to his fathers and a polite request would go forward to the authorities of Earth Government in Mars Port to furnish the Borrodrones with another electrician, to replace the last one, "who has met with an unfortunate accident." The Borrodrones would be polite about it. They needed an electrician. The representatives of Earth Government in Mars Port would be polite too. They would furnish the electrician—if they could find another volunteer—and they would not make indiscrete inquires about the way the last one had died.

Everything would be handled very politely. Nobody would ever admit that under the politeness was hidden sudden death.

"What this thing do?" Jevnar asked. He pointed to the microphone.

"You talk into that," Kirkham said. "Very busy now, Jevnar." If he could get rid of the green man.

"Busy? What mean that?"

"Got work to do."

"Oh," Jevnar's uninterested face said what was the point

in working so hard? "Let it wait." He bent down until his nose was almost thrust into the radio set.

Kirkham fervidly hoped it would shock him. "Elfrone himself is interested in these walkie-talkies." Since Elfrone was the supreme ruler of the Borrodrones, just the mention of his name ought to send any green man on his way in a hurry.

Jevnar showed signs of strain at the name of Elfrone. His face turned a shade less green. Lights glittered in his eyes. "You tell him radio not working yet, he won't know any better." He bent again over the radio set.

Kirkham suppressed profanity. From the bench, he picked up a screwdriver. "You don't seem to have a very high opinion of Elfrone," he said.

Instantly he had Jevnar's agitated attention. "Have most high opinion of Great One. He our father, our friend, our saviour."

KIRKHAM KEPT his grin to himself. Since any green man who expressed a low opinion of Elfrone would not be likely to live long, the shoe was very much on the other foot now. Tapping the screwdriver in the palm of his hand, he watched Jevnar writhe.

"Elfrone very great person," Jevnar repeated.

"You very big liar," Kirkham said.

"Oh, no!" For a moment, Kirkham thought the green man was going to have a heart attack. Kirkham dropped the screwdriver. Jevnar bent instantly to pick it up. When he straightened up with it, the screw was gone from the top of the bench.

"I was just teasing you," Kirkham said. He could afford to be generous now. "I know you are a loyal subject—"

"Most loyal," Jevnar said.

"Sure," Kirkham answered. With the screw in his

possession, he felt almost safe. "Did you want something in particular, Jevnar, or did you just come to talk?"

The green man's face registered a double-take. "I get so interested talking to you, I almost forget. Sure, want something. Captain of guard send me for you."

"What does he want?"

"Wants you to talk to man."

"What man?" Kirkham's voice rose a notch. So far as he knew, he was the only human being in this whole vast fortress city of the Borrodrones. "Men don't come here unless invited. It is forbidden."

"This one came," Jevnar answered. "Guards catch him in lower city."

"Why don't you talk to him?"

The green man's face showed traces of embarrassment. "I did. He said he couldn't get what I was saying. Guard captain send for you."

"Who is he?"

Jevnar shrugged. "I not know. You come talk?"

"I guess so," Kirkham answered. He wondered who the man was and what he was doing here. Some stubborn, daring fool who had ventured across the desert spaces separating Mars Port from the city of the Borrodrones, some obstinate ass who didn't have better sense than to go into forbidden lands. A trader, perhaps. Possibly a damned fool risking his neck on Mars for the sake of the publicity he might get back on Earth, if he ever got back to Earth. The Borrodrones had got him, of course. Kirkham swore silently. He wished the fellow had stayed where he belonged but now that the idiot was here, there were two reasons why he had to talk to him.

The first reason was simple. Nobody in his senses would refuse a request from the captain of the guard. The second reason was more complex but it involved his feeling that he had an obligation to help even a damned fool out of a spot, if he could. He rose to his feet. "Okay, let's go."

Jevnar's eyes went carelessly over the workbench, came up quickly and questioningly to search Kirkham's face, then were instantly veiled. The human felt a touch of chill. Had the little devil noticed that the screw was gone?

There was no way to know. All that could be done was to wait and find out. And, if the answer was wrong, die.

"Come now," the green man said politely. He led the way. Sweat again greasing the palms of his hands, Wade Kirkham followed.

CHAPTER TWO

THEY WALKED through the heart of the fortress. Actually the fortress was a gigantic granite mountain that had been formed when Mars was still a steaming, warm planet, before the water vapor began to slip away into the sky, before the dry winds began to blow eternally across the deserts. When this mountain had been in the process of formation, bubbles of gas in the mass of molten granite had created holes in it, long tunnels, vast chambers where a whole tribe could take refuge. Later, when this molten mass had become a granite mountain rising up out of a chain of mountains, whole tribes had taken refuge in the vast caves. The frescoes they had left behind them on the walls, the stone tools on the floors, their bones also, were still visible on the lower levels. Kirkham had seen them there, mute relics of the long history of the Red Planet. The cave men themselves were long since gone, swept aside by some marauding tribe that had wanted the shelter of these great caves.

For twice ten thousand years this mountain had been inhabited. In it and around it the whole history of Mars had been written. In its early days it had been a place of refuge. Then, as each succeeding tribe that had conquered it had added something to its defenses, had extended the caves, deepened the subterranean water reservoirs, invented new weapons, pursuing its leisurely quest of the eternal mysteries of life and death, getting first hand information about the latter as some new tribe of desert-hardened warriors had overwhelmed its masters, this mountain had become a mighty fortress.

The legend, the tradition, and the fact had been well established—who ruled this mountain ruled Mars.

The green men had been the next to last masters of the mountain. They had gone down to defeat before the race that had discovered what they called, with considerable reason, the weapon of the gods, and which the green men called the Elsar beam. At just the thought of that grim weapon, Wade Kirkham was aware of perspiration appearing on his face. His mind going back to the tiny screw that had been on his workbench, he wiped the sweat from his face.

"You jump," Jevnar said, beside him.

"I—uh—"

"On your mind is something?" the green man asked. The tone of his voice showed concerned anxiety. His friend was worried, therefore Jevnar was worried. Or was his anxiety actually malicious mischief? Had he seen the screw on the bench and was he leading this human, like a lamb to the butcher, to sudden death? Kirkham did not know. There was no way he could find out.

He put the thought out of his mind. He told himself that Jevnar had always seemed friendly, that Jevnar had always listened eagerly to his descriptions of Earth. They had even talked of going to Earth together, to see the green forests and the blue seas, to smell the rain, to taste wind with no trace of dust in it.

So far as Jevnar was concerned, this talk was pure poppycock. Jevnar was a slave. A trusted slave given the bitter task of driving his own kind to menial tasks, to destruction, and to death.

Kirkham suspected from time to time that torment existed in the mind of Jevnar. He felt now and again an odd sympathy for the green man, but he knew better than to extend that sympathy to trust. A human likes to stay alive too.

"On my mind is nothing," Kirkham said.

THE PASSAGE widened in front of them, branched in two directions. A grilled window looked down over the lower city. Down there in a huddle of buildings lived the wretched remnants of every face who had once ruled this fortress. Of all the races that had once lived here, perhaps the cave men were the luckiest. They were all dead.

Kirkham had always imagined he could feel a mist of hate rising from the lower city. Whether or not he could feel it, he knew the hate was there. But the means to implement it were missing. The Borrodrones had the weapons of the gods.

Nor was the arrival of the human race on Mars likely to change this situation. A hundred thousand men and a hundred atom bombs could not make a dent in this citadel. The human race was on Mars on sufferance. They had crossed space but they were not the rulers of the Red Planet. Nor were they ever likely to be, unless luck intervened. There was a languid trade between the two races. When the Borrodrones saw a human product that they could use, they tried to buy it. If it was not on the secret list, they got the product, radio sets, electrical gadgets. But no weapons. They had not asked for weapons. What need was there for such things?

Scientists asked permission of the Borrodrones to explore and investigate the planet and received that permission or did not receive it, as the whim of Elfrone indicated. Between the humans and the Borrodrones there was a sort of guarded truce, they watched each other like strange dogs that might be friends—and might not, depending on which way the wind blew and which way the bitch went. If Elfrone chose to order all humans from the Red Planet, the humans would be well advised to go. There was the Elsar beam.

But the Borrodrones had not yet chosen to order men from Mars. They weren't sure as yet how big were the teeth of the other dog. Officially there was peace between the two races but this peace existed only at a high diplomatic level. On the level of a single man, there was no peace.

Two races were meeting. Each was trying to make up its mind what to do about the other one. In the process, a few casual throats would be cut, a few heads would be broken, which made no real difference one way or the other, except to the man whose jugular vein felt the keen edge of the steel. When races collided, individuals counted for less than nothing.

Wade Kirkham could feel the edge of the knife at his throat.

"This way," Jevnar said politely. The corridor turned. Before them appeared a bank of elevators.

The sight of these elevators always made Kirkham a little homesick. They had come from Earth. Riding in them, he could imagine he was in some big department store back on Earth. "First floor. Gown shop. Lingerie, hosiery, shoes. Watch your step."

The Borrodrones had never invented elevators but they had liked the idea, once it had been explained to them. Since Earth Government could see no reason for objecting, the elevators had been installed. Jevnar led the way to three elevators aside from the main bank, pressed the button. These three were reserved for green men, slaves, servants, humans, and such cattle.

THE CAGE slid to a halt, the doors opening automatically. Stepping inside, Jevnar pressed the down button, and closed his eyes.

"Jump—jump always goes stomach."

"Some day you will get used to it," Kirkham answered. The cage dropped like a rock falling down a well. The green man gulped and grabbed his middle. Air hissed and the cage stopped, the doors opening. Jevnar opened his eyes. "Some day it won't stop. Then what happens?"

"I suppose the electrician will be blamed and will meet with an accident," Kirkham answered. "How many electricians have you had up to now?"

"Six, maybe seventeen. Don't know."

"What happened to the last one?" Kirkham questioned.

Jevnar shrugged. "Not know. Heard he went down to lower city and got drunk—"

"What do you *think* happened to him?"

"Think?" Jevnar fingered the word mentally, deciding on its exact meaning. "Think he got nosey." Something like a shudder passed over his body. "Why you ask?" His keen eyes turned toward the human.

"Just curious," Kirkham answered.

"Curiosity not good," Jevnar spoke. He patted Kirkham's arm. "Believe me, please."

Kirkham was silent. There was no doubt in his mind that curiosity in this place did not tend to increase the life span.

Jevnar unlocked a door. "In there. You talk to him."

"Where's the captain of the guard?"

"Back later, I guess. You talk."

The room Kirkham entered had been carved from solid granite. Light from the distant sun poured through a barred window. The door closed behind Kirkham: The man, a slender fellow dressed in whipcord trousers and a floppy brown shirt, looked up.

Kirkham took one glance and blinked astonished eyes. There was no doubting what was hidden behind that floppy brown shirt. There was no mistaking the tilt of the chin, the startled expression in the gray eyes, the red lips. Jevnar had probably not known the difference between the sexes but the "man" was actually a woman.

She came quickly to her feet, a little cry of gladness forming on her lips. It was a sound that said she had been all alone here in this place and terribly frightened but now that he was here, she was no longer alone and not frightened at all. She started toward him.

Kirkham had the dazed impression that he knew this woman. Back when he had been a senior in the University he had known a girl— But that was impossible. He nodded cheerfully. "Hello. In trouble?"

"I was."

He could see the fear on her face. It was going away now. Back of it he could see such courage as women usually do not possess. "How did you get here?"

"I came with a dothar caravan from Mars Port."

"Did you get permission?"

"No."

"Then why in heaven did you come?"

THE EXPRESSION on her face said she did not like the tone of his voice. What right did he have to demand her reasons for being here? Her chin tilted, then came back down, a gesture which said she had changed her mind about giving him the answer he deserved and was going to be polite to him even if he wasn't polite to her; "I came here to get material for a book on Mars."

"You came here— A lady author! I don't believe it!"

Amazement held him. Behind the amazement there was disgust at such stupidity. A man alone on Mars lived by his wits and his strength. If he had a shortage of either, the desert got him, or a wandering tribe of green men took care of the job, or a Borrodrone patrol picked him up, for questioning.

"What's wrong with being a woman, and a writer?"

"Nothing. Both are fine, in their place, but their place is not here."

"How can you write about Mars if you don't come here?"

"How can you write about Mars if you're dead?" He snapped the words at her, then fell angrily silent. His anger stemmed from his knowledge that he was going to have to try to protect her, if he could. Woman's place was not on Mars. True, Earth Government trained and used women for many purposes, he did not in the least doubt that they would use women, or anything else that would enable them to ferret out the tightly-held secret of Borrodrone power, but a woman here was a complicating factor he did not want.

She said her name was Paula Wilson. "And I think I know who you are. I saw a picture in a magazine—"

"When did you reach the lower city?"

"Just a few hours ago. This picture—"

He could feel the pound of his pulse rising suddenly in his veins. "How did you get away from Mars Port?"

"Why—" She was surprised and angry again, at his tone.

"Did you get permission from the authorities to leave Mars Port?"

"No."

"Then you are a damned idiot."

He had never seen a woman so angry. "You don't have to shout at me."

"I'll shout when I feel like it." In his pocket, his fingers unconsciously sought the spring gun. His eyes searched the walls, seeking the microphone that probably was hidden somewhere. She started to speak. He interrupted. She started again. He interrupted again.

"I never knew a man as rude as you are!"

He did not answer. If the mike was there, it was well concealed. His actions caught her attention. As she realized their significance, the color fled swiftly from her face. "Oh!" she gasped. It was a tiny frightened sound in the stillness of that stone cell. He found a package of cigarettes in his pocket, stuck one in his mouth, lit it, then remembered the girl. She took the precious rolled tobacco he offered her. He leaned forward to light it. "You never heard my name in your life," he said. His lips hardly moved to form the words and the sound of his whisper could not have been heard a foot away.

She shook her head. Her eyes came quickly up to his. Her eyes said she was a fool and that she was sorry.

He decided maybe he liked Miss Paula Wilson. He had read a book she had written about life on Venus and it had been a good job. While she had a high and mighty opinion of her own importance, she could think fast. Her lips formed almost inaudible words. "Is it as bad as that?"

He nodded over the cigarette.

Her face went blank, carefully so. Her tone was suddenly casual. "Well, it is nice to meet a human being. What is your name, by the way?"

He told her his name.

"What do you do here?"

He told her he was technically an electrician but that actually he was a jack of all trades and that his job was to keep in working order all equipment the Borrodrones had purchased from Earth. "A mechanic?" she said.

He nodded.

"Well, I guess all there is for me to do is to ask you to notify the authorities at Mars Port where I am."

KIRKHAM LAUGHED, a brittle burst of harsh sound. "I'll write them a letter," he said. "We'll send it by camel caravan to Mars Port. When the authorities there get it, they will inquire politely of the Borrodrones what they wish to do with you. If the Borrodrones say they wish to keep you—or that they never heard of you—that will be the end of the matter."

Her face was perplexed. "But—"

"This is Mars," he said, his voice still harsh. "You came from Earth and like every other human being, you probably think of yourself as something of a little tin god. For generations we have taught our children that the individual does not matter a damn. Unless he happens to be a Borrodrone. You can die here and nobody will lift a hand to save you. You can be raped here, a thousand times, and nobody will care that much." A snap of the fingers explained how much he meant. "You probably think that the minute the authorities learn where you are, they will send a fleet of space ships hot-footing through the sky after you. Get it out of your mind. They won't even send a boy in a jeep, not because they don't want to, but because they can't."

Her face was carefully blank.

"When the Borrodrones conquered this fortress, they kicked the ruling class of green men out of the top windows, everyone of them, men, women, and children. Seventy-five per cent of the green people were massacred in a single night."

"Aren't you being—a little rough?" Paula Wilson said.

His eyes searched the wall. A wind, blowing through the grill, brought with it the far-away odor of the desert, the dry, tangy smell of dust.

"If it is as dangerous as you say, why did you come here?" the girl spoke:

He shrugged. "It was a job."

In the door, a lock clicked. A guardsman entered. Following him, tall helmet nodding as he stepped under the low doorway, was the captain of the guard. Kirkham had never seen this particular captain before, which made no difference. When you had seen one Borrodrone, you had seen all of them.

"What was he doing here?" the captain spoke to Kirkham, in his own language.

The human knew enough of the Borrodrone tongue to be able to understand and to answer. "He is a poor, stupid fool, sire, so stupid he did not know that coming here was forbidden." He was glad that Paula Wilson could not understand what he was saying about her. How her chin would go up in the air if she knew he was calling her a stupid fool.

"I see," the captain said.

"He intended no wrong when he came here," Kirkham spoke. "The intrusion was the result of accident and ignorance." Obviously the Borrodrones had not realized that their prisoner was a woman. He saw no reason to enlighten them on this interesting fact. Kirkham knew enough about the Borrodrones to know that this captain had the authority to do as he saw fit with this prisoner. He could order her held for Elfrone, for further questioning, or he could literally have her thrown out the window.

KIRKHAM, moistening dry lips with a tongue that seemed to have turned to sandpaper, tried to think what he was going to do. The gun in his pocket was useless now. If he used it, as a last desperate resort, he might gain the girl and himself an extra hour of life—and he might get both of them blasted to charred lumps of flesh. Keep your mouth shut, Kirkham, and think.

"What did you tell him?" Paula Wilson spoke.

"I told him, if you opened your mouth again, I would stick my foot in it."

Her jaw dropped in astonishment.

"So try to keep your mouth shut, will you? It might be as important as your life."

The captain of the guard was trying to make up his mind what to do with this prisoner. To him, it wasn't a really important decision. Watching him, Kirkham saw that it wasn't important. "If the captain pleases—" he spoke quickly.

"Yes," the Borrodrone grunted.

"If no one has any use for the prisoner, give him to me." Kirkham spoke the words casually, almost indifferently. His tone and his manner indicated that this matter was of slight importance to him too, something that might be settled out of hand and forgotten.

It was an odd little drama that was being played out here. Probably if Paula Wilson had caught even an inkling of what Kirkham had said, had grasped the slightest hint of his meaning, her reaction would have ruined whatever chance he had of saving her. The thought that she might be given away, as one gives a pair of old shoes to an obliging janitor, would have horrified her. But she didn't know what had been said.

The captain knew. Kirkham had his complete attention. "Of course, if the captain has some other use for him, or if some other Great One wants him—"

Kirkham spread his hands in a gesture which said that, of course, under these circumstances the matter was settled. But if—

"What do you want with him?" the captain challenged.

"Oh, perhaps he could run errands for me," Kirkham answered. "I could keep him busy, doing one thing or another—"

"Oh, I see." The captain was completely deceived. He

shrugged the matter away. "Very well. I'll give him to you for a slave."

Grunting to the soldier with him, he strode out of the room. The door was left unlocked, indicating that so far as the captain was concerned, this matter was settled.

Ahead of Wade Kirkham was the problem of explaining to Paula Wilson just exactly what *had* happened.

CHAPTER THREE

SHE DIDN'T take the news like a lady should. For a moment, Kirkham thought she was going to explode. He was surprised. He had gotten her out of trouble, hadn't he? What more did she want?

"Do you mean to tell me that that over-dressed boy scout who was just in here gave me to you as a slave?" she demanded.

"Sure," Kirkham said. "To own slaves is the custom here. He had the authority to do what he pleased with you."

"He had no right to do anything with me."

"Maybe not, but he had the *power*. He could have kept you for himself if he had wanted to."

She was quiet for a moment while she thought about that. But only for a moment. "Just exactly what is included in this business of giving me to you?"

"Anything and everything I want it to include," Kirkham answered. He leered at her. "I've been here almost a year and you're the first woman I've seen."

"You dog!" she said. "You dirty dog."

"Wolf," he corrected. He leered again. "Look, honey, you came here without asking anybody's leave. You might just as well prepare yourself to take the consequences." He was very lofty about it, very condescending.

He thought she was going to spit at him. "That pompous

fool had no right—"

"I told you maybe he didn't have the right but he had the power."

"He wasn't even armed!"

"He wasn't?" In spite of himself, Wade Kirkham shivered. He shook his head. "Look, honey, you're in a new world. Things aren't always what they seem to be around these parts. You're going to run head-on into a lot of new ideas and you might as well start getting used to them." He grinned wickedly at her, moved toward the door. "Come on," he tossed the words over his shoulder.

"What makes you think I'm coming with you?" she demanded.

He shrugged. "You can stay here, if you like it better."

She came in a hurry. Her voice followed him. "I'd like to know what right—" The tone was rising.

Ahead of them, at the bank of elevators, the captain and the guardsman were waiting.

"Shut up..." Kirkham spoke quickly. She didn't shut up. "Do you feel all right? Or are you having delusions? What makes you think you can tell me to shut up."

"Please!" he said. His eyes were on the captain. He shrank back against the wall. She saw the captain. The anger in her boiled over. She started forward.

Kirkham grabbed her. "You little idiot, what are you trying to do?"

"I'm going to give that over-dressed thug a piece of my mind. Let go of me."

Smack! Her open hand came up across his face. He grabbed her hand.

The struggle ended in a way that neither had anticipated.

The elevator had been slow in coming and the captain had been visibly growing more and more impatient. When it arrived at last, the doors opened automatically. A green man scuttled out. He saw the captain and stopped.

Perhaps the green man had been in a hurry to get from one level to another. Whatever the reason had been, he had taken the chance of riding in one of the forbidden elevators. And had been caught in the act. When he saw the captain of the guard he fell forward on his face, screaming.

"I had orders, sire, to take the elevator. Mercy, sire. I had to obey."

Possibly he had had such orders but the fact didn't help him now. The Captain of the guard had caught him in a forbidden spot. "In that case, your master wished to be rid of you," the captain spoke.

The slave screamed. He knew what was going to happen. The captain rested both hands on the broad belt at his waist—and stared at the slave.

A FLASHING burst of binding electrical fire roared out of nowhere and struck the green man. It came in a second, struck the green slave, and was gone. The scream died.

Lying on the floor of the corridor in front of the bank of elevators was a charred chunk of still smoking flesh. The captain looked meditatively at it as if he was considering his handwork, then he stepped daintily around it and entered the elevator, the guardsman following him. Neither took a second look at the smoking object on the floor.

"Call the clean-up squad," the captain grunted, to his aide. The guardsman nodded. The elevator door closed behind them.

Paula Wilson clung to Wade Kirkham. All argument had gone out of her. Her face was ashen, bloodless, her mouth a splotch of twisted red. "What—what was that?"

Kirkham shook himself. The voice that came from his lips sounded as if it came from a man far away. "That—? That was the god weapon."

"But—where did it come from?"

"The captain turned it loose. The slave was in the wrong spot. The captain caught him. Bingo!"

"But—"

"You thought the captain wasn't armed. Remember?"

Her face said she remembered.

"In the captain's opinion, you were about as important as that green slave," Kirkham continued.

"You mean he would have done the same thing to me?"

"If you had given him either a reason or a pretext, if you had annoyed him, or if you hadn't shown the proper respect."

Her face was a twisted mask of fear. He watched her try to put that fear aside. She didn't succeed, the first time. He watched her try again. She did better this time. He squeezed her arm. "Stout girl," he said softly. Her eyes thanked him. She found her voice. "How—how does that thing work?"

"The Borrodrones claim they are descended from gods and that they have the powers of a deity. They say the lightning of the gods flashes from their eyes and destroys anyone they wish to destroy."

"That sounds like hot air to me." Paula Wilson came from a world that had scant respect for superstition, from a world where men believed more in the operation of natural laws than in the will of mythical deities. "A god weapon?" Scorn crept into her voice. "Who hides behind the god?"

"The Borrodrones, in this case," Kirkham answered. He found he was admiring this girl. She had seen a miracle and she had shoved aside soul-shaking fear and was seeking cause and effect.

"But how does it work?" she questioned.

"I wish to hell I knew!" he answered. "There are times when I think it would be simpler to believe the Borrodrones."

"You mean you have tried to find out?"

"I don't mean anything," he answered quickly. An odor

was snaking along the corridor, the foul smell of burned flesh. "Come on," he said. She followed him without question this time.

They used the elevators reserved for the green slaves. The odor followed them into the cage, reminding them of what they had seen here, what they could never forget.

A green slave had died. In the history of Mars, the death of a green man was not an important event. They had died like flies. But this one had died in a searing flash of blinding fire that had apparently sprung from nowhere, in response to the will of the captain of the guard. The god weapon!

The race who held this fortress ruled Mars. The race who owned the god weapon might rule space as well as Mars.

KIRKHAM sank down on the stool in front of his workbench. He wiped the stains of sweat from his face, saw that finally his hands had stopped trembling. Reaching under the bench, he changed the position of the switch there.

"So far as I know, there are no mikes hidden around here," he said. "If anybody comes along the corridor, there are two photoelectric cells and two beams of invisible light hidden around the turn. The bell will warn us in time."

Paula Wilson sank down in the chair beside the bench. She accepted a cigarette, lit it. Her eyes went over the workbench to the door that opened into the rooms beyond. The first room contained a table and chairs, cooking equipment, supplies of food in cans that had come all the way from Earth. Beyond the kitchen was a bedroom. Her gaze came slowly back to where

Kirkham sat watching her intently. "Welcome home," he said.

"I'm to live here?"

"I'm sorry," he said gently. "I'll fix up a private room for you. There is no other place. If you are worrying about morals—don't." He didn't know whether she liked what he had said or whether she didn't. Her face was expressionless.

"I'm not worrying—much," she said. Something in her tone caught his attention.

"What do you mean—*much?*"

"I mean I am not worrying about morals and about you. Even if you do seem to think you own me, I think you will find very good reasons for taking care of me." Her tone was casual, her eyes guarded.

Kirkham was aware of a cold spot down at the base of his spine. "I don't get what you mean," he said.

"I keep remembering a picture I once saw in a popular magazine," she answered. "I have a good memory for a face. Above this picture were three words—*Earth's Top Scientist.* Below it was a name." Her voice trailed away into the thin air.

Like a huge amoeba, the cold spot extended itself farther up Kirkham's spine. He growled unintelligibly beneath his breath. "What's that got to do with morals on Mars?" he said.

"Perhaps nothing. But I keep wondering what the captain of the guard would do if he knew that the top scientist on Earth was masquerading here as an electrician..." Her eyes went over Kirkham's shoulder to the blank wall beyond.

The cold spot seemed to explode up the big man's spine. His fingers gripped the edge of the bench. "Now who's a dirty dog?" he said.

"Bitch would be the better word," she corrected. Her face was the color of desert dust, and her gray eyes showed vivid flecks of green.

"Would you turn me over to the Borrodrones?" His voice had a rasp to it that would have moved a dothar, the Martian camel, to a burst of speed.

"Would you claim me as a slave?" Her voice sounded like

paper tearing.

"No," he answered quietly.

Her eyes came down to his face. For the first time, he saw the tears there. "And I wouldn't tell the Borrodrones who and what you are, no matter what you did to me." He did not know how it happened, but a split second later, her nose was buried in his jacket and her lithe body was shaking with sobs. He patted her shoulder, awkwardly, because he didn't know much about women—had never had time to learn. "There, there Paula…"

"I wouldn't do it. No matter what I said, I wouldn't do it."

NOT UNTIL then did he realize that under her brazen exterior there was hidden a timid, frightened, little girl. She had had the courage to come to Mars, to evade the authorities at Mars Port, to come here to a forbidden world, but she didn't have the courage to turn traitor. Her arm went around his neck, the heavy strap watch that she wore ticked in his ear.

"Wade Kirkham, Earth's top-drawer physicist, working as an electrician in the forbidden city of the Borrodrones," she whispered. "What are you after? No. Don't answer that. I don't want to know."

"And I don't want to tell you," he answered. He didn't like the fact that she had recognized him. It added one more possibility of a bad roll to dice that were already badly loaded against him.

"And all the time you were talking to me in the guard cell, you were afraid I was going to blurt out who you were?" she questioned.

"Afraid is a little bit too weak a word for the way I felt," he answered. "The odds were about nine to one there was a mike hidden somewhere in that room." His eyes went past her, down to the heavy box under the bench.

A spider with a thousand legs of ice climbed over every vertebra of his backbone.

A wire-end hung out of the chest.

An instant later he had jerked open the lid. The chest had been searched, thoroughly. The radio set that served as a hiding place for the helmet was open.

The helmet was gone.

He dropped the lid of the chest hack into place, rose to his feet.

"What's wrong?"

He did not know the girl had spoken. The spider had raced all the way up his spine and now was turning somersaults inside his skull.

"What's wrong?" the girl repeated. The words beat against the wall of his concentration.

"We're leaving," he spoke.

"Leaving ?"

"I came here after something. I got part of it. I had it hidden in there." His hand waved toward the chest. "It's gone."

"Well—" She didn't understand.

"I'm in trouble."

She still didn't understand. "You are one of Earth's top scientists. If you are here as an electrician, it must be with the knowledge of Earth Government. Won't they protect you?"

"Protect me?" His laugh was harsh. "They won't lift a hand. They can't, I'm a spy. Don't you know that?"

HER FACE said she knew it. "Officially, they can't admit that I am anything but an electrician. Any other admission might get the human race exterminated on Mars. They can do nothing to protect me or to help me. I'm on my own. If I get what I came after, they will give me enough medals to cover my chest a foot deep. If I get caught, they can't even help dig my grave."

"What—did you come after? No, I wasn't supposed to ask that."

"You've probably guessed it. The god weapon."

Her nose wrinkled at the memory of that horrible blasting discharge and of the burning odor that had followed it.

"I had a part of it, I think, in that chest. It's gone. That means I've been discovered."

Human scientists had nothing to compete with the god weapon. Nor did they, actually, want to compete with it or with any other weapon. They wanted to live in peace with Earth's neighbors in the sky. Their space ships had reached Venus and Mars but no other planets as yet. To reach the other planets, a firm base had to be established here on Mars. Jupiter was next on the list, three hundred and forty-two million miles away. To cross that gap of space, a ship had to start from Mars. Earth scientists were already dreaming of the day when Jupiter would be reached, Saturn, Uranium, Neptune, finally Pluto. When Pluto's frozen globe had been reached—well, after that might come flight to the stars. But that was only a dream as yet, and might remain a dream for centuries.

With a universe waiting to be explored, who wants to fight with his neighbor? On the other hand, nobody but a fool will leave himself in a position where a quarrelsome neighbor can cut his, throat. With the god weapon in the hands of the Borrodrones, with that quarrelsome race likely to order all humans off the Red Planet at any moment, no space ship could mount from Mars toward the far-off reaches of the sky.

"We'll go to the lower city," Wade Kirkham spoke. "You can buy anything down there, if you've got the price. We'll go in disguise from there."

"Into the desert?"

He nodded. "We'll have a better chance in the desert than we will here—"

The flashing death of the god weapon or the slower but probably equally certain death on the Martian desert? The frying pan or the slow fire? Neither was good but Kirkham was glad they had at least a choice. He moved swiftly to the rooms he occupied. Gold would be needed. Well, Earth Government had seen that he was plentifully supplied with that. It was the most they could do for him.

Outside in the corridor, like a warning from fairyland, the tiny bell chimed. Again the soft liquid note seemed to apologize to each air molecule for the disturbance made in passing.

Wade Kirkham swung around, the spring gun ready in his hand.

CHAPTER FOUR

THE BELL rang again, more urgently now. Kirkham held the spring gun concealed in the palm of his hand, its muzzle covering the turn in the corridor. He felt like a pop-gun armed hunter facing the charge of an elephant. If the captain of the guard came around the turn, or a squad of Borrodrone troopers, he might get needles into them before they knew they were being attacked. And might not! If it was just the captain and his aide, both might possibly be struck by needles before they knew it. Torguline acted fast. If there were more than two, he did not think he had any chance at all.

Running feet rustled on the floor.

Around the corner came—Jevnar.

"Kirky! Kirky!" The green man was out of breath. He looked over his shoulder, then called again for Kirkham. The human turned his hand, concealing the spring gun. "What is it, Jevnar?" he called softly.

The green man found him in the doorway. "Ske—ske—" He was out of breath and his eyes were rolling, either from unaccustomed exertion or from fear. He groped for an unfamiliar word. "Skedaddle you."

"Eh?" Kirkham said. He had forgotten using this word once in Jevnar's presence, then spending a half-hour trying to explain what it meant. "What are you talking about?"

"The air, take you!" the green man panted. "They listen while you talk to him." He nodded toward the girl behind Kirkham. "They not like what you say."

The words were fumbling but the meaning back of them was clear enough.

"Thank you," Kirkham said. He already knew he had to take the air, fast. But one thing he had not known and had not anticipated—that Jevnar would come to warn him. "Why do you do this, Jevnar?"

"Do what?"

"Tell me I am in danger. You're risking your own neck, you know."

The green man writhed away from the questions. "What I care? You my friend. I come to help you. Come with me. No talk. Come."

"Eh?" Kirkham blurted. Was bread that he had cast upon the waters in the form of kindness and consideration and patience coming back to him in the form of help?

Jevnar was tugging at his arm. "Know place where Borrodrones never find you. Take you there."

"What if we don't make it to this place?"

Jevnar's hand slid across his throat. "Any place suitable for dying. Come, friend."

Wade Kirkham made up his mind. "It's a deal," he said. His heart jumped as he realized they had gained a valuable ally. Jevnar knew the peoples and the customs of Mars, he knew what to say and what not to say, what to do and what not to do. In the lower city, be could hide them where they could not hide themselves. On the desert he could show them how to stay alive where otherwise they would perish. Jevnar was worth his weight in gold.

But what was the green man getting out of this? Jevnar was risking his life for the sake of friendship with an alien, a foreigner, a man who had come from a world across the skies. Did friendship rise to such exalted heights as this?

Kirkham felt doubt rise, a small gray cloud in his mind. He pushed it aside. When the devil rides behind, a man takes what help he can get where he can get it. The two humans followed the green man.

"Must hurry fast," Jevnar urged. "No, not elevator. Use old stairs. Not many people there."

AS THEY moved down the dark passage toward the old stairs, Kirkham, looking back, caught a glimpse of an elevator opening. From it came the captain of the guard who had questioned Paula Wilson and had given her as a slave to Wade Kirkham.

The captain moved straight toward the passage where Kirkham had his quarters.

"We miss by not much," Jevnar hissed. "Hurry fast now."

The green man did not say what they had missed by—not much. But deep in his heart, Kirkham knew. He pushed the doubt in his mind still farther away.

"At first, they wait for you in your quarters," Jevnar whispered. "They think you will come back. Later, when you not return, they start looking. We will go the old ways to the lower city."

"When we leave the lower city—what?"

"To my people," the green man said. "Later, we slip through to Mars Port. You take me back to Earth with you?"

"I do that," Kirkham promised. He wondered if Jevnar's

real motive in helping him lay in the desire of the green man to see Earth.

To Kirkham it seemed they walked for hours, always going down, before they reached the lower level and passed out of the fortress. Night had fallen. Above them the sky blazed with the light of a million stars. Here in this thin air the stars seemed brighter and nearer and much more numerous than they did when seen from Earth. Over toward the western edge of Mars was one bright star that caught his eye. He felt the tug of homesickness, the urge to know again the old familiar human things. That star was Earth.

In a vast circle around them, saw-toothed mountains lifted up jagged peaks toward the moons of Mars like a many-fanged monster whose wide-open mouth threatened to engulf all space. Above them the tremendous granite peak rose up—up—but not to the clouds. Millenia had passed since the thin air of this ancient planet had known its last cloud. Around them, huddling close to the granite base of the fortress, stretched the lower city. Here and there lights were visible but most of the city was dark—and had never been lighted. Martians who had to go through these narrow streets at night took lanterns and guards with them. Wise Martians did not venture here at night, not even the Borrodrones. What good is chain lightning striking in response to your wish if you already have a knife in your back?

Jevnar moved confidently forward. The humans followed. Kirkham could feel Paula Wilson tremble. She stayed close to him. He wondered, if she was frightened now, where she had found the courage to come here in the first place. Hadn't she known what this city was?

Jevnar knocked on a door. It squeaked and opened. Light streamed out. A green man looked at them. He started to close the door. Jevnar spoke rapidly to him in his own tongue. The green man grunted and opened the door wide.

The three entered.

In the days of the old west, when the United States of America were surging westward across the plains and the mountains of America, this place would have been called a saloon—a house where men drank and gambled and idled. It served the same purpose here but the men who drank here were green. They fell silent as the two humans entered. Eyes came up questioningly, hands moved toward knives hidden at the belt. Jevnar spoke again, a quick sentence of explanation. Or was it an order to cut their throats?

It might have been either.

"Come," Jevnar said. He moved toward the rear. Kirkham shrugged, followed. They entered a back room. A smoky lamp burned on a rough table. It did not give off much light, but what it lacked in this direction, it more than made up in stink. Paula held her nose.

Jevnar grinned from ear to pointed ear. The smell did not bother him. "We safe. You stay. I go make plans for leave." He slid out the door.

THE LAMP continued to stink. Paula said something through her nose, which Kirkham did not understand. He thought: Through such dives as this, through such stinks, men must go to reach the pathway to the stars.

Aloud he said: "I wish they hadn't taken that helmet—"

Escaping from the Borrodrone fortress without the helmet had been a gadfly buzzing in the back of his mind. He could have learned a lot from it. The god weapon needed an elaborate set of radio equipment in the helmet of the user. That much he knew now. What else was needed? A lot. The tiny coils and condensers he had found in the helmet might possibly control the flashing lightning but they could never generate it. Where was it generated? How was it generated? Questions pressed in on his mind until he thought that perhaps the simpler explanation would be to believe that the Borrodrones claimed to be true, that their's was actually a god weapon responding to their wish and their will alone. "I'll be damned if I believe that…" he said aloud. Paula Wilson looked questioningly at him but did not ask for an explanation. He did not bother to try to give her one.

He had lost the helmet. The next spy that Earth government sent here would have to try to remedy his failure.

With a wrench, he realized that probably never again would the Borrodrones bring in a human technician who might possibly pry into their secrets. Hereafter the towering fortress of the Borrodrones would be off limits to the human race.

But men would come here, even if it was off limits, they would come through stinking dives as this, along these mean and narrow streets, seeking the secret of the god weapon. It stopped them, that weapon did, from doing something that they wanted to do. They would never give up trying to lick it. They never gave up!

As individuals they gave up, they quit, they laid down and died in droves, but always there was one who came back at last—and got what he wanted.

They had wanted to sail around the water surface of the Earth, and one man had done it, in ships blown by the wind, they had wanted to fly around the planet. They had done that too. There was the moon in the sky, an eternal challenge. They could not let that pass. So—the moon.

After the moon—well, here they were with a toe-hold on Mars.

Out in the night the stars blazed their eternal challenge. Always one step led to another step that could be taken. Would they never give up? Perhaps, when the stars talked one to the other, saying: "We have seen their rocket trails against the evening sky," perhaps then they would give up.

But no sooner.

Jevnar entered, grinning. With him were two green men. "Fix up—good."

Kirkham finally fathomed that the purpose, of the green man was to disguise them. He submitted. They went to work with some soft plastic. When they had finished, he had the head and the face of a green man. He wouldn't go undetected in a thorough search—he was two feet too tall, for one thing—but he might get by in a dim light.

Paula Wilson stared at the final product. Her face said she didn't like it. "You look as if you belong in a side-show," she said.

"Silence, woman," Kirkham answered. "Please remember that you belong to me." He ducked the chunk of plastic that she had thrown.

WITHIN AN hour they were on their way out of the lower city. Jevnar had worked miracles. He had provided them with the equipment they would need in the desert, with food, with an escort of green men, doing so thorough a job that Kirkham had the feeling that all of this had been arranged beforehand. They rode on dothars, the slow, tireless, Martian equivalent of Earth's camel. Jevnar had provided these too.

With the plodding beast moving slowly under him, Kirkham wistfully wondered if Jevnar could not work another miracle and provide them with a jet plane, but he knew that the wish was useless. Because the thin air would not support flight readily, birds had not evolved on the Red Planet, the grim competitive struggle for life had eliminated all such attempts in this direction. Without birds as models and as living proof that it could be done, the Martians had not achieved flight through the air, had not known that it was possible.

The first jet plane, designed for use in this thin air, had been brought from Earth within the past year. The Martians had been as much astonished by the sight of it as they had been by space ships, perhaps more so, for a space ship was a monstrous bulk that came roaring in from the far reaches of space, landed and did not move again until it took off. A plane was much easier to understand.

The Borrodrones had promptly made efforts to buy the jet plane but, for one reason and another, they hadn't had any luck.

Jevnar was very pleased with himself. "We lick Borrodrones, beat 'em to hell, mow 'em down." He shook his fist back in the direction of the granite fortress.

All night long they rode through barren mountains where the only sound was the crunch of sand under the pads of the dothars. At dawn they stopped, long enough to eat a hasty meal of something that tasted like cheese. Then they went back into the saddle.

"When are we going to rest?" Kirkham asked.

"When we're dead," Jevnar answered. "Make much distance today. Tonight we rest—if we're still alive."

With the coming of day, Jevnar's apprehension seemed to increase. No more did he boast what they would do to the Borrodrones, no more did he shake his fist back at the granite fortress beginning to fade away into the sky behind them. Instead, he watched the hills. He kept his caravan low in the valleys.

"Guard stations many places," he explained. "Also maybe patrols out looking for us by now."

All day long they moved forward through a vacant world under an empty sky. As night approached, they reached a spot where moisture seeped out at the base of a tall cliff, forming a tiny trickle of water that slipped down into a ravine and was soon lost. Where the moisture existed shrubs grew green. To Wade Kirkham, accustomed to the luxuriant vegetation of Earth, this spring was hardly worth noticing, but to the green men it was almost a holy place. For generations, desert wanderers had slaked their thirst there.

By signs in the sand, Jevnar determined that a Borrodrone patrol had been here and gone on. "We safe now," he said.

"Are we?" Kirkham answered. "What about that?"

He nodded toward the slope at the left.

Coming down the slope were three Borrodrones on dothars. The leading Borrodrone wore a tall helmet of the type Kirkham had once examined, the two others had round helmets.

"Patrol cut back!" Jevnar gasped. He cursed harshly, in the tongue of the green men. "Act stupid, act know nothing. Maybe they think we are just tribesmen."

It was a hope, maybe it was a prayer. Jevnar's face had lost all trace of its green color. "Drop flat on sand when they come up," the green man whispered. "I do all talking. Watch one with tall helmet. If fight starts, try for him."

"Okay," Kirkham said. They could not run and they could not fight. He nodded to Paula Wilson. "It was nice knowing you," he said.

"It was nice knowing you too," she answered.

WHEN Kirkham went to the sand to prove that he knew as well as any green man the proper course of conduct in the presence of a Borrodrone, the little spring gun was snuggled out of sight in the palm of his hand.

If worst came to worst, maybe he could take one with him, the one with the tall helmet.

The patrol came up. Tall helmet remained in the saddle. In a hard but disinterested tone of voice, he began to ask questions. The other two Borrodrones slid to the ground.

Jevnar, lifting both hands and bowing repeatedly, got to

his knees. Kirkham caught parts of what he was saying. "We hunt the wild dothar, sire."

"You don't seem to have caught any," Tall Helmet said.

"No luck as yet. Dothars very scarce this season. Hope to do better tomorrow." The tone Jevnar used made hunting wild camels the most important activity in the life of a green man. Kirkham wondered where Jevnar had learned so much about hunting dothars. While their leader was talking, the two Borrodrones were making a careful search of the baggage. They were being damned casual how they treated the property of other people—ropes were slashed, tied bundles were kicked open—but they were also being thorough in their search.

Kirkham was aware that Jevnar, while he was outwardly giving his complete attention to Tall Helmet, was actually watching the two Borrodrones searching the baggage. The other green men were turning their heads an inch at a time to watch. Was there something hidden in the baggage?

"Has the great one seen any dothars?" Jevnar spoke.

He did not get his question answered. As he spoke, one of the searchers leaned forward and picked up an object he had kicked out of a bundle of clothing. A sharp exclamation of surprise burst from his lips.

As the Borrodrone cried out in surprise, a green man rose to his feet and buried a knife in his back.

TALL HELMET opened startled eyes. This had started out as a simple search of the baggage of a party of hunters. It had taken a new twist. No green man, no matter what the provocation, ever tried to resist a Borrodrone. Under no circumstances did a green man stab a member of the ruling race of Mars.

Not and live long afterwards.

Nor did this green man live long. Tall Helmet hesitated

just long enough to make certain he had seen what he had thought he had seen.

During that split second, Kirkham lifted his hand and pressed the stud of the little weapon hidden in his hand. The gun throbbed.

Tall Helmet had at least five tiny steel needles in him without knowing he had been hit. But the torguline, fast-acting as it was, wasn't as fast as something else, nor was it fast enough to save the green man.

Before the torguline could act, Tall Helmet had turned loose the god weapon.

The air crackled. Lightning flashed. The startled dothars reared and tried to run. Little flickering rivers of fire so bright it hurt the eyes danced over the body of the green man. He flung himself backward and up in the air, screaming. The fire followed him. The scream died. The green man threshed on the sand, dying. The stink of burned flesh filled the air.

Tall Helmet turned his head to look for the next victim. A vacant expression settled on his face. He lifted a hand to his eyes, pitched forward from the saddle and lay face down on the sand.

The third patrolman had started to run. "Get that one!" Jevnar yelled. "He not have Elsar beam. Get him!"

In obedience, two green men rose and started after the fleeing Borrodrone.

Jevnar's eyes swiveled to Kirkham. "How—did you do that?" He pointed to Tall Helmet.

"With this," Kirkham said, revealing the spring gun. He was not interested in answering Jevnar's questions. Something else was holding his attention.

On the sand, the knifed Borrodrone twisted and sighed, then was still. The green man who had knifed him was already still. His face was losing its twisted grimace and was settling into peace. Kirkham walked around both of them, picked up the object that the Borrodrone had found in the bundle of clothes and which had caused his death.

He stared at it. It was the helmet he had hidden in the chest under his workbench back in the Borrodrone fortress.

Somewhere near him, he was aware that Jevnar was making apologetic noises.

CHAPTER FIVE

"HOW DID this get here?" Kirkham said.

Jevnar writhed. His hands made circling motions in the air. An expression of deep chagrin showed on his face. Words rattled from his lips. "I bring," he said at last.

"You bring!" Kirkham said, explosively.

Jevnar's face indicated a strong desire to crawl under a rock and hide, anything to get away from the hot eyes and the brittle, accusing tone of the human. "I steal," he said.

"You steal!" Kirkham repeated. In this moment he could cheerfully have wrung the neck of this green man, he could have kicked Jevnar's round behind all the way back to the Borrodrone fortress. "Then the Borrodrones did not know I had this helmet?"

"They know," Jevnar said.

"Huh? How did they know?"

"I tell them," Jevnar answered.

"What?"

"I slip them the word," Jevnar repeated. "First, I steal helmet from you. Then I slip them the word. Then I tell you they are coming—"

"The devil you say!" the amazed human gasped.

If Jevnar had been a dog, he would have been crawling up to Wade Kirkham to get the licking he knew he had coming. He gave a good imitation of a dog now, a dog that has been caught sucking eggs in the hen house. "I steal helmet," he said. "Then I steal you."

"Me?"

"I need helmet, I need you."

"Why in the name of hell do you need the helmet and why do you need me?"

"Helmet part of god weapon," the green man answered. "I need it for that reason. You smart man. I need you to make the helmet work."

Kirkham's mouth hung open. "I'm an electrician—"

The ghost of a grin showed through the chagrin on Jevnar's face. "You tell that to Borrodrones," he answered. "Not tell same to me. I know better. You very smart man. You also after the same thing I was after—the god weapon. Not fool Jevnar."

"It looks as if I didn't fool anybody!" the perturbed human answered.

Jevnar shook his head in agreement. "Not much good as spy. Better as something else. You come with me to my people. We make welcome. When we make god weapon work, we turn it loose on Borrodrones. Make them hard to catch."

THE WORDS that Jevnar used were the slang of Earth that he had picked up from Kirkham but the hate that appeared on his face when he spoke of using the god weapon on the Borrodrones was strictly his own. In that blast of hate, Kirkham saw the motive for all of Jevnar's actions. The green man was fighting for his people, he was trying to bring back to the position they had once occupied the race that the Borrodrones had conquered and turned into slaves with such a goal as that, treachery and lying and theft, and possibly murder too, could be condoned. With this goal, Kirkham was in complete sympathy. He came from Earth, where men were free, but he knew that even on Earth, freedom was a hard-bought thing, purchased by men who had lone what Jevnar was now doing.

"You forgive Jevnar?" the green man spoke.

"I forgive," Kirkham answered.

"You help with god weapon?"

"I help," Wade Kirkham said. With such a goal as this, a human and a green man could find themselves in complete agreement. But—wasn't Jevnar overestimating a little his abilities to make the god weapon work? Kirkham thought the green man was overestimating by a couple of country miles.

The two green men who had followed the fleeing Borrodrone returned, dejected, spreading their hands in a gesture that has the same meaning among all races.

"He got away," Jevnar interpreted. "That is much bad. We rest short time, then hurry on to my people." His eyes went down to the patrol leader. "Got two helmets now."

To Kirkham, it seemed that he had barely sunk down on the sand when he was aroused again, to climb sluggishly into the saddle and to ride through the bright moonlight of the Martian night. For long stretches, he dozed. Near morning, the dothars were halted and the riders dismounted. They were taken into some sheltered place, Kirkham knew. Jevnar showed him a pile of skins on the floor of a room. The two humans were asleep before their heads touched the skins. Kirkham dreamed he was back on Earth.

It was a pleasant dream. In it a girl was singing. The song broke off and the girl said, "Damn," as if she meant it. The damn sounded much too real to belong in a dream. Kirkham opened his eyes.

Light was streaming through a square opening in one side of a room that seemed to have been hollowed from solid rock. For a moment he had the impression he was back in the fortress of the Borrodrones. Then he saw the pile of skins: Apparently they formed a bed of sorts and were a green man's idea of a good place to sleep. Humans, accustomed to foam rubber mattresses, had other ideas on this subject. Kirkham considered the possibility of forming a company to import foam rubber mattresses to Mars. He was still half asleep.

"Good morning," the girl said. Kirkham sat up. The girl was sitting on a bench beside the pile of skins. She had removed the plastic material from her features and was now engaged in vigorously washing her face in a basin that contained about a pint of water. She grinned at him, through the soap on her face. "The trouble with these green men is that they would rather give you their right arm than a little water," she said.

"They think more of water than they do of both arms," he answered. "Water is scarce and precious on this planet."

HE THOUGHT for a moment of the contradictions of Mars. Probably few Martians had ever had a bath, simply because water was much too scarce to waste on so unnecessary a personal foible. But in a world where they didn't have enough water to bathe, they had a weapon that struck like the lightning strikes. Martian scientific development had been uneven. In some fields they had run far ahead, in others they had lagged behind. They knew nothing of the science of social relationships or how different races learned to live together. There wasn't an airplane on the whole planet, except the one jet ship the humans had brought, they had electricity, they didn't have the internal combustion engine, but they had—the god weapon. Some of them had it anyhow.

Slowly these thoughts were forced out of Kirkham's mind and another thought intruded. The arrangement of the skins caught and held his attention. They revealed a fact that startled him.

"Hey!" he said. He looked at Paula Wilson. "Hey," he repeated softer. Mutely he nodded toward the arrangement of the skins.

"Yep," she said. "I slept there." Behind the soap her eyes mocked him.

His face was still covered with the plastic that had been used as a disguise. His features revealed nothing but his eyes must have hinted what he was thinking. The girl laughed. "Are you worrying about what Jevnar will think?"

"Well—"

"Don't let it bother you. Green men have no morals."

"Uh!" Kirkham said. "I wasn't worried about Jevnar. I was wondering if I had done any—uh—sleep walking maybe?"

Her eyes were demure. "How would I know? I was asleep."

"Uh…" Kirkham said.

"Disappointed?" There was a trace of a taunt in her voice.

"I don't know. Should I be?"

"What do you think?"

Jevnar appeared in the door. "I'll think about that later," Kirkham said. He turned his attention to the green man.

"How feel?" Jevnar inquired. "Rest good?"

"Feel fine. What time is it?"

"Morning the next day. You sleep all day and all night. I not bother. Would like talk now. Would like show something."

"First, get this off of me," Kirkham fingered the soft plastic that hid his features. "Second, shave. Third, eat. Then look and talk."

"Sure. I fix." Jevnar motioned to someone following him. A green man carrying a small basin of water entered.

Kirkham, with a yelp of satisfaction, got busy making himself clean. Watching him use the precious water, Jevnar's face revealed that the human might just as well have been using his heart's blood. But, expensive as it was to use water for washing, Jevnar was apparently determined to be the perfect host, no matter what it cost. Not once did be open his mouth while Kirkham was shaving, but his tight lips revealed what he was thinking.

WHEN THEY had finished eating, Jevnar motioned to them to follow him. He led them through an intricate series of passages carved out of solid rock. "This last fortress of green men," he explained. Pride appeared in his voice.

Apparently Jevnar was a person of some importance in his own land. When other green men came along, they bowed respectfully to him.

"I—how you say it?—small-sized big shot here," Jevnar explained. "Go now to secret place. Must hide eyes."

From a pocket of the cloak he wore, he produced strips of soft tanned skin. By motions, he indicated he wanted to blindfold them. Kirkham, dubious of the situation, hesitated.

"No one except most trusted green men ever see place I am taking you," Jevnar said. "Better you not see way there. Later, if something go wrong, you can't tell what you don't know."

It was a reasonable request. The two humans assented. After the blindfolds had been placed on their eyes, Jevnar led them by the hand. They moved forward interminably. Twice guards challenged sharply, Jevnar replying in the soft slurred language of his people. Twice they went through heavy doors. Then they entered, by the feel of it, a large open space. Muted voices sounded around them. Somewhere a heavy generator droned. There was a feeling of electric tension in this place. Kirkham felt his skin prickle. The blindfold was removed.

He was in an immense room. Lights ran across the ceiling. Off to one side was a workshop and through an ached doorway, he caught a glimpse of an immense laboratory where green men were at work. In the center of the room was a single hulking piece of machinery, a generator of some kind. It looked like a dynamo but it was unlike any dynamo ever constructed on Earth. Five bulky leads ran from a bulky wheel mounted beside the generator. This wheel was in motion. As it spun effortlessly on its axle, Kirkham caught a glimpse of a maze of coils mounted on the rim. Rising from five points were heavy copper rods. A current of some kind was flowing out through them, leaping from the ends into space. The air around them appeared distorted as if by heat waves A blue halo circled the tip of each rod. Energy of some kind was flowing up these rods and was passing from them into—what?

What was this generator?

"This generator makes the god weapon," Jevnar said. "Generators like this in Borrodrone fortress. Juice controlled through helmet."

"Radio power," Kirkham said. So that was the secret of the god weapon. When he had examined the helmet, he had had the suspicion that it was something like this. But was the god weapon straight radio power as humans knew it?

"How did you get this generator?" he asked.

"We steal it, a piece at a time, over many years," Jevnar explained. "Green men working as slaves in Borrodrone workshops carry away one piece one day, get another piece later. Maybe memorize part, draw picture of it, pass picture along."

"The devil you say. How could they steal something like this right under the nose of the Borrodrones?"

"Not easy," Jevnar said. "Many green men die." Sadness

crept into his voice and lines appeared on his face. "When the last green man dies, we give up."

IN SUCH words, he voiced the defiance of his people for their conquerors. For generations, Jevnar's people had been considered as slaves, as vermin to be crushed under foot. Heavy had been the foot of the conqueror on their neck, tight the grip around their throat. Jevnar himself had gone into the fortress of the Borrodrones, knowing that if he said the wrong word, if he used the wrong tone; if even the expression on his face indicated he might be thinking the wrong thing, his life would be snuffed out.

"Come, I show you how helmet work," Jevnar said.

On the workbench were two tall helmets. Jevnar pointed to a stud on the belt they had taken from the Borrodrone patrol leader. "This switch control the distance at which beam is to strike, the helmet control the direction. They look at you, beam aimed at you. Press power button—Boom!" His hands spread to indicate what happened then.

It was an ingenuous and an amazing device. To anybody not in on the secret, it seemed that the lightning struck in response to the wish of a Borrodrone, that the Borrodrones had the destructive power of Jove. Probably they had fooled the green men with that weapon for a long time. Certainly they had impressed the humans arriving on Mars with superstitious awe and dread.

"I see why you wanted a helmet," Kirkham said. "But you said you also wanted me. Why?"

"Need you too," Jevnar said. "Need someone, hope you are the one. We have generator, now we have helmet. But we do not understand how generator is supposed to work, in fact, cannot make it work. Something wrong somewhere." He spread his hands in a helpless gesture. "You can make it work for us, we hope."

"Hell on wheels!" Kirkham gasped. The problem was enormous. They expected him to make a generator work when they could not make it work themselves. Yet Jevnar and the other green men were looking hopefully and expectantly at him, as if they thought he could do anything. He was a man, wasn't he? He was a member of the race that had crossed space. Men could do anything!

"I'll—I'll try," Kirkham said. The expression on the faces of the green men said they thought he was their fairy godfather who could wave a wand and turn out miracles on order.

An hour later, he knew he was tackling a problem as tough as the first atom bomb. Or so it seemed to him. By the time the day was finished, he knew he was tackling something that might be tougher than the bomb. A few things he had learned, none of which made his job any easier. The first was that the generator did not produce electricity. When he had seen the lightning flash, he had assumed that electricity was the force involved. He learned now that he was not dealing with electricity but with some new and hitherto unknown force. Some Borrodrone genius had discovered this force and had learned how to generate and control it, but the laws that governed it were not in any text book published on Earth.

"The blasted thing scares me," Kirkham admitted. It scared the green men too. When the generator was in operation, they walked very gingerly around the laboratory. The force created odd and unpredictable effects. Tools would rise up from the workbenches, hang suspended in the air for a few moments, then come gently back to their resting place. Some vagrant, unpredictable current accounted for this phenomenon. But what current? The first time it happened to Kirkham it scared him almost out of his wits. He had been working with a screwdriver and had laid it down for a moment. When he reached for it, he discovered it was floating six inches above the bench. His hair rose on end at the sight.

"Happens often," Jevnar explained. "It is the effect of the force." Apparently this explanation satisfied him and the other green men. They were accustomed to the effect and they saw nothing strange about it. But Kirkham was not accustomed to it and he saw it as something utterly strange— the defiance of gravity. Under other circumstances, he would have given everything he possessed for a chance to investigate this one effect.

THE SECOND problem was how the force was projected from the generator. Generated in one spot, it could be made to appear miles away, with dramatic suddenness. How did it get there?

Kirkham did not know and did not care. It got there. The important problem was how to get this equipment into operation. Scientists could argue for generations about how the force was propagated. The green men could not wait for generations. Maybe they could not even wait until tomorrow!

Late in the afternoon a green man was admitted to the lab. He spoke rapidly to Jevnar. His words produced a stir among the green men. Kirkham did not understand what had happened. Jevnar reluctantly told him.

"Borrodrone patrols near us. The one who got away at spring, bring them on our trail."

Kirkham listened with half an ear. The generator was in operation. On the workbench a metal stool was slowly lifting into the air. Fascinated, he stared at it. Invisible demons seemed to be tugging at it. He could almost hear the demons grunt! "Any danger of the patrols finding us?" he asked.

"Maybe, maybe not. They hunt long time for sure."

Kirkham did not ask what would happen if the patrols

succeeded in finding them. The demons had grown tired of the struggle and had released the wrench. Kirkham started to speak, stopped. A gentle-fingered giant was taking hold of him.

"Cut off the generator," he yelled.

As the green men hurried to obey, the giant lifted him an inch from the floor, then, patting him as a man pats a child, released him. He went down to his knees as his normal weight hit again. His hair was standing on end, each charged strand standing separate and distinct from all the rest.

"I don't like this," he said.

A day later, he was liking it even less. Perhaps he felt a little as had the first scientists who developed the atom bomb that he was meddling with basic forces of the universe about which he knew little or nothing. The giant who had lifted him an inch from the floor might lift him a thousand miles, and drop him, for all he knew to the contrary. Meanwhile he was aware that the green men in the laboratory were apprehensive and uneasy.

"What goes on, Jevnar?" he asked. Jevnar was a shadow who rarely left his elbow. If he wanted a tool, Jevnar saw that he got it. If he made a suggestion, the green man saw that it was instantly carried out.

"Nothing," Jevnar answered. "What think if we made this change?" He pointed out a different way the leads might be brought from the generator.

"You'd short the whole damned business," Kirkham answered. "Why is everybody so nervous today?"

"Not nervous," Jevnar answered. "What do next?"

"Next—stop lying," Kirkham said. "Why is everybody so nervous?"

Jevnar, writhing, evaded the question. Eventually Kirkham forced from him the admission that green warriors trying to defend this last place of refuge of their people had fought a pitched battle with the Borrodrone patrol, and had lost it.

"How in the devil did they fight the god weapon?"

"With knives in dark," the green man answered.

"Knives against *that?*"

"Knives all we got. Either fight with knives or give up. Do you think the generator will work soon?"

"You kind of want to get the generator working, don't you?"

"Kind of want to keep on living," Jevnar said.

It was as simple as that. Green men armed with knives might have the magnificent courage to go out into the dark and tackle a Borrodrone patrol. If they were lucky, they might slip between the sentries, if every green man struck at the same instant and drove home his knife the first blow, they might possibly wipe out a small patrol. But the odds were nine to one against.

"Courage like that deserves better weapons than knives," Kirkham said.

"Need god weapon," Jevnar said. He tried to keep his features imperturbable, he tried to indicate by his manner that this was a small matter, but even his superb control of his features was beginning to fail. "Spies report Borrodrone army moving in this direction. Hurry, my friend, and make generator work."

The expression in his eyes said he was expecting a miracle.

CHAPTER SIX

WHETHER it was a miracle or not by the time the nearer moon of Mars had reached the zenith of the sky that night, the generator built by the green men from stolen parts and stolen plans was under control. That control was faulty and erratic, the control device was improvised, the tall helmet of the Borrodrones was not and could not be used, but the gadget that focused the beam and brought it into existence at the desired spot was simple and workable.

When the first test had been run, the excitement of the green men in the laboratory made Kirkham think of a crowd at a basketball game when the home team has just put the winning basket through the loop. They did everything but kiss him and they would have done that if he had let them.

"Now we fix the Borrodrones!" Jevnar exulted. As he spoke, a shout sounded in the lab. Came running a green man. What had happened to him was obvious. His clothing was gone and his burned flesh was falling away from his back in layers. The god weapon had grazed him.

He gasped words to Jevnar.

"Borrodrones inside fortress."

"How did they get in?"

"Once they find path, no way to stop them," Jevnar said. He spoke the truth. Armed with the god weapon, the Borrodrones were lords of all they surveyed. They walked where they pleased and none could stop them.

"Can they get to us here?" Kirkham questioned.

"In time they can, when they find the way," Jevnar answered. "The god weapon at full discharge burns down any door, eats through solid rock. Slow but gets through."

"How much time before they can get to us here?"

"A day, maybe two days. Who knows?"

"How many discharge controls can your technicians construct by dawn tomorrow?"

Jevnar wrinkled his face in thought. He consulted with the technicians. "Can make twenty-five," they decided at last.

"Can you find twenty-five green men who will volunteer to use them against the Borrodrones?"

"Twenty-five?" Jevnar snorted his contempt of this question. "Five hundred, a thousand. I myself will lead them."

"Get twenty-five and you yourself won't lead them," Kirkham answered. "I need you."

Sometime before dawn came a green man with the news that the patrol that had penetrated the fortress had drawn off. They had not been forced to withdraw by the resistance offered them, they had simply become tired of hunting through dark cavernous tunnels for inferior creatures that threw knives at them from the dark and fled away without fighting. Perhaps they got tired of killing. At any rate, they withdrew.

Other Borrodrone forces were moving up. Fresh warriors could take off the task of exterminating these vermin in their nest. They had located the hidden nest. That was the important thing. All that remained now was the usual mopping-up operation.

FROM A hidden niche high up on the face of a gigantic cliff, Wade Kirkham, Jevnar, and Paula Wilson watched the resumption of the process of extermination. Below them was a broad valley. To the south was a long, barren ridge. Tents were visible along the top of this ridge and dothar-riding troops were moving casually into position. They made no effort at concealment—why should they hide from green men?

A column of troops detached themselves from the main group and rode up to a dark opening at the bottom of the cliff. Blast marks on the rock showed where the patrol had forced an opening the night before. The troops dismounted. Hostlers took the reins of their mounts, the troops formed a precise column. It was all very military and very efficient. Three abreast, tall helmets waving over their head, a strutting officer in the lead, the column advanced into the opening.

"All they need is a band and they will be ready to pass in

review," Kirkham muttered. He was worried, fretful. Long hours of hard work and no sleep had scoured the insulation from his nerves. He felt raw all over. Down there an army was moving into position against a handful of green men. What chance did they have?

The strutting officer was within ten feet of the opening when the lightning hit him and outlined him for an instant in a halo of sizzling flame.

Even though he was a quarter or a mile away, Kirkham could imagine he heard that officer fry.

Another bolt followed the first one, striking straight down the middle of the advancing column.

As if a giant had driven a wedge through its heart, the column split apart. Panic hit the Borrodrones. One second the column was all spit and polish, the next second it was not a column but was broken mass of panic-stricken warriors each fleeing for his own life.

For the first time in history, the Borrodrones had run head-on into their own weapon.

They didn't seem to like it much.

Beside him, Kirkham could hear Jevnar breathing heavily. For the green man, this was a great day, the day when his conquered people struck their first blow for freedom. All his life, Jevnar had lived in anticipation of this day. He had lived for it, talked about it, probably dreamed about it. Now it had come.

Or had it?

Down below, the troops responded quickly to the first shock of surprise. The fleeing warriors found every available spot of cover. On the long ridge, there was a flurry of movement as Borrodrone troops there, seeing what had happened down below, got themselves out of sight.

"They recover fast," Kirkham growled. "Too damned fast."

Messengers were seen running. Inside the fortress the green men held their fire. Kirkham cursed beneath his breath. This was not the way to use the god weapon. The green men had failed to take advantage of the possibilities of surprise, they had not been ready to move instantly to the attack, to strike hard at the Borrodrone forces before they had time to reorganize.

The green men had broken one column. They had left an army intact.

Already that army was moving to attack.

THIS TIME it was not advancing as a column in regular order but as a formation of skirmishers. Slipping from cover to cover, individual fighters were advancing, one warrior running forward while his comrades protected him.

Meanwhile the advanced troops were pouring charges of deadly lightning into and around the opening in the cliff.

The green men inside were firing back but every time a charge flashed outward, a dozen explosive bolts of white-hot fire came in reply.

"It's hopeless," Kirkham ground out the words. "There are thousands of disciplined fighters against twenty-five green men. We can hold them for a day or two, we can make them advance cautiously into the tunnels, but in the end they are certain to win."

Jevnar's haggard face revealed that he too, recognized the truth. His great day had come—and gone. For him it was the moment when dreams falter, when the house of cards comes tumbling down.

"Sorry I am that I brought you here," he spoke. "Time now for you to go."

"Eh?"

"I take you out by secret path. You get away—save life."

"You mean there is a way we can escape from this place?"

Jevnar nodded. His face was wretched. "A way for a few to go. I take you two."

"To Mars Port?"

"You two go to Mars Port," Jevnar answered.

"Where will *you* go?"

"I come back here," Jevnar said.

Kirkham's voice rose harsh and angry. "You mean you want us to run away while you stay here and die?"

"You not green man," Jevnar answered. "Quarrel of green men not your quarrel. You get away, take with you knowledge of god weapon. Maybe there come another day when you come back." Fire flashed in the green man's eyes. In the belief that there might come another day when somebody else fought the Borrodrones, he could die happy.

"I don't think there is a chance to get away," Kirkham said slowly. "If the Borrodrones are as smart as I think they are, they will have this whole area surrounded. They will challenge and search every six-legged bug, every sand flea trying to get away."

Jevnar's troubled face said that this might well be true. In the silence Kirkham was aware of Paula Wilson speaking. "Is there a place here where a plane can land and take off again?" The girl was talking to the green man.

"Plane?" Jevnar had to have this word explained to him. Kirkham listened. There was turmoil inside of him. A chance to escape, a chance to live! Down below the Borrodrones were maintaining almost continuous fire against the opening of the cave.

"This mountain has flat top," Jevnar said. "Plane could land there." His voice said he didn't understand this foolishness. Kirkham didn't understand it either. "What sense does this make?" he growled.

"I was thinking that a plane could get you over the patrols of the Borrodrones," the girl answered.

"So it could. So what? There isn't a plane on Mars."

"There is one."

"Oh. Yes." He had forgotten the jet ship. Now that he remembered it, he could not see what difference its presence made. It was in Mars Port.

"Within fifteen minutes after taking off, the plane could be here," Paula Wilson pointed out.

"So it could, if the pilot knew where to come, if we could get word to Mars Port, if—" Exasperation sounded in his voice. "This is silly talk."

"Is it?" Paula Wilson rolled back the sleeve of the floppy man's shirt that she wore, revealing the heavy strap watch on her wrist. From some place beneath her clothes, she took that piece of equipment that no woman is ever without, a pin. The end of the pin fitted neatly into a tiny hole in the watch case. She slipped the watch from her wrist, moved the winding key. Kirkham and Jevnar stared at her, the human in dubious doubt, the green man with polite though strained interest.

"What are you doing?" Kirkham said.

"This watch happens to be a compact, high-frequency radio transmitter," Paula answered.

"What? Let me see that." Kirkham reached out his hand.

SHE HELD the watch away from him. The pin projected upward like a tiny antenna.

"Back in Mars Port there is a receiver in continuous operation. It is tuned to this transmitter and only to this transmitter. When I wind the key, the receiver in Mars Port will pick up the signal. It has been adequately tested and will work. As soon as the signal comes in, the plane will take off. The pilot will home on the beam from this transmitter." She sounded very technical and very sure of herself. "Within twenty minutes after this receiver goes into operation, we'll have a jet plane landing for us."

Jevnar nodded. Probably he didn't understand one word in ten but he got enough of it to know that a plan was being made to rescue the humans. Wade Kirkham understood everything—and nothing. His eyes sought the girl. Again he had the haunted feeling that he had known her somewhere before. But where? The impression was gone before he could quite catch it.

"I don't get this," he said. "How does it happen that you have a transmitter tuned to bring to your rescue the one jet plane on Mars?"

Her face was quiet. A smile lurked in the depths of her eyes. "It might be that the people I work for think it is worth something to help me when I need it."

"The people—"

"Earth Government," she answered. "You've heard of them, I imagine."

"The hell!" He felt pressure move inside of him. "Then you must be—"

"A spy too," she answered. "All three of us are spies." Her nod made this the most matter-of-fact statement she had ever made in her life. "You didn't actually believe my story about the Borrodrones capturing me, did you? Of course, they captured me, but it wasn't an accident. They were supposed to. There was hardly any other way I could have gotten inside their fortress."

"You took a risk like that?" He was having trouble believing his own ears.

"Earth Government thought the risk was worth while. I don't imagine you will have any difficulty in understanding that."

He had no trouble whatsoever in understanding. The game was worth any risk. That was not the hard part. "But a woman—" he said.

"Paula Wilson had worked for Earth Government for some time," the girl answered.

Kirkham swallowed. He let the idea that this girl was a secret agent filter through his mind. "What did they send you after?"

"They had the strange idea that two humans were better than one," she said. "So they sent me after the same thing you were after. They also had the strange idea that you might get into trouble and that it would be worthwhile to have someone on hand who could send for help, fast."

"What?" he gasped. "They sent you to help me?" His eyes went through the slot in the wall. Movement on the slope indicated the presence of thousands of Borrodrone troops. "They should have sent a couple of armies."

"They took a chance that you might need help in escaping," the girl pointed out. "Jevnar says the plane can land on the mesa above us. So it looks as if their chance might pay off—"

Some part of Kirkham's thoughts must have appeared on his face. The girl's soft cry was loud in the silence as she seemed to grasp what he was thinking. "You don't mean you're not going—"

"I mean exactly that," Kirkham answered.

"But you've got to go!" She was really frightened now, more frightened than she had ever been. "You know how the god weapon operates. You've simply *got* to get that information back to Mars Port. There is no argument about it." She was winding the watch.

"What about Jevnar?" he asked.

"But that is different!"

"There is no difference that I can see. These people are my friends. Do you think I am going to run away to safety while they stay here and die?"

"But—"

"As to the information about the god weapon, Earth Government will get that sooner or later, somehow or anyhow. They've already sent at least four men. They will send a hundred, if necessary. But I am not going to turn out on my friends. This fight is not over."

HE WAS ALMOST hysterical. Inside of him he was aware of the pounding of his heart. He knew how desperately he wanted to allow this girl to send for the plane, to seek safety in flight, but if he ran away, the face of Jevnar and the other green men would follow him all the rest of his life, haunting his dreams, torturing his waking moments. Forever he would have the feeling that he had played the part of a coward. "There's no argument about it." A man has to live with himself. He shook his head decisively.

The eyes of the girl were on him. Something was shining in them, tears he thought. Why should she be crying now?

"I thought you would say that," she whispered.

It did not occur to him to wonder why she had thought such a thing. "But—" He started to speak, stopped.

She dropped the tiny transmitter. The tinkle of breaking glass sounded as it struck the floor.

"Hey!" he yelled.

She lifted her foot and brought the heel of her shoe down heavily, on the transmitter. A tangle of broken parts was all that was left when she had finished.

"Why did you do that?" he stammered. "I was going to say *you* could call the plane, *you* could escape."

"I knew you would say that, I knew you would make me do that, if you had the chance. I—I stopped you."

"But—" He was appalled.

"If it is all right for you to take a chance, it is all right for me to take the same chance," the girl spoke.

"I—" He did not know what to say. She had no reason

for her actions, or none that he could see.

The tears in her eyes were plainly visible now. *"Wade, haven't you recognized me yet?"*

His mind swept back across the years and across the miles of space to the time when he had been a lordly senior in college. He had spent a summer with his folks in a cottage on the Maine coast. Next to them had been a cottage occupied by new people. There had been a girl, in the awkward age, skinny as a beanpole, with more freckles than he had ever seen in his life, who had dogged his footsteps that summer. If he went swimming, she was there. If he played tennis, she chased the balls that went over the backstop. His friends had teased him, his parents had mentioned the crush this child had on him, until he had come to hate the sight of her…almost. He had not seen her again after that summer, he had forgotten about her, but somehow she had not forgotten about him.

"Skinny Velma," he whispered. "And still tagging after me."

"Not skinny any longer," she answered. "But still tagging after you, I guess."

"But—"

"Paula Wilson is a pen name of a writer who works, actually, for Earth Government. When word came through that they were looking for a volunteer to come here, I didn't pay much attention. Then—" Her voice a thin whisper. "I learned that *you* were the spy that was already here. So—"

"You volunteered." He saw now why she had come to the fortress city of the Borrodrones, why she had taken the chances she had taken. It was the same reason she had tagged after him during that golden summer so long ago.

"When I learned you were here, I found I still remembered. So I came."

HIS HEART was jumping very strangely. "I'm a lucky man," he said. "I ought to have had enough sense, a long time ago, to know how lucky I was."

The tears in her eyes had turned to stars.

On the plain below, the first of the Borrodrone troops had penetrated the opening into the cave.

On the floor, the broken radio transmitter was an unrepairable tangle of broken parts.

Jevnar watched uncomprehendingly. Perhaps this was the way all humans acted before they died. He regarded all humans as great people but he was not familiar with their rites. They were laughing and crying at the same time and holding each other very close. Perhaps it was not good manners to watch them. Turning his back, he moved to the observation slot, looked out.

The scene below him was of death closing in, coming closer and closer. He tried to estimate the strength of the Borrodrone troops on the farther slope. They were as plentiful as sand fleas on the desert, their numbers beyond comprehension.

He could hear the humans laughing and crying. He tried not to listen. A voice spoke.

"Come on, Jevnar. It may be that the giants of Mars will fight on our side yet."

The green man did not understand about giants. There were no such creatures on the Red Planet. Were the humans giants? He had often had the idea that they were. Were they?

"I guess not," Kirkham answered.

"You've got one giant here," the girl spoke. "A giant in the field of science."

"Nonsense," Kirkham said. He was embarrassed.

The girl's eyes said she wasn't sorry and that she wasn't flattering him. She had always thought he was a giant.

"Not understand," Jevnar spoke.

"Come on," Kirkham said. "I don't understand either, but I am betting I am right. I've *got* to be right."

Jevnar still did not understand but since the human seemed to wish it, he led the way back to the hidden laboratory of the green men.

Giants?

What meant that word?

CHAPTER SEVEN

LATE THAT same day, Elfrone, supreme high priest and military commander of the Borrodrones, arrived at the hideout of the green men. He had come to direct the activities of his troops and to make certain that this nest of vermin was wiped out of the last screaming occupant. He had been surprised to learn that the green man had dared to build a secret hiding place. Would the fools not learn what happened to rebels?

Arriving at the scene of action, Elfrone was even more surprised to learn from his perturbed generals that the green men, by some means, had managed to master the god weapon and were using it against his troops.

When Elfrone grasped the fact that his underlings had been keeping secret from him the fact that the green men had unquestionably been stealing parts of the god weapon generator for years, there was for a time merry hell in the camp of the Borrodrones. Five generals were executed forthwith and a proportionate number of colonels, majors, and captains. After this execution was finished, Elfrone surveyed the situation.

Had effective measures been taken to make certain that no one escaped from this area?

A quaking general, in desperate fear of his life, detailed the precautions. A continuous circle of troops had been set up five miles away from this hideout. Roving patrols were moving now to take up positions twenty-five miles away, from which they would endeavor to check the flight of any green men who might escape the first net. Other patrols were moving out to a distance of fifty miles, to catch anybody who managed to elude the first two lines.

Even Elfrone considered these precautions adequate. What steps had been taken to storm the hiding place itself?

The general, breathing a little easier, gave him the number of fighters engaged in this operation, the numbers in reserve, and their disposition.

"Double the attackers," Elfrone ordered.

"Yes, sire."

Elfrone was now fairly certain that the situation was secure.

"There are rumors, sire, unverified, of the presence of two humans with the green men," the general told him. It was better to tell this now than to risk letting Elfrone find it out later.

"Two humans!" Again the supreme leader considered the situation. He was aware of the potential danger to the Borrodrone dynasty by the human race on Mars. He was aware, also, that the humans were excellent scientists. They had achieved space flight. That one fact made them dangerous. If two humans were with the green men, then presumably they knew something about the operation of the god weapon. The last thing Elfrone wanted on Mars was information about this hellish weapon to reach human minds.

"Double the attackers again," he ordered. "Let the major assault be made in the middle of tomorrow's morning."

"It will be done, sire," the general answered.

WHEN THIS had been done, Elfrone felt at ease in his mind. Now, no matter what happened, the situation was under control. The cursed humans at Mars Port would not dare ask questions about the killing of any number of green men. Nor would they, considering the circumstances, dare take any action about the death of two members of their own race. Or ignore action that could not be shrugged off.

Elfrone, anticipating the slaughter of the morrow, spent an easy, restful night.

On the middle of the next morning, carefully out of sight behind the long ridge—he wanted to take no chance of exposing his august person to a blast from a god weapon in the hands of a green man—Elfrone prepared himself to await the arrival of messengers telling how the slaughter was going.

The first messenger arrived, panting.

"An advance by our forces has been achieved at the main entrance."

"Good," Elfrone said. "What of the defense?"

"Only one green man, a suicidal volunteer, attempted to stem the attack. He was destroyed. The troops have now reached the hiding place of a second volunteer and are engaged in burning him out."

"Only one at the main entrance?" Elfrone said.

"That was all, sire."

A little uneasy, Elfrone dismissed the messenger.

Later a second messenger arrived, telling that the second green man who had tried to stay the advance had been burned from the rock niche where he had hidden himself.

Elfrone let the messenger go. From where he sat, behind the long ridge, the flat top of the mesa into which the green men had dug themselves, was visible. Elfrone had the impression that he had seen something move on the mesa top. He looked again, straining his eyes. No, there was nothing to be seen.

The attack was going well. That was the main thing. Perhaps several days would be needed to penetrate to the final secret place where the stolen god weapon generator was in operation but his troops would reach their goal. Time was not important. Elfrone noticed a stir among the staff officers surrounding him.

They were all looking toward the flat-topped mesa. He followed the line of their gaze. His first thought was that his eyes were blurring.

Either his eyes were deceiving him or something was moving in the air above the mesa top. It looked like—

"A green man," Elfrone whispered. No! That was not possible.

As he watched, he saw two objects appear in the air, then three, then many.

The stir that ran through his own staff was unmistakable.

"Look, sire," a general said. They too, had seen the things in the air.

Moving with erratic, hovering motions, the objects rose a thousand feet above the mesa. From their height, Elfrone's camping place was plainly visible.

One object seemed to slip and fall away. Elfrone saw it go out of sight. If it was a man, the fall had certainly killed him. Elfrone watched. The other objects moved toward him. He was aghast.

What were these things that looked like green men? How did they move through the air? What was their purpose?

A FEELING of chill rose in him, a coldness that seemed to appear from nowhere. The objects came nearer. They were still high in the air but not beyond the range of the god weapon.

Elfrone lifted his hand to order them knocked down, then stayed the impulse. Wait a minute? What is happening here?

The objects were almost directly above him. They hovered there. A stir and a murmur of superstitious awe ran through the ranks of the watching Borrodrones. One of the objects began a slow descent.

Its identity was clearly visible now.

It was a green man.

The green man dropped slowly until he was only fifty feet above Elfrone. The ruler of the Borrodrones had the impression that he had seen this particular green man somewhere around the fortress palace of the Borrodrones. He dismissed the idea from his mind. The green man slowly descended another twenty-five feet.

The strange apparatus covering his body was clearly visible now. He seemed to be inside a wire cage.

"Do you wish to surrender, Elfrone of the Borrodrones?" the green man asked.

"Surrender?" It was a word no Borrodrone had ever spoken. Nor did Elfrone intend to speak it now.

"Blast that slave out of the sky!"

In response to his command, from a dozen sources the god weapon lashed out.

Lightning lit the sky. Lightning struck to the right and the left of the green man hovering there, struck above him and below him, but did not strike him. Thunder roared. He bobbed in response to the air currents sent up by the flashing lightning but he did not burn and he did not fall.

"Get him!" Elfrone spoke. There was a touch of hysteria in his voice. At this range, the god weapon could not possibly miss. The aiming was automatic, it was only necessary to look at any object to strike it down.

The lightning formed a halo of fire around the green man.

It did not strike him, did not touch him, did not come near him. He seemed to carry some invisible "No Trespassing" sign that the lightning recognized and obeyed.

The green man's hand moved on his belt.

In that moment, the truth must have come home to

Elfrone of the Borrodrones. The ruler's hand jabbed at his own belt. The god weapon that he carried was most potent. His tall helmet glinted as he looked upward. The lightning flared.

Like all the other bolts, it recognized the "No Trespassing" sign and stayed away.

Instead, lightning came back down from the green man, came back from the sky, came in a flashing, gleaming bolt of dreadful fire, struck and ringed Elfrone, surged through him in a mighty blast of roaring flame.

Elfrone did not have a chance to scream.

A million green men who had died in the blast of the god weapon over the preceding generations must have enjoyed the way Elfrone sizzled.

As Elfrone died, from the sky dropped other green men who had remained hovering there. From them poured deadly blasts of white-hot fire. Gathered here in this spot was the core of the Borrodrone administrative setup, the heart of their ruling organization.

WITHIN two minutes after the first blast struck, the only Borrodrones left alive of that central core were the ones who had thought first to run. Green men, looping lazily through the air, were following them.

Up high in the sky, Wade Kirkham watched. He saw the break-up of the Borrodrone headquarters.

A green man rose up beside him.

It was Jevnar, who had launched the first blast against Elfrone.

"Broken," Jevnar said, nodding toward the ground below. "They'll never recover. We strike next at the main fortress."

"Strike fast," Kirkham said. Don't give them time to discover how to deflect the god weapon."

"We won't," Jevnar said.

"Did the shielding work?" Kirkham asked. This had worried him more than he cared to admit. A thousand things had worried him, the shielding, the control of the lifting force, would the hastily improvised controls for the lifting power of the god weapon function properly? There had been no time for adequate tests.

"Perfect," Jevnar answered. "Lift work too, like elevator, mighty good. Blow hell out of Borrodrones." To Jevnar, the accumulation of generations of wrongs against the green men was being repaid here. The gratitude in his eyes as he looked at Kirkham was a living thing. "The giants walked." He was still awed by that fact.

Wade Kirkham grinned. Both the Borrodrones and the green men had missed the fact that the powers of a giant lay hidden within the god weapon. He thought of the screwdriver that had been lifted from the workbench. That had been the clue to the miracle of the giant. But to him the real miracle was the fact that in such a short amount of time they had been able to devise a way to control this giant.

"Go back now," he spoke to Jevnar. The green man nodded.

Under the manipulation of the switches held in their belts, the power locked in the generator back there under the flat-topped mesa began to carry them back.

Far in the sky overhead a gleaming object moved—a space ship coming in for a hazardous landing on Mars.

"One day this giant will lift you," Wade Kirkham thought, watching the space ship.

To him, this was the real importance of the god weapon, perhaps its only importance. If it could warp space in such a manner that a man could be lifted, it might also be used to lift a space ship.

The day would yet dawn when a ship equipped with such giants would lift off from Pluto on a flight to the nearer stars.

Two worlds had met. Out of that meeting had been born a giant with the strength to carry a ship across the void between the stars.

Floating beside Kirkham, Jevnar grinned. This was a great day for the green men. He tried to say as much, was aware that his companion was not really listening.

Off on the flat top of the mesa, Kirkham could see a figure—a girl waving. In that gesture, calling him home, he sensed that in one way at least it was also a great day for one man—Wade Kirkham. With a great night coming. He felt his pulses surge at the thought.

THE END

If you've enjoyed this book, you will not want to miss these terrific titles...

ARMCHAIR SCI-FI, FANTASY, & HORROR DOUBLE NOVELS, $12.95 each

D-1   **THE GALAXY RAIDERS** by William P. McGivern
SPACE STATION #1 by Frank Belknap Long

D-2   **THE PROGRAMMED PEOPLE** by Jack Sharkey
SLAVES OF THE CRYSTAL BRAIN by William Carter Sawtelle

D-3   **YOU'RE ALL ALONE** by Fritz Leiber
THE LIQUID MAN by Bernard C. Gilford

D-4   **CITADEL OF THE STAR LORDS** by Edmund Hamilton
VOYAGE TO ETERNITY by Milton Lesser

D-5   **IRON MEN OF VENUS** by Don Wilcox
THE MAN WITH ABSOLUTE MOTION by Noel Loomis

D-6   **WHO SOWS THE WIND...** by Rog Phillips
THE PUZZLE PLANET by Robert A. W. Lowndes

D-7   **PLANET OF DREAD** by Murray Leinster
TWICE UPON A TIME by Charles L. Fontenay

D-8   **THE TERROR OUT OF SPACE** by Dwight V. Swain
QUEST OF THE GOLDEN APE by Ivar Jorgensen and Adam Chase

D-9   **SECRET OF MARRACOTT DEEP** by Henry Slesar
PAWN OF THE BLACK FLEET by Mark Clifton.

D-10   **BEYOND THE RINGS OF SATURN** by Robert Moore Williams
A MAN OBSESSED by Alan E. Nourse

ARMCHAIR SCIENCE FICTION CLASSICS, $12.95 each

C-1   **THE GREEN MAN**
by Harold M. Sherman

C-2   **A TRACE OF MEMORY**
By Keith Laumer

C-3   **INTO PLUTONIAN DEPTHS**
by Stanton A. Coblentz

ARMCHAIR MASTERS OF SCIENCE FICTION SERIES, $16.95 each

M-1   **MASTERS OF SCIENCE FICTION, Vol. One**
Bryce Walton—"Dark of the Moon" and other tales

M-2   **MASTERS OF SCIENCE FICTION, Vol. Two**
Jerome Bixby—"One Way Street" and other tales

If you've enjoyed this book, you will not want to miss these terrific titles…

ARMCHAIR SCI-FI & HORROR DOUBLE NOVELS, $12.95 each

D-71 **THE DEEP END** by Gregory Luce
TO WATCH BY NIGHT by Robert Moore Williams

D-72 **SWORDSMAN OF LOST TERRA** by Poul Anderson
PLANET OF GHOSTS by David V. Reed

D-73 **MOON OF BATTLE** by J. J. Allerton
THE MUTANT WEAPON by Murray Leinster

D-74 **OLD SPACEMEN NEVER DIE!** John Jakes
RETURN TO EARTH by Bryan Berry

D-75 **THE THING FROM UNDERNEATH** by Milton Lesser
OPERATION INTERSTELLAR by George O. Smith

D-76 **THE BURNING WORLD** by Algis Budrys
FOREVER IS TOO LONG by Chester S. Geier

D-77 **THE COSMIC JUNKMAN** by Rog Phillips
THE ULTIMATE WEAPON by John W. Campbell

D-78 **THE TIES OF EARTH** by James H. Schmitz
CUE FOR QUIET by Thomas L. Sherred

D-79 **SECRET OF THE MARTIANS** by Paul W. Fairman
THE VARIABLE MAN by Philip K. Dick

D-80 **THE GREEN GIRL** by Jack Williamson
THE ROBOT PERIL by Don Wilcox

ARMCHAIR SCIENCE FICTION CLASSICS, $12.95 each

C-25 **THE STAR KINGS**
by Edmond Hamilton

C-26 **NOT IN SOLITUDE**
by Kenneth Gantz

C-32 **PROMETHEUS II**
by S. J. Byrne

ARMCHAIR SCIENCE FICTION & HORROR GEMS SERIES, $12.95 each

G-7 **SCIENCE FICTION GEMS, Vol. Seven**
Jack Sharkey and others

G-8 **HORROR GEMS, Vol. Eight**
Seabury Quinn and others

If you've enjoyed this book, you will not want to miss these terrific titles...

ARMCHAIR SCI-FI, FANTASY, & HORROR DOUBLE NOVELS, $12.95 each

D-81   **THE LAST PLEA** by Robert Bloch
THE STATUS CIVILIZATION by Robert Sheckley

D-82   **WOMAN FROM ANOTHER PLANET** by Frank Belknap Long
HOMECALLING by Judith Merril

D-83   **WHEN TWO WORLDS MEET** by Robert Moore Williams
THE MAN WHO HAD NO BRAINS by Jeff Sutton

D-84   **THE SPECTRE OF SUICIDE SWAMP** by E. K. Jarvis
IT'S MAGIC, YOU DOPE! by Jack Sharkey

D-85   **THE STARSHIP FROM SIRIUS** by Rog Phillips
FINAL WEAPON by Everett Cole

D-86   **TREASURE ON THUNDER MOON** by Edmond Hamilton
TRAIL OF THE ASTROGAR by Henry Haase

D-87   **THE VENUS ENIGMA** by Joe Gibson
THE WOMAN IN SKIN 13 by Paul W. Fairman

D-88   **THE MAD ROBOT** by William P. McGivern
THE RUNNING MAN by J. Holly Hunter

D-89   **VENGEANCE OF KYVOR** by Randall Garrett
AT THE EARTH'S CORE by Edgar Rice Burroughs

D-90   **DWELLERS OF THE DEEP** by Don Wilcox
NIGHT OF THE LONG KNIVES by Fritz Leiber

ARMCHAIR SCIENCE FICTION CLASSICS, $12.95 each

C-28   **THE MAN FROM TOMORROW**
by Stanton A. Coblentz

C-29   **THE GREEN MAN OF GRAYPEC**
by Festus Pragnell

C-30   **THE SHAVER MYSTERY, Book Four**
by Richard S. Shaver

ARMCHAIR MASTERS OF SCIENCE FICTION SERIES, $16.95 each

MS-7   **MASTERS OF SCIENCE FICTION AND FANTASY, Vol. Seven**
Lester del Rey, "The Band Played On" and other tales

MS-8   **MASTERS OF SCIENCE FICTION, Vol. Eight**
Milton Lesser, "'A' is for Android" and other tales

A WORLD GOVERNED BY GENIUSES!

The shadow of a horrific Atomic War had never really lifted. Atomic research had been outlawed for well over four hundred years. In this world of the future the first rule was simple—no Atomics! Secondly, only people of the highest intelligence would ever be allowed to rule the planet Earth.

But then a minor police agent from the backwaters of the South Pacific, Max Krull, was given the job of investigating a man's death from strange radiation burns. Someone had been playing with the atom again! Espers—who were mutants with extraordinary talents— were thought to be at the bottom of it. But what could their motive possibly be? And what incredible revelations would Krull's investigation lead to?

CAST OF CHARACTERS

MAX KRULL
Peace and quiet was what he wanted, but as an investigating police agent that was next to impossible.

BEN YARGO
He was the Prime Thinker, the most powerful man on Earth—and he had a secret to keep.

HERMAN BOK
President of the Espers. He couldn't really change destiny, but he could certainly help it along!

JORDAN GULLFIN
This special agent was as cruel and sadistic as they came. His weapon of choice—a rubber hose!

IVAN SHEVACH
Arrogant and ruthless, his twisted mind lusted for power—lots of power.

MERRYWEATHER
This Public Relations man had a smile for every occasion—even when the occasion was murder.

THE MAN
WHO HAD
NO BRAINS

By
JEFF SUTTON

ARMCHAIR FICTION
PO Box 4369, Medford, Oregon 97501-0168

*For more information about Armchair Books and products, visit our
website at…*

www.armchairfiction.com

Or email us at…

armchairfiction@yahoo.com

CHAPTER ONE

BEN YARGO, 90th Prime Thinker of the Empire of Earth, broke the fateful news to the World Council of Six at the planet capital in Sydney, Australia, on 26 November, 2449 A.D.—

An atomic conspiracy had been discovered.

History does not record the reactions of the individual Council members. However, such a conspiracy directly violated the First Law of Mankind—*There shall be no atomic research*—as decreed by Edward Crozener, who founded the Empire of Earth some 450 years earlier, in 1999 A.D., resurrecting it from the remnants of human civilization which survived the day-long Atomic War of 4 July 1970. Crozener's decree, intended to prevent another such holocaust, had been the Empire's most rigidly enforced law. Such a conspiracy, at the time, was unthinkable. Yet the Council did not order a sweeping investigation.

Curiously, a single agent was assigned to look into the incident...

Blak Roko's
Post-Atomic
Earthman.

* * *

KIM LEE Wong was last to enter.

He came through the tall gold-embossed doors of the Council Chamber hiding his nervousness behind a mask of calm. The other members of the World Council of Six already had gathered—statue-like and silent, waiting around the long polished table. Enigmatic. By the wall he saw the ascetic, arrogant face of Ivan Shevach, World Manager, and wondered why he was there. Council meetings were usually secret, restricted to members and of course, the Prime Thinker, who ruled the planet.

An emergency?

The thought frightened him. He nodded deferentially while he took his seat, conscious again that his official intelligence (IQ 208) placed him as the body's junior member. Eve Mallon (IQ 213), mathematician and only woman on the council, inclined her head. The others didn't acknowledge him, nor did he expect it. He returned her greeting almost gratefully (she represented North America) before flicking his almond eyes around the table.

Taussig of Europe...
Lincoln of Africa...
Serrano of South America...

Sociologist, lawyer, educator—faces of power and prestige—power won at the polls by virtue of intelligence. Each represented the most brilliant mind in one of the world's six major political subdivisions. Around them swirled the angry tides of politics, lapping at the throne of the Prime Thinker. He looked last at...

Kingman of Anzaca...

The face of the representative of the powerful Austra-New Zealand bloc was thin, harsh, veined, with tight bloodless lips and eyes that were implacable black pools. His long narrow hands were white talons gripping the arms of his chair. Wong shivered involuntarily and looked at the ornate clock set high on the rear wall, facing the one empty chair at the head of the table. Eight fifty-seven, three minutes before the Council would come to order. More precisely, it would open with the arrival of Ben Yargo, the Prime Thinker, for he was as punctual as the clock itself. A revolving scale below the center of the dial face showed the date: 11:26:2449.

At exactly 8:58 a.m., the tall doors opened—opened and closed behind Ben Yargo, who crossed the wide expanse of floor with the easy steps of a man who ruled a planet. The Council and the Manager rose with one accord. Wong watched covertly.

Yargo was middle-height, stocky, with short-cropped iron-gray hair, undersized ears pinned tight to his skull and a face of hewn granite in which the sculptor had not learned the art of polish. The skin was swarthy and rough, the nose crooked, the lips full and sensuous. But it was the eyes Wong saw—chill, ice-blue, hard as diamonds, nestled deep under jutting orbital ridges and, for some reason, he thought of a panther staring out from the dark places of a cavern. His apparel, knee-length green shorts with matching short-sleeved shirt under the flowing purple cape of office, revealed heavily muscled arms and legs. Little in his appearance suggested his background—philosopher and ecologist—nor the fact he was, by official test, earth's greatest intellect. He had won office with an astounding IQ 219 the last two terms.

THE Council members watched him with varying expressions: Eve Mallon's eyes were tender, Taussig's appreciative, Kingman's vindictive; Lincoln and Serrano appeared vaguely puzzled. Wong cast a side-long look at the Manager; Shevach's arrogant face held undisguised hostility. He wondered again at the powerful forces swirling around the planet's ruler, and thought: Only the Prime Thinker stood between the Manager and supreme power. Yargo was chief world executive, Shevach its manager and, as such, subject to executive power. Shevach was a whip, but Yargo was the arm that wielded it.

Yargo nodded curtly to the Council and fitted himself into the well-cushioned chair set on a slightly-raised dais. The members resumed their places and waited expectantly. The clock struck nine, a muffled beat in the huge chamber; it died away and Ben Yargo said:

"Council is in session."

He paused, looking slowly around the circle of faces before resuming. "I wish to apologize for calling this extraordinary session, especially"—he smiled at the Chinese biochemist—"just as Wong was starting his vacation. I hope I haven't caused too much inconvenience."

"It's an honor," Wong murmured politely.

"Hardly that," Yargo countered gravely, "but an extraordinary emergency has arisen." He paused to let his words sink in.

Lincoln, the dusky-skinned lawyer, looked faintly perturbed; Kenneth Kingman, the engineer, curled his lips in a slight sneer and Taussig, the sociologist, raised his eyes inquisitively. Yargo caught Ivan Shevach's bemused look and said slowly:

"There is evidence of atomic research."

"No!" Surprising, he thought, it was Lincoln who denied the statement. He looked inquiringly at him; the lawyer recognized the invitation to speak.

"Perhaps I should apologize for the expletive." He bowed politely. "But the fact is, I was merely surprised—still am." He shook his head incredulously. "I can't imagine that anyone…anyone would break the First Law." His words carried a denial meant to reinforce his belief.

"But someone has," Yargo countered softly.

"The proof?" Kingman interjected harshly.

"Damning." Yargo scanned the intent faces. "A man was found dead in a Sidney hotel room yesterday—dead of radiation burns."

Someone gasped and Serrano asked sharply: "Who?"

"Identity has just been made, only moments before this meeting. The victim's name was—" Yargo watched the ring of faces carefully— "William Bixby Butterfield." There was no change of expressions; no change, either, in Ivan Shevach's black eyes, nor his slightly sardonic expression.

"Who was Butterfield?" Serrano pursued. He licked his lips nervously.

"A physics professor on the faculty of the University of Palmerston North…before he disappeared."

"Disappeared?"

"Some five years ago, the fall of 2444," Yargo supplied.

"Could the burns have occurred any other way, perhaps excessive X-ray treatment?" Lincoln asked dubiously.

"Not in this case."

"Why?"

"Expert medical opinion," Yargo replied bluntly.

Lincoln shook his head hopelessly. "It's bad."

Taussig broke the following silence. "The point is, what are we going to do about it? Or what can we do? If the news became public..." He left the words dangling, watching the Prime Thinker curiously.

"The news won't...can't be made public," Yargo declared emphatically. "The coroner is bound to absolute secrecy." He added: "So are all persons present."

"The public would be highly disturbed," Eve Mallon said.

"But we must investigate immediately," Lincoln insisted.

"Of course, that's why I called this session. The Council is—after all—advisory in such matters."

Kingman tersely said: "I suggest an immediate all-out investigation; that the Prime Thinker order the full resources of the Government's agents of police to pursue that end."

Yargo remained poker-faced. "Any other suggestions?"

"The suggestion has merit," Wong ventured.

Yargo nodded. "Any others?"

Lincoln pronounced with great solemnity: "What alternative do we have? Atomic research means world destruction. We can't risk that, gentlemen."

"Lincoln's right," Kingman agreed. He shifted his head, caught Shevach's eye and continued: "I realize it's irregular but I'd like the Manager to express his views...if any."

"Certainly." Yargo's voice was tinged with annoyance. "Would the Manager have any comments?"

"THE Manager would," Shevach promptly replied. He rose, a slim elegant man of middle-age with a high-domed forehead and sharp pale features. He was the only non-elective official present, an appointee of Yargo's predecessor. As such, he could be removed from office only by the Prime Thinker with unanimous Council assent, a move Kingman had repeatedly blocked. He spoke easily without taking his eyes from Yargo.

"As world Manager, I am naturally concerned with public reaction. No one needs reminding that the ban against atomic research is our First Law; nor does anyone have to be told of the unrest—if not riots—that might occur if the information we have becomes public. Still, I heartily endorse the views expressed—an immediate, thorough investigation." He smiled thinly and continued:

"With the Prime Thinker's permission, I would be happy to launch such an investigation immediately." He let the words fall and sat down. Silence.

Yargo studied each person in turn; he looked last at Eve Mallon and his eyelid drooped, just a trifle. There was a bustle and she rose from her seat, a slender, gracious woman in the late thirties, gowned in a golden-colored semi-transparent tunic that showed the lines of her body in sharp relief. Her blond hair, lacquered in a high bun, sparked with jewels. She spoke with assurance.

"With the Prime Thinker's permission?"

"Certainly." Kingman's lips curled as Yargo half-rose in a courtly bow. She was reputed to be his mistress.

"First, we can assume a conspiracy, or at least the beginnings of one. Atomic research isn't a one-man operation. But even so, I must oppose the proposed plan." Her voice was a gentle ring, soft but incisive. "I can give at least three reasons."

"Name them," Kingman snapped irritably.

"An all-out investigation would alert the conspirators, assuming such a conspiracy exists. It could in that case drive them underground—I believe that's the historical phrase for going into hiding. Secondly, we can't have an all-out investigation without alarming the public." She half-turned and smiled at Ivan Shevach. "After all, that is one of the Manager's prime concerns, isn't it?"

Kingman demanded: "What else?"

"If there is a conspiracy, we don't know who—or how many—are involved," she said quietly. "Perhaps persons high up…"

Kingman sprang up. "I can't see the argument; but I can give an excellent reason for an immediate full-scale investigation regardless of public reaction."

Yargo said softly: "Give it."

"Espers!" He snapped the word. "This has all the earmarks of an esper conspiracy—one that we've got to root out and crush before we wake up and find the damned peepers ruling the world."

WONG gave an audible gasp, Yargo smiled faintly. The esper problem was Kingman's pet whipping post. Since the Sawbo Fang affair he'd used it on innumerable occasions in attempts to ram through pet legislation. The quiet voice of Taussig with its soft inflection broke in.

"There are only a few thousand espers in the world. With exception of a few hidden cases, all are on public record. While they have, shall we say, full privileges of citizenship, the possibility of danger is recognized; they are watched carefully." He hesitated, then continued:

"I don't believe it's any state secret that esper activities are closely monitored, even to the extent of tapping their homes and businesses. Then, too, we have the...searchers." He seemed to hesitate over the last word. "The Manager can testify to that," he concluded.

"That is correct." Shevach rose languidly. "However, that in itself means nothing."

"Explain that," Taussig demanded.

"Certainly." Shevach's face took on a condescending look. "What do we really know about the espers?"

"Plenty."

"We know they possess the power of telepathy, the ability to read minds, but we are prone to forget they are mutants..."

"What has that got to do with it?" Taussig challenged.

"The psychmasters point out the ability to read minds is just one facet—the beginning phase—of their eventual evolution. How about Sawbo Fang? How do we know where the rest of the espers stand on the evolutionary ladder? What of clairvoyance...psychokinesis?" He asked the questions in rapid sequence. "I say they're dangerous."

"Poppycock," Taussig snorted indignantly. Mass peoples and cultures were his business and he clearly didn't like Shevach's venture into his field. He faced the Manager and spoke tolerantly.

"Telepathy is a confirmed fact, yes, but the Sawbo Fang affair was mass hysteria, born of ignorance." Kingman started to interrupt but he waved him to silence. "Sawbo Fang was a Burmese boy of eight. A rumor started that he had wild talents...could lift stones by mental powers, stir trees, even keep his body suspended in air; but we've go to remember his background. The boy lived in a small mountain village whose people were ridden with superstitions and beliefs in black magic..."

"And died," Kingman sneered.

"But not because of Sawbo Fang," Taussig said pointedly. "An earthquake leveled the village; he was blamed, killed by a mob, but that didn't make him a psychokinetic."

"Then why the searchers?" Kingman cut in.

"You know the answer as well as I do," Taussig replied. "The affair created a public clamor that started witch hunts; thirty legal espers were stoned, burned, shot. The world was in an uproar demanding action, so we acted. We created secret agents...searchers...to comb the world, searching for hypothetical pk's. That satisfied the public. Personally, I'd like to remind my fellow council members that the witches of pre-atomic Salem weren't really witches, but they were burned." He smiled bemusedly and sat down.

Kingman said angrily: "Reputable psychmasters have testified that Sawbo Fang was a psychokinetic..."

"We're getting off the track," Yargo broke in. "We're here to discuss a possible atomic conspiracy, not espers."

"I say it's the same thing," Kingman half-shouted. A vein in his neck throbbed visibly.

"Rubbish," Taussig said, "there's never been a clairvoyant or pk outside of TV science fiction." The Prime Thinker broke the strained silence that followed.

"I believe the arguments in favor of an all-out investigation have merit. However, I have decided against such action on the grounds offered by Council member Mallon. I believe a covert investigation would serve better."

"I take it you intend to direct the investigation yourself?" Kingman challenged.

"That is correct."

"But irregular."

"Irregular?"

"Investigation is a police function."

Yargo waited.

"The police function under the administration of the Manager," Kingman continued belligerently.

"Yes, for the purpose of administration," Yargo corrected, "but the Prime Thinker may, at his discretion, assume full direction of the police agency. For any reason whatever," he added.

Kingman half-turned and looked inquiringly at the lawyer. Lincoln's dark face was forcedly thoughtful and it was a moment before he spoke.

"Prime Thinker Yargo is correct. The Archon ruled in favor of Joseph Zwolinski, the sixty-third Prime Thinker, when he took direction of the agents during the worker rebellion in the submerged city of Molokai in the early part of the last century."

"One other point," Kingman persisted.

"Name it," Yargo snapped. He leaned forward in his chair without any effort to conceal his cordial dislike of the Anzaca representative.

"It seems unwise for the Prime Thinker to embark on an investigation which he may not be able to finish." He spoke the words with a faint sneer. Yargo contemplated him coldly—he knew very well what the engineer meant. Elections were less than three weeks away and, this time, he faced formidable opposition in Ivan Shevach who, at IQ 217, was considered his leading contender. The Manager was not only brilliant but seemed to possess an uncanny ability to assess political situations. His hand was everywhere, at exactly the right time, and he had surrounded himself with a hard corps of fanatically loyal lieutenants. Now he was making a stab to rule the planet. In a short time they would face each other at the polls in a battle of intelligence, a battle Yargo couldn't afford to lose. UPOP, the Universal Public Opinion Poll, gave the Manager as his strongest competition. The faces around the table watched him, assessing his thoughts. Yargo spoke succinctly:

"In event of a change in office, I would naturally acquaint my successor with all the facts in the case, I can't see any problem there." He looked slowly at each person in turn; only Kingman was openly hostile. Shevach, in the background, smirked.

"Any other questions?"

Silence—broken only by the faint sound of Wong shuffling his feet under the table.

"Council is adjourned."

The Council of Six rose as a body. Ben Yargo gripped the edge of the table with strong, stubby hands and pushed himself back with a quick glance around, then left as he had entered—with easy steps, looking straight ahead, apparently already forgetful of the session just closed.

CHAPTER TWO

MAX KRULL languorously moved his arms in a slow breast stroke, feeling the pressure of the cool water against his flesh with almost sensuous pleasure. Above him the rays of the tropic sun struck the lagoon in dawn—slanted blows, giving the water a delicate shade of green. It darkened, becoming a deeper forest color in the shadowy depths where grotesque sculptured coral heads jutted from the ocean floor like calcareous ghosts. A school of small fish, with oddly bulging eyes and narrow orange fins high on their saucer-shaped bodies, swam past his faceplate and disappeared in a canyon of twisted rock.

He zoomed deeper, swimming between ledges of white coral and fronds that swayed with the passage of his body until he reached a small amphitheater formed of rock and fronds. He entered it and let his body drift, studying the familiar forms of bottom life, now just feet below his faceplate: small red crabs poised on shell-studded rocks, the black beads of their eyes unmoving; large spider crabs that scuttled past with an odd sideways motion; hordes of shell creatures of all shapes and colors. It was a world he loved—had loved since his assignment to Waimea-Roa three years before. He knew every foot of Abiang Lagoon, named for the chain's principal atoll, just as he knew every sandy cove of the twenty-two mile-long L-shaped string of atolls which formed the Waimea-Roa group. They lay on the breast of the South Pacific like a carelessly-flung string of pearls, except that their pearl-luster sands were dotted with waving cocoanut palms and the lesser foliage of fern, pandanus, mulberry and breadfruit. He knew its beaches and villages and people, knew them and loved them and devoutly hoped he would never be transferred. Not that it was likely with his IQ rating.

He rolled on his back and lay for a long while watching the silvery bubbles of expired air shoot toward the paler surface waters. Finally he pulled his water watch close to his face and sighed. Seven a.m.—time for work. He twisted around and swam leisurely, breaking surface close to the shore, pausing to admire the beauty of the sundrenched lagoon. Tall wind-bent cocoanut palms shaded beaches which gleamed like ropes of coral sand. On the opposite side, by the low-lying barrier reef, the ragged yellow sails of Paha Jon's outrigger lay idle in the still air.

He contemplated the scene with quiet satisfaction. Waimea-Roa was a peaceful oasis in a turbulent yet strangely stagnant world, where the future seemed but a mirror-reflection of the past. The centuries had passed it by. The atolls remained much as they had been at time of the Atomic War, nearly 500 years before. And how many centuries before that? Elsewhere men were mining and farming the sea-bottoms, building domed cities on the ocean floors—living in crowded mainland communities, packed so close together that, for the workers, all semblance of privacy had long-since vanished. Elsewhere people were rigidly separated according to caste—LIQ's and MIQ's and HIQ's, the low, middle and high IQ's; a man's standing was determined by his brain or, more correctly, the IQ rating that was as much a part of his ego as his name. But not here. Waimea-Roa seemed almost forgotten by the bustling outside. It was the backwash of the world.

HE raised his eyes. Several miles beyond the reef Black Chimney Rock jutted high above the sea. The morning light gave it a brilliant sheen, more like a man-made artifact than anything created by random nature. It was, he knew, the hard core of a small volcanic mountain whose softer shell had eroded away. A black dot moved reef-ward from the rock, splitting the combers like a playful dolphin until, finally, it vanished beneath the waves. August Cominger riding his torp, returning from one of his frequent explorations of the sea-bottom, he thought. Cominger was a hermit who had appeared in the atolls years before, building a small house on the bluffs of Te-Tai, a miniature atoll adjoining Abiang. He had sought neither friends nor acquaintances and, in time, had become almost a legend. Krull felt a tinge of envy. Torps were costly. The hermit owned the only one in the atolls. He was free to scour the seas, adventures Krull could but dream of. Maybe, perhaps, he'd have a torp someday; but it didn't appear likely on his salary.

He remembered the time, sighed and swam the remaining few strokes to the beach, removed his gear and started along a well-worn path leading inland through the dense foliage. The greenery abruptly thinned and he came to Abiang's central village, a scattering of native huts and plastic houses along the atoll's single road, which ended in a central square.

Krull's house—a standard green plastic portable model, as befitted his station as an agent of police—stood at one end of the square immediately adjacent to a cubical concrete and plasto-glass building whose entrance bore the legend: Headquarters, Agency of Police, Territory of Waimea-Roa. A smaller sign under it read: Martin Jonquil, Inspector—Agent in Charge.

He entered his small bachelor quarters, stripped and ducked under a shower. His strong slim body was burned to the mahogany color of a native, a far cry from the comparative whiteness of his skin when he had lived along the wind-swept shores of Cook Strait, in his native New Zealand. His thoughts were mellow. To an aspiring young agent the atolls represented the end of the line, the end of promotions, the end of everything. He grinned ruefully. There was no question why he'd drawn the atolls. He had stood at the foot of his class, IQ 113 on SPIM, the Standard Police Intelligence Measure. His classmates had drawn Greater London, New Berlin, Tokyo Two, Nome, Sydney, the massive California, all the large centers of population and intrigue; and he had been sent to Waimea-Roa. He was glad.

He dried himself and slipped into a pair of thigh-length tan trousers and matching short sleeved shirt, put on a sun helmet and sandals. Finally—it was a regulation requirement—he donned a shoulder holster containing his snubbed service revolver and flinging the black cape of office around his shoulder walked next door to the station.

MORNING, Derek." A small wizened half-breed of indeterminate age and a perpetually-cheery smile returned the greeting.

"The old man's waiting for you."

"Thanks." He flung Derek a mock salute and crossed the small room, knocking lightly on the Inspector's door.

"Come in."

He entered, idly wondering what was in his superior's mind. "Good morning, Martin."

"Morning, Max." Jonquil briefly glanced up from a paper he was studying. "Sit down—be with you in a second."

"Thanks." Krull slid into a battered chair and idly studied his superior, a middle-aged stocky man with slivers of silver coursing through his black hair. His nose was prominent, beaked, his lips full and square chin cleft. His fingers drummed restlessly on the desk while he read, a sign he was disturbed. Krull's thoughts were pleasant. There had been a deep friendship between them from the start. In a way, it was a father-son relationship, yet more comradely. They swam the lagoon, dived, fished, drank together, and shared a mutual hobby, art. Krull rated himself as fair, excelling in figure sketches; he rated the quiet Jonquil as tops. The Inspector's forte was seascapes executed in sweeping strokes. Jonquil rated unusually high for an agent: IQ 172. He could have been almost anything, Krull thought. But he had chosen the police; ironically, he had been shanghaied to Waimea-Roa.

The Inspector finished, pushed the paper aside and contemplated the younger man a moment before speaking, his dark eyes grave and brooding. Krull grew uneasy.

"Max, you're going to leave the atolls…for a while."

"Why?" Krull asked, startled.

"Orders." He indicated the paper on his desk.

The younger agent breathed deeply. "I suppose it had to come some day," he said simply, "but I won't like it. I'd always hoped to stay here."

"It's just a job—a special job. You'll return when it's over," Jonquil encouraged.

"That's something," Krull said, relieved. "Where to?"

"Sydney."

"Sydney?"

"The House of the Prime Thinker."

"What!"

"You'll report to him direct." His eyes met and held Krull's. "It's a confidential job."

He sat back and stared at the Inspector. No, Jonquil wasn't joking; he meant it—every word. A minor police agent from the backwaters of the South Pacific was ordered to report to Ben Yargo—in person!—the most powerful man on the face of the globe. It didn't make sense. It was a moment before he could put his disbelief into words.

"There must be some mistake."

"There's no mistake."

"Look, Martin"—he leaned forward and spoke with tumbling words—"I'm a plain agent, IQ 113, with all my duty in the atolls. There's got to be a mistake."

"No mistake," Jonquil reiterated.

"But…"

Jonquil cut him off with a shake of his head. Krull looked reproachful. "Okay, there's no mistake, but explain it," he implored. "It doesn't make sense."

Jonquil leaned back and stared thoughtfully at the ceiling while he fished a cigarette from his pocket, lit it, and blew a cloud of smoke upward.

"I'm not informed of the details," he said. "You know how orders are—pieces of paper with times and dates and destinations. But I can surmise. I suppose the Prime Thinker has some sort of investigation in which he can't use local police. Perhaps the police are the subject of it; I don't know. Perhaps it's a job that requires an outsider, someone not committed to local politics. Those are my surmises."

"But why me? I'm IQ 113. Why not a high-rated agent?"

"IQ 113's not bad," Jonquil reproved.

"Don't sell me, I'm not sensitive on the score." Krull grinned weakly. "Besides, it's a matter of public record—and 113's not enough to solve a rape in a cage with two rabbits."

"I don't know what the job is, but you can handle it," Jonquil replied confidently. "The Prime Thinker wouldn't tab you without reviewing your record."

"What record—tossing a wife-beater in the cage for the night?"

"You can handle it."

"Okay, so I can handle it. When do I leave?" A tremor ran through his body, and he tried to suppress it.

"Tomorrow morning."

"So soon?" Krull asked.

"On the nine o'clock carrier. Reservations are made." Jonquil smiled briefly. "Why not take the day off, rest up."

"Thanks." Krull answered bleakly. He urgently needed to escape. "Think I'll go swimming."

KRULL managed to keep his composure as he left the station. He nodded casually to Derek, remarking he wouldn't be back for the day and returned to his house. He stood for a while with his hand still on the doorknob, looking at a sketch of Paha Jon's granddaughter, Rea. She had large almond eyes above a straight nose, a heart-shaped mouth. Her hair was long, straight, and wisps fell over one shoulder. She wore a provocative smile—and little else. He knew the meaning of the smile—knew it well. He sighed and donned his trunks, then picked up his swim gear and headed for the lagoon.

The cool green water felt good again, particularly after the session he'd just been through. He swam beneath the surface until he reached a particular coral head he knew—he and Rea sometimes played tag there—and allowed his body to relax and drift. It was clean down under the lagoon, clean and quiet, a place where a man could think.

He thought and felt the tension come. Tension and fear. It nibbled at his mind, tugged at his nerves, ran through his brain and gave birth to the beginning of panic; he banished it with effort. Years ago he had learned to live with the fear; then, in the quiet backwaters of Waimea-Roa, it had vanished, replaced with peace and security. Now it was on him again.

Esper. He was an esper. Worse, a hidden esper. If they caught him now he'd have to undergo surgery, have the mind power removed. Not that he would mind that—he very seldom used it—but it would cost him his job, place him under a social stigma, make him an outcast. Paha Jon's granddaughter—no woman—would have him. Not an esper!

He looked across the years, resurrecting fragments of memory, his first knowledge of what an esper was—what it meant. He had been playing games with his mother. What games? He forgot now; but suddenly she had looked strangely at him. He could see her eyes (they were brown) grow strange, then fearful. He remembered his parents' whispers far into the night, their odd behavior. There were more games, guessing games.

His mother had appeared unnaturally constrained; her smile was a mask of sorrow.

What am I thinking of, Max?

A big ship. You're thinking of a big ship, Mama.

Now what?

Mr. Krinker's toy store. He's standing in the doorway.

Now who?

He didn't know. The pictures, never sharp, had faded away again as they so often did; but his mother persisted. He remembered his parents' looks, the tears in his mother's eyes. Finally they told him, explaining what a mutant telepath was in the simple kind words parents use when they try to explain things to children. Esper—he was different.

There had been countless admonitions.

Don't tell anyone.

Don't play guessing games.

She reminded him before school, questioned him every evening. Cautioned him.

Don't put down what the teacher is thinking on tests. Don't...don't...don't.

Little Max didn't. He had understood the meaning of some of the tests from the teacher's thoughts. So he grew, silent, alone, shunning his playmates until his mother warned him it was dangerous.

Don't be different.

HE decided early in life he couldn't shield his talent forever. If he erected a mindshield—a simple thing for an esper, he later learned—the shield was the give-away. If he didn't, the risk was equally great. Sooner or later he would encounter a legal esper; and legal espers shunned their hidden cousins, perhaps through envy of the greater freedom they enjoyed. Greater freedom'? No, it was a hunt, a constant hunt, a life of fear. In the end he hid another thing—his IQ. At an early age he figured that the smart kids would be placed with smart kids—greater danger. But if he were just a dumb kid... No matter, he hid his IQ as carefully as he hid his wild talent (the term they used). He tried to push the knowledge he was an esper from his mind, deny it by never using it. In time he scarcely realized he was any different from his playmates. Most of his school tests were ridiculously easy, but he seldom managed more than a passing mark. It was fun, in a way, the careful calculations to determine the range of scores he should make—the balancing to keep in the safe level of low-normals.

He made one more decision while still a boy: he would be a police agent. Police agents were mainly low MIQ's, low middle IQ's; a few—like those at the top—were superior. But he wouldn't be at the top, or anywhere near it. He made his decision for just one reason: the safest place to escape detection would be among the agents—he thought. And so he applied for admission to the World Police Academy.

Well, he was an agent now. But he was stepping into Ben Yargo's house, working under the eyes of the most brilliant mind on the planet. How long could he escape detection? How long? The question drummed through his brain.

CHAPTER THREE

EDWARD CROZENER, founder of the Empire of Earth, made Sydney, Australia, the planet Capital in 1999 A.D. (The old name Australia refers to the largest land mass in the world state of Anzaca, which includes the former New Zealand and adjacent South Pacific islands).

It was the logical choice.

Like other Anzaca metropoli, it escaped the severest blows of the Atomic War due to down-pole winds which held back radiation-polluted air. In the dark decades following the war (1970-2000 A.D.), it became the largest citadel of civilization—a beacon in a shattered world. Crozener decreed the Capital should never be moved. He wrote:

It shall remain as a symbol of human triumph over the madness of the atom.

Crozener's Second Law of Mankind—*The world shall be governed by intellect*—shaped planet government. Under his plan a Prime Thinker, who competed for office in publicly administered machine-scored intelligence tests, headed the planet. A Council of Six, elected in similar manner, with each member representing one of the planet's six major political subdivisions served as the advisory arm.

Under Crozerian principles the peoples of the world gradually fell into three classes determined solely by genetics—the low, middle and high IQ's (commonly called the LIQ's, MIQ's and HIQ's). Crozener's famous "60-35-5 proclamation" existed for generations: sixty percent manual laborers (LIQ's), thirty-five percent professional workers (MIQ's), and five percent representing the higher sciences, arts, administration and upper-government levels (HIQ's).

His edicts remained supreme, for centuries.

Blak Roko's
Post-Atomic Earthman.

* * *

THE great bluffs of the Sydney Heads—sheer sandstone cliffs towering over the sea—wheeled toward him below the seaplane carrier. Sydney Basin, enclosed on three sides by flat highlands, spun into view; the city was below. Wharves, jetties, beaches, factories, the neat geometric patterns of colored houses reaching to the far horizon whirled by; the harbor was alive with the ballooning spinnakers of sailing yachts. A long train of ore ships, their decks awash, threaded in through the narrow channel from the sea, towed by a powerful subtug. Their cargo, Krull knew, would be manganese, cobalt, iron and nickel ores from the ocean-bottom mines off Melville Deeps, a submerged city off the coast of Brisbane. He watched curiously. It was headed toward the southern side of the port, a section of the city which housed both the larger industrial plants and the residences of the LIQ's, mainly laborers of less than 100 IQ. It was a sprawling, dirty, crowded dark area, quite unlike the clean tree-shaded northern part of the city where the intellectual elite lived. The vastness of the city awed him. Fifteen million people. He smiled. There had been less than four thousand in Waimea-Roa. The stewardess' voice broke into his thoughts.

"Fasten your seat belt, please."

The plane banked, dropped toward the harbor, straightened and raced over a thin channel of water lined with docks; the pontoons touched down with a slight jolt and they taxied toward a float based at the bottom of a wide gangplank leading to street level. Krull loosened his safety strap and waited until the cabin was empty before picking up his bag and leaving. He stood for a moment among the milling people, trying to orient himself by the City's skyline. He would be met by an agent named Cranston ("Don't seek him out, let him find you."), his hotel quarters had been reserved; he would be escorted to the House of the Prime Thinker; he wouldn't wear police garb; he would be provided with essential papers. Just like that, all neat and wrapped up. He felt a trifle bitter. The details were too elaborate for Jonquil to know as little as he had proclaimed. Still...

"Mr. Krull." A hand tapped his elbow and it wasn't a question—it was a statement. He turned, staring at a short, rotund man wearing a wide smile that amply exhibited his dentures. His eyes were sky-blue, jovial, and although he wore a weave hat Krull guessed he was bald—it was that kind of face and figure.

"I'm Cranston." Krull gripped the almost dainty hand—it felt moist—and he winced. "Come along, I'll show you to your quarters."

Krull followed him up the gangplank. Cranston drove through a crowded thoroughfare, past pastel-tinted stores jammed by early afternoon shoppers. Krull was curious. He had almost forgotten the LIQ section with its dirty narrow streets, jammed shops and noise. Most of the people wore the somber grays or browns of workers, the men in sandals, shorts and open shirts and the women in simple tunics. Here and there he taught the flash of scarlets, emerald greens and lavenders, clothes which marked their wearers as middle or high IQ's. Not that dress was a matter of law, but few LIQ's could afford the luxury of color. Occasional huge photographs plastered on buildings reminded him that election was only two weeks away. He studied them curiously.

Yargo…Shevach…Harshberg…Sherif: the faces of the candidates for Prime Thinker stared out over the crowd in black-and-white, color, and a few were animated for sound.

Sherif's face intrigued him. It was a peasant face, hard, square and dark, but even in the photographs the eyes seemed alive. He remembered hearing he was anti-Crozener, a man who wanted to rebuild society and erase all class differences. (A dangerous trait!). He had been stoned, berated, but refused to budge from his principles. Krull found himself liking the man's looks. A huge cube suspended over one intersection displayed Yargo's face on each facet. The lips moved and a voice intoned:

Good government for all the people…Good government for all the people…

A monorail slid by, momentarily drowning the voice. Noisy street hawkers peddled their wares from plastic handcarts, competing with small dark shops that clung to the edges of the street like rows of kennels, each distinguishable only by its signs and displays of wares on outside racks. They came to another talkie photo of Yargo promising good government.

Supposing he loses Krull thought. The possibility momentarily startled him. What then?

THEY came to an area where the stores were spacious, well-lighted, almost stately in appearance. The streets were broad, lined with graceful eucalyptus trees and free of the numerous public TV screens found in the LIQ quarters.   The crowds had vanished, the noisy hawkers gone, replaced by a scattering of unhurried shoppers. The men wore pastel-colored shorts, open shirts and sheer capes that seemed to serve no purpose other than to testify to the affluence of the wearers. The women wore sheer clinging tunics (yellows and pinks were in vogue) designed to reveal more than conceal, and elaborate lacquered hair-styles—knots, buns and conical designs sprinkled with gems. All wore colored sandals. Sleek white bubble-topped Capricorns and luxurious Regals lined the curbs while uniformed chauffeurs passed the time watching dashboard TV's. Most of the buildings were topped with copter landings and a number of the small craft were darting between the building-formed canyons. Even the air seemed cleaner, as if it had been magically filtered.

Cranston kept up a steady line of chatter, pointing out the highlights as if Krull were a complete stranger to the world capital. The wide thoroughfare narrowed, the trees vanished and they entered a busy area that seemed a curious mixture of LIQ and MIQ, with businesses of all varieties.   Cranston turned abruptly down a ramp leading to a subterranean garage.

"The Edward Crozener Hotel, not fancy but comfortable." He turned the car over to an attendant and led Krull to a lift. The room assigned him proved light and airy, with a view overlooking St. George Avenue. It contained beside the few pieces of furniture a small private bath, the inevitable wall TV and a movie box with portable screen. Cranston caught his glance.

"Any kind of pix you want, from pornos to classics. Just ask the desk." He casually inspected the room. "Take it easy for the afternoon. I'll pick you up at nine tonight—sharp." He tossed the keys to Krull, gave a toothy smile and departed.

That's that, Krull thought, everything according to schedule, including a night visit with the ruler of the world. Personally he'd rather be swimming the waters of Abiang lagoon with Paha Jon's granddaughter. Or something. He sprawled in a chair to think things over. Something told him he'd better think straight.

After a while he turned on the TV. The screen glowed to life—a cream-faced man who looked like a cross between a mortician and an educator was making a pitch for distinctive clothing. He idly listened to the purring voice:

"Zarkman's clothes of distinction are the mark of high IQ. Look about you. When you see a man dressed in Zarkman's super togs, chances are he's IQ 150 or above. Remember, Zarkman's clothes come in all pastel shades—darker if desired—and are tailored to fit all occasions. Zarkman's clothes mean high IQ...Zarkman's clothes mean high IQ...Zarkman's clothes mean..."

He reached over disgustedly and snapped off the set, looking ruefully at his own dress. He didn't think they gave the impression of IQ 150.

THE knock came at the door at precisely 9:00 p.m., followed by the single spoken word: "Cranston." Krull opened it and the fat man beamed at him. "Ready?"

He nodded, closed the door behind him and followed Cranston to the car. They drove slowly through traffic, then faster as they reached the outskirts of the city where the crowded noisy streets gave way to wide tree-lined avenues and large well lighted homes set beyond park-like lawns. He turned onto a tree-lined lane spiraling upward toward a massive house, its lights agleam against the starry sky. He stopped at a sentry box, nodded genially without producing credentials and drove up the hill, parking under a portico. Nodding familiarly to a guard, he led Krull directly into the house. He had no time to look around; the agent made directly for the stairs.

I'm here. The thought startled him. Somehow he was there without being prepared for it. Did Yargo keep a peeper agent? Inwardly he was shaken. He had heard such rumors. He suppressed a touch of panic. Watch yourself...be on guard, every second. He had to keep unbidden thoughts from his mind.

No mind shields, no mind shields. Don't think the word esper.

Think of the lagoon, he told himself. Think of formless swirling waters, fish schools, sea fronds and coral. No, that was no good. It wasn't natural. An esper would recognize such thoughts in a place like this as an evasion, a deliberate effort to mass tangible symbols.

Don't think of espers.

Cranston started up the stairs with Krull at his heels. He felt sweaty, nervous and anxious, all at the same time; fearful he would make a slip.

No mind shields.

Think of Rea Jon—that day on the beach—how you tried to capture her provocative smile in a sketch. They were halfway up when a woman appeared above them and started down the stairs. Krull had the impression of youth, vitality, a well-formed body.

No mind shield. Think of Rea Jon.

Cranston nodded familiarly to her, then she was past. Krull heard the tattoo of her sandals suddenly cease, had the feeling she had stopped, turned—was watching him!

No mind shields.

The thought popped unbidden into his mind and he desperately tried to concentrate on Rea Jon as Cranston led him through a door.

A square man with dark—was there some silver?—hair rose from a desk at the far side of the room and the agent halted.

"The Prime Thinker...Agent Krull." Cranston wheeled and left, with as little ceremony as that, leaving Krull to stare at the solid figure advancing toward him. For an instant he was speechless.

YARGO extended a hand and smiled. Krull grasped it feeling bewildered. He looked so natural, so friendly—not at all like the stern visage so often seen on the TV s; not like the world's number one brain. What was it? IQ 219. Yargo indicated a seat across from his desk saying something about being happy he had consented to the assignment. Consented? He answered automatically:

"It's an honor. Sir."

His eyes dropped to the desk and he saw a thick volume with the name Alexander embossed in gold across the cover. Yargo caught his look and smoothly swept the book to one side without appearing to do so, then went through the formalities, went through them nicely. Krull thought. He asked a few questions about the atolls, hoped Krull would enjoy his present assignment—stated he had chosen him on the basis of his record. All very smooth. The name Alexander popped into his mind while Yargo talked. Alexander—who was Alexander? Alexander the Great was an obscure figure in pre-atomic history; it must be some other Alexander. He dismissed the thought and returned his attention to the square face with the pale blue eyes.

Yargo offered him a cigarette, which he accepted, extending a light in return. The older man leaned back and took a few puffs.

No mind shields.

The thought popped into his mind and he tried to banish it by concentrating on the figure opposite him.

Don't think it...Don't think: it...No mind shield.

There, he had thought it and Yargo hadn't batted an eye. Concentrate, don't think that word. *Esper*—the word formed in his brain and he concentrated harder on the features of the man sitting opposite him: thick neck, heavy shoulders, small ears, squat...

Yargo's expression altered, became serious and Krull tried to follow his words, feeling all at once easier. Of course Yargo wasn't an esper. He had nothing to worry about. Unless Yargo kept an esper guard. The Prime Thinker was saying he had chosen him because he needed an agent with no local ties—Jonquil's words!—either with the police or other government officials. Krull felt his tensions melt. The Prime Thinker paused, then added:

"Before I describe your present assignment I would like to caution you on the need for absolute secrecy."

"I understand."

Yargo hesitated, then said slowly: "It's an investigation into the possibility of illegal atomic research."

Krull started imperceptibly, but Yargo didn't appear to notice. He related the evidence, and Krull made a mental note of the name, William Bixby Butterfield, the radiation victim, thinking it might provide a starting point.

"There are a few points you might consider," Yargo pointed out. "The police intelligence appears to know nothing of the situation. Assuming that's true, and assuming there is some sort of conspiracy involving atomic research, it must be small. Also, for obvious reasons, it must be centered in a fairly remote place. Finally, it must be restricted to the research phase because of the obvious impossibility of building an actual reactor without the knowledge leaking out." He finished speaking and studied the agent casually, but Krull had the distinct impression he was being dissected atom by atom.

"In other words, the Prime Thinker doesn't believe the danger is...perhaps...critical?" he asked, after an interval of silence.

"Any atomic research is dangerous," Yargo replied. "If it exists, I don't believe it has reached an advanced state. But that's why you're here—to keep that from happening." He hesitated, and described the reaction of each Council member to the proposed investigation. "That's so you'll get a clear mental picture," he added.

Krull nodded and he continued:

"One other thing, I realize it'll make your task much more difficult but you'll have to mask your activities. We can't afford to alarm either the conspirators—if they exist—or the public. No one must know what you're looking for. No one but myself, and of course the Manager and the Council."

Krull readily saw his point but remembering his supposed IQ managed to retain a blank look. Yargo waited, expectantly, and when he didn't speak, said softly:

"Dope—you'll be investigating a supposed dope ring. You're working for me because the ring may involve members of my Government. But don't give any explanations unless you have to," There was a note of pity in his voice—the pity a genius might feel for a moron, Krull thought. He allowed a look of comprehension to cross his face and exclaimed:

"Dope, of course, I'm glad you thought of it. A perfect cover." He hesitated, as if momentarily confused. "What kind of dope?"

"Heroin," Yargo snapped impatiently.

"Yes, heroin," Krull echoed slowly. The interview closed with Yargo's repeated caution to maintain secrecy; he rose, pumped Krull's hand again and escorted him to the top of the stairs, Cranston was waiting at the bottom. Krull started down. *No mind shield.* He began hurrying, as if anxious to return to the cover of night.

THE door had scarcely closed behind him before the girl he had passed on the stairs started toward the library with rapid steps. She knocked at the door and opened it without waiting for an answer. Yargo looked up inquiringly and his face softened; in the eight years since his wife had died his daughter had become his whole world. Or almost.

"Father, who was that man who just left?"

"Why?" He looked curiously at her. Jan seldom bothered with his visitors and was even less seldom disturbed; now she was visibly agitated.

"He's an esper," she announced.

"What?" Yargo rose from his chair, incredulous.

"Yes, he's an esper." Jan repeated calmly. "I saw it in his mind when I passed him on the stairs."

He looked alarmed. "Do you think he…?"

"No," she cut in, "he wasn't paying attention to me."

Yargo gave an audible sigh of relief. Jan was a telepath. Fortunately, he had discovered it when she was little more than a babe, had tutored her so well that no one had ever suspected. Now, that her mother was dead, only he knew. Not that it was a crime to be an esper. Still…

"Is it bad?" she asked worriedly. Yargo brought his thoughts back to the present.

"Yes, it's bad," he said simply. "Tell me exactly what you saw—or should I say read?" He smiled faintly.

"He was scared—tried to keep thinking about mind shields."

"What else?"

"He was trying to mask his thoughts, keep them innocuous—tried to resurrect strong memories in an effort to over-ride the word *mind shield.*"

"What thoughts?"

She hesitated. "The information may be important," Yargo said sharply.

"A Polynesian girl on a beach—a naked girl."

"Oh." Yargo masked a smile. "At least our esper appears normal."

"Can I be of any help?" she asked tentatively.

"You stay out of this," Yargo observed quietly. "You can't take any chances now."

"I wouldn't be," she replied. "I know how to use mind shields even if your visitor doesn't."

"Maybe," he relented, "we'll see."

He watched her leave engrossed in thought. No, it wasn't a crime to be an esper, but it carried a heavy social stigma. Hidden espers when discovered were subject to surgery to remove the mind power, the penalty of their deception. Fear of the mutant's talent was strong, tenacious. He thanked God she had learned to use mind shields.

HE finally stirred, reached into a desk drawer for a dossier and began scanning it, information he had already digested. But there might be a clue. His eyes flashed down the sheet. Max Krull, IQ 113, graduate of the World Police Academy, Sydney Campus, class of 2446 A.D., 5'10", 170 pounds, dark short-cropped hair, muscular, small mole on lobe of left ear. He dropped his eyes: Unimaginative, steady, loyal, dependable, unsophisticated; no highly placed friends or relatives, no political affiliations; normal sex life, friendly, unobtrusive…only talent appears to lie in art—a good hand at sketches; excellent memory for detail. He read to the last line. *Capable of only limited mental work.* The dossier was signed:

Martin Jonquil.

Inspector-Agent of Police.

Territory of Waimea-Roa.

He thoughtfully tucked it back into the drawer. So, Max Krull, IQ 113 was an esper—a hidden esper. No doubt the IQ rating was as false as his talent was real. He cursed softly. He had gone to great pains to pick the exact man for the job. Now he was committed—Krull knew the details. And Krull was an esper! The over-riding fact burned in his mind: the investigation was of first magnitude importance. The future of mankind, perhaps, hung on the agent's performance; what he did, whom he saw, what he said…*what he found.* He had needed just the right man, one whose every move was predictable. And he had got Krull. Only Krull was a fake, a man traveling under a mask, a man who wasn't what he was supposed to be.

The fate of the world hung on an esper.

He held his hand out and studied it curiously. Steady. Strange, it should be shaking. He forced Krull from his mind and picked up the thick volume he had been reading before the agent's arrival. Its archaic cover proclaimed it a pre-atomic publication: Alexander. He read far into the night. Alexander the Great.

He had use for Alexander.

CHAPTER FOUR

IVAN SHEVACH, World Manager, thoughtfully pursed his lips while scanning a photostatic copy of a dossier on his desk. His face, pale under the indirect lighting, was vaguely puzzled, as if some obvious fact were eluding him. He reached the end of the record and backtracked, picking out isolated hits of information of particular interest. Max Krull, Agent of Police, Territory of Waimea-Roa, had, it seemed an IQ 113. Then there was the end notation: *Capable of only limited work.* It didn't jibe with his idea of the kind of agent needed for such a job. After a while he looked up. Jordan Gullfin, his chief of special agents, was watching stolidly. The Manager contemplated his flat face, smashed nose and heavy sensuous lips before murmuring :

"Interesting—very interesting."

"That's what I thought." Gullfin's voice was a husky horn in the small office, Shevach continued his musing as if he hadn't heard him.

"Why did Yargo pick an IQ 113 agent? And why one from Waimea-Roa?" He raised his voice. "Why that particular man?"

"Maybe he didn't want someone too bright. This guy sounds like a fishbrain."

"I can understand a use for that kind of agent."

Gullfin failed to detect the sarcasm. "He's a fishbrain," he repeated.

"That's the whole point." Shevach looked up sharply. "You're keeping him under constant surveillance?"

"Not around the clock. I didn't think it was that important."

"I do. From now on it's around the clock—and let me do the thinking. I want to know every move he makes, everything he learns, every contact—and the reason for the contact. It's important, Gullfin." He smiled narrowly. "It could make the difference whether or not you become Chief of World Agents."

"You'll get it," Gullfin promised quickly. "He won't get a second of privacy."

"Are his rooms bugged?"

"They will be."

"Cameras?"

"We'll even have them in the bathroom."

"You're keeping Yargo covered?"

"Every move," Gullfin boasted. "We got Saxon, his confidential secretary, in the bin."

"You can trust him?" he asked. Gullfin grinned evilly. "With those pleasure palace photos we got of him, we sure can. He'll come through, all right, and he's got Yargo's complete confidence…"

"Excellent," Shevach cut in. "I want to know every development, immediately, and that applies to all of Yargo's contacts."

"You'll get 'em." Gullfin rose to go, then stood with a faintly puzzled look in his eyes. "Personally, I think this guy Yargo is loose upstairs, at least according to Saxon."

Shevach became instantly alert. "How so?"

"Hell, he goes to sleep nights reading about some stiff that's been dead a century, at least."

"Oh…?" The Manager looked curious. "Who?"

"Alexander—some bird named Alexander."

"Alexander the Great?"

"Yeah, that's the guy. Like I said, he's been dead a long time."

Shevach watched his lieutenant depart, engrossed with his last bit of information. "Alexander the Great." He thoughtfully snapped on the intercom.

"Gelda, get me all the books and tapes available on Alexander the Great—biographies, histories, everything." He cut the connection and sat musing. After a while he got up, walked across the room and opened an inlaid paneled door, staring for a moment at the array of dials exposed. He moved a switch, punched a button, and a counter began spinning. Behind the panel a selector moved across tables of random numbers and finally stopped: the number 11234 appeared in a glass window. He moved his hand to another circular dial and spun the number on the indicator reading. Something whirred inside the machine and a small booklet popped into a slot at the base of the console.

He picked it up and eyed it curiously: CLOIM, the Crail-Levy-Osman Intelligence Measure. He returned to his desk, read the instructions on the first page, slid out the answer sheet, glanced at his desk clock and went to work. He finished with three minutes left to go, sighed with satisfaction, then returned to the machine and inserted the answer sheet in another slot. A mechanism hummed to life as electronic scanners scored the paper. Within seconds a red light blinked above another window and the number 216 appeared. IQ 216 on a randomly selected subject wasn't too bad, he thought. Still, he had to do better than that at the polls. He closed the panel and returned to the desk.

HABIT was stronger than comfort. Krull awoke at dawn despite the fact the city still slept, elated with realization he was on his own. It was his second full day in Sydney. He had spent the first getting acquainted with the city again and, incidentally, learning the names of leading government officials he might have occasion to contact. Yeah, he was on his own. He had a job to do—clear cut—and no one to tell him how to do it. Not even Yargo. The Prime Thinker had done little more than suggest, had appeared content to let him steer his own course.

He relived the interview over morning coffee. There were things he liked—and didn't like. But he definitely liked the feel of freedom. Cranston's last act (Who was Cranston, by the way?) had been to deliver his official credentials, together with a short speech. He couldn't forget the speech. Summed up it gave him full freedom of action—to go where he wanted, see who he wanted, request assistance and a lot more. The credentials witnessed the fact the roly-poly Cranston hadn't exaggerated. They gave him the full stamp of authority; they also bore the Prime Thinker's official seal and counter-signature. All that was good. Against it rested the fact he knew virtually nothing of the task confronting him; only that a man had died of radiation, an atomic conspiracy might exist—somewhere in the world. That could mean Antarctica, Tibet, the upper

Amazon, Sydney, or one of the floating or subsea cities. It could be anywhere. Yet Yargo must have realized the magnitude of the task. *But why had he picked an IQ 113 agent?* He'd probably find out, he thought ruefully.

Krull was at the door of the Bureau of Public Records at 8:00 a.m. sharp, much to the annoyance of the LIQ clerk, a gaunt middle-aged woman with a tired face. She reluctantly contemplated her steaming cup of coffee before deciding in his favor.

"Good morning," He smiled cheerfully. "I'd like to see the autopsy report on the death of William Bixby Butterfield." He gave the place and date of death and watched her disappear between two ceiling-high rows of ledgers. He noticed a picture of Shevach tacked to one wall underscored by the words:

I promise government reform.

The reminder of the coming election caused him to grimace. He wasn't certain he wanted to be in Sydney when the event occurred, or in any large city for that matter. The election of the Prime Thinker was a world holiday for all except skeletal maintenance, police and public utility crews. It was a day when all laws except those governing felonies were suspended, when revelry and debauchery reigned. It was the one day of every five years when all class distinction was cast aside—when LIQ's and MIQ's and HIQ's intermingled indiscriminately in public and private celebration to hail the new ruler; a time when the elite HIQ's of both sexes demonstrated their democracy by seeking LIQ partners for the night. There would be brawls, riots, jubilant merriment, and a lot of headaches the next day. He wasn't at all certain he was prepared for it, especially after the quiet of the atolls. He saw the clerk returning with a puzzled look.

"Mind repeating that name?"

"Butterfield—William Bixby Butterfield."

"That's what I thought you said." Her face wrinkled in thought followed by startled comprehension. "Just a moment." She briskly turned away and headed for an office at the far end of the room. He watched her curiously. The name had clicked—had set some wheels in motion in the gaunt clerk's head. He was pondering it when she emerged from the office followed by a man he thought must be her boss.

Her boss?

He took a second look and decided against the conjecture. The fellow accompanying the clerk was tall, thin; a lantern-shaped face with a beaked nose and livid slash across one cheek giving it the impression of a perpetual sneer. His eyes were black beady gimlets, his ears small and close-cropped. A hard face, Krull decided. He took a second look. A LIQ or MIQ who lived for the semblance of authority he enjoyed over his fellow men, he thought. An agent. He instinctively noted the man's clothes—tan tropic shorts and open-necked shirt with a light brown cape clasped at the neck. He wore sandals and his knees were knobby; but the clothes didn't fit the face. They reached the counter and the clerk stepped deferentially aside. Her companion fixed Krull with gimlet eyes and rasped:

"You the fellow asking about Butterfield?"

"That's right." Krull didn't like his tone.

"Why?"

"That's my business. It's a public record."

Hardface's lips wreathed in a sneer. "Maybe it's my business, too." He reached up and moved his cape back, displaying an agent's badge—and a small automatic in an underarm holster. He looked at Krull as if expecting him to flinch.

"Okay, so you're an agent," Krull said calmly. "Now just trot out the ledger like a nice fellow."

"Maybe you don't know it but you've got some questions to answer," Hardface barked.

KRULL sighed and reached toward his pocket—Hardface's body stiffened. His hand came back with his credentials and he shoved them under the agent's eyes.

"Okay, there they are," he said. "Now let's get the files, like a good public servant."

Hardface glanced at the credentials, took a longer second look, then squinted at Krull. "Don't mean a thing to me. I don't work for the gent."

Krull was taken aback. He hadn't expected that. "Okay, gimme your boss," he snapped. "Maybe he's heard of Ben Yargo."

"Maybe," the agent said, and added: "I work for Jordan Gullfin." He stared at Krull as if the name should have brought awed recognition, and appeared disappointed when it didn't. "He's the Manager's special agent," he added.

"The Manager works for my boss," Krull said drily.

"He won't—after this month." Hardface spun on his heel and moved toward a phone. So that's it, Krull thought, the Manager's boys are already savoring victory. Hardface dialed, spoke briefly into the instrument, cupping the mouthpiece with his hand. He finished and came back.

"Gullfin says okay." He gave Krull a malignant look, nodded toward the clerk and vanished back into the office.

The file on William Butterfield was interesting. William Bixby Butterfield, age 52, had checked into the New Empire Hotel at 7:00 p.m. on November 23—the last he was seen alive. A curious maid found him dead in bed. Reason for the death: Coronary occlusion. Well, the doc, whoever it was, had had the sense to falsify the record and contact Yargo immediately. But if the real reason for his death was secret, why Hardface? It was obvious the Manager didn't intend to keep the file secret. He merely wanted to ascertain who might he curious about it— and why.

Krull picked up the details: identification, physical description, IQ, occupation, and all the facts that survive a man who departs the world via the coroner route. Further down: survived by George Henry Butterfield, IQ 138, public works engineer. His address was listed as Number 27, Cell A-15, Benbow Deep, which he knew was a submerged city lying below the shallow waters of the Pacific west of the Mala Take Atolls. So, William Bixby Butterfield had a living brother. He whistled. Yargo hadn't mentioned that. He studied the notation carefully. It was made in a slightly different hand and there were faint differences in the intensity of stroke and color of ink. Might not mean a thing, he reasoned. The information might not have been available at time the original record was made. He made a few pertinent notes, slid the ledger back across the counter, smiled at the clerk's suspicious look and departed.

His next stop was the Bureau of Missing Persons. He didn't expect it to yield much—it only included local disappearances—but it was a start. The Bureau turned out to be under the charge of a beetle-browed agent with heavy jowls and a cigar shoved deep into his mouth. As in the case at the Bureau of Public Records, his request was passed from the clerk to the heavy-faced man now staring at him. The latter eyed him suspiciously while he gave his request: a look at the files of persons who had dropped from sight during the fall of 2444. The agent looked incredulous.

"That runs into the hundreds." He spoke with the tone of a man humoring a child.

"I know."

"What's your reason?"

"Do I have to have one to look at a public record?"

"You do—in this case." Hard piggish eyes weighed him warily.

Krull sighed and produced his credentials. The agent stared at them, then back at Krull. His eyes were cold and hostile. "Your reason?"

"An investigation," Krull snapped.

"Of what?"

"That's my business."

The agent dropped his eyes to the credentials again and a look of fear suffused his face. Why? Krull took a chance and did something he had seldom done before: he peeped him.

Fear, formless chaotic fear mingled with hate, a kaleidoscopic pattern of shifting emotions without clear form or content; fear and hate and suspicion, welded together and reaching out to engulf Krull. A name flashed into the mental pattern, blinking on and off like a neon sign: Gullfin…Gullfin…Gullfin. The thought-pattern jelled and the name was accompanied by the imagery of a bullet-skulled man with mean black eyes, a smashed nose and a forehead that reminded him of pictures he had seen of ancient cavemen. His mouth was heavy-lipped, sensuous, his skin swarthy, splotched and unhealthy.

Gullfin!

THE name screamed in the brain of the agent sitting opposite him. Krull felt his hands grow sweaty and recoiled involuntarily, quickly withdrawing from the hateful mind. It was like suddenly returning to consciousness again—he became aware of the agent staring oddly at him. Momentarily he felt scared. Risky…penetrating another person's mind. He wouldn't try that again; not until he learned more about the esper talent he had so seldom used—not until he learned the tricks. But he had learned something: Gullfin had his slimy fingers in a lot of pies. Gullfin—or his master, the Manager?

"All right," the agent snarled. Suddenly he stopped. He was staring past Krull's shoulder with a look of half fear, half respect. He started to say something but couldn't seem to get the words out.

"Mr. Krull?"

He turned at the well-modulated voice and looked at an extremely tall thin man with a lean, almost skeletal face, framed by shaggy locks of gray hair. He topped Krull by a good six or eight inches.

"I'm Peter Merryweather." He stuck out a large bony hand, smiling pleasantly. Krull shook it automatically.

"Let's step into a private office and have a chat." Krull started to ask why and bit the question off. Merryweather's face was open, honest, clearly devoid of any guile. Almost too forthright! He felt an instinctive liking and trust of the man, yet tinged with doubt. He nodded and followed him into a room marked Albert Skoda. Captain-Inspector of Agents. A short burly man rose at their entrance, his face immediately respectful.

"Mind if we use your office a moment, Al?"

"Not a bit, Mr. Merryweather." The agent's deferential tone told him his host was a person of standing. As the agent slipped out the door, Merryweather motioned to a chair and sat down behind the desk.

"You're probably curious, Mr. Krull." His eyes twinkled. "Gullfin reported your encounter with Agent Cathecart at the BuPub-Records. I thought you'd probably show up here so I came over."

Krull made a mental note of Hardface's name. He asked:

"You are…?"

"An assistant to the Manager, sort of public relations function. At least that's one of my jobs." His lips wrinkled pleasantly. "By Crozener's ghost, work for the government and they pile the jobs on until you really don't know what you're doing. But I don't think I can complain."

Krull masked his surprise.

"I know what you're thinking: What the hell am I doing in the act?"

"Something like that."

"When Gullfin told me about your credentials, I figured Cathecart probably gave you a rough time. Thought I'd better step in and smooth the path."

"Why?" Krull challenged. Merryweather seemed too smooth.

"Public relations," he explained. "If you've got a job to do, I'm here to help, not hinder. Just let me know how I can be of aid."

"Sounds good," Krull admitted. "How about…Gullfin?"

"To hell with Gullfin." He continued amiably. "He's playing politics—thinks Shevach's due to win the election and he's trying to butter himself up for the post of Chief of World Agents." He caught the surprised look on Krull's face and smiled.

"I serve the Manager, too," he said slowly, "but I'm honest and try to do a conscientious job. Shevach's not really a bad sort when you get to know him. If he seems hard, it's because he's got a tough job. You can't penalize a man for being ambitious."

"No—I suppose not."

"Anyway, the doors are open. If you need anything—or run into any obstacles—just give me a buzz. You can catch me at this number." He tore a sheet off the desk pad, scribbled briefly on it and shoved it across the desk, then rose. Krull pocketed the paper and scrambled to his feet, trying to assess Merryweather's role. His ready admission that the Manager was his master was in his favor. Only something was wrong. The tall man was too genial, too ready to help. Help? Well, he'd see…

"We'll start in by clearing the way for you to get access to all the records—every damn one." Merryweather promised. "Follow me." He led the way to the outer reception desk, gave brief orders to the beetle-brewed agent in charge and waved toward the files.

"They're all yours. Webster here will be glad to help you." He shook hands with him and left. Krull turned to face the scowling agent.

He quickly found Webster had been right. People seemed to be disappearing by the scores—for the most part, harassed, debt-ridden fathers who just gave up the struggle; to a lesser extent, drunks, the unstable and ill. In the end he wearily closed the file, thinking he would check again when he had more time. Just now the lead on Butterfield seemed too hot to let hang.

KRULL got off the monorail from Tonga surface station and looked curiously around the main station of Benbow Deep. He had never been to a submerged city before, although he had seen them often enough on TV. He felt momentarily uneasy. For one thing, he could look up through the cell's plastitex ceiling—the monorail station was located in cell T-12—into the ocean. It was a darker shade than the clear bottom waters of Abiang Lagoon but, he thought, the city was built on a sea bottom plateau at the hundred meter level. The long reds and yellows of the spectrum had been filtered out, leaving only the deepened blues. He searched the ceiling—carefully until he caught movement. It was true, then, you could see the marine life from the city streets. He had heard that. He recalled that the first subsea city had been made of opaque materials and mass claustrophobia had resulted. Since then transparent materials had been used. Everyone was happier—so the psychmasters claimed—but he wasn't so sure. The idea of three hundred feet of ocean pressing down on him wasn't exactly reassuring.

He studied his surroundings curiously. The cell had a long rectangular shape beneath its cylindrical roof and narrowed abruptly at either end where it joined adjacent cells. The narrow street running down the center of the cell was lined with businesses on one side—extremely crowded by surface standards—while the monorail station occupied the other. In case of disaster, each cell could be isolated by electrically-controlled doors fitted in slots below street level where the cells adjoined. The entire system was monitored at a central station where watchmen scanned the city's warning devices around the dock. If he were asked to describe the general topography of Benbow Deep, he would liken it to a string of sausages, he decided. The cell was illuminated by soft indirect lighting; the temperature was pleasantly cool and the filtered air clean and fresh. Life under the seas had its benefits as well its dangers. For one, there was perfect control of the environment. Weather, to the dwellers of the deep, was an almost forgotten topic. A cab drew up.

"Transport, sir?"

"Yes, thanks." The rear door slid open and he sank into a deep foam cushion, noting the small vehicle was equipped with a panel which, if desired, could be raised to afford complete privacy.

"Where to?"

He gave Butterfield's address and settled back as the vehicle jerked into motion. He watched the passing cells with interest. Each was dedicated to a specialized activity—seafarm products processing, commercial business, a milling cell where great trains of carriers traveling on sea-bottom rails came through the locks bearing manganese, cobalt and nickel ores from the depths beyond the city. They passed through a clinical cell containing a hospital and small mental ward and, adjacent to it, an educational cell which housed the city's schools at all levels. Most of the buildings were of plastic materials in various pastel shades; a few were ornamented in solid brick, coral block, and synthetic stone and wood. His interest picked up when they reached the recreation cells. One was devoted to swimming and aquatic sports; another to gymnastics and games; a third, constructed of pink plastitex, was illuminated by indirect rose lighting.

"Pleasure cell," the driver informed him. "Want to stop?"

"Maybe later." Krull grinned. "Just now I'm a working man."

"What's your tastes?"

"What do you have to offer?" Krull countered.

"Everything," the driver said pridefully. "There's nothing in the world we haven't got right here in Benbow Deep. Nothing." He smirked over his shoulder. "Cell R-22 is a good one—a girlie cell."

"I'm just a looker," Krull laughed.

"Then you'll like R-22. It's called peep heaven." Krull didn't reply. They entered the residential cells. The houses were much like any others except for the scale; miniaturization was the rule. The cab abruptly slowed down. in front of a small plastic house that was distinguishable from the others only by its number. He dropped a bill in the driver's hand, got out without waiting for change, and headed for the door.

GEORGE HENRY Butterfield was prim, slender, with a narrow face, pointed jaw and thin lips. A fringe of gray hair circled a shiny pate and, together with face lines, added up to about fifty years. He looked inquiringly at Krull, his body braced against the partially open door. Krull stated his mission, clearly, everything but his real reason. He finished and waited expectantly.

"You came all the way from Sydney to ask about my brother?" Butterfield asked incredulously.

Krull nodded cheerfully. "It's not far."

"Why?"

"Because we need answers," Krull stated calmly.

Butterfield hesitated. "What do you want to know?"

"All about him—his life, hobbies, friends, what he did and said and believed; any letters you might have."

"I can't see the reason for all that," the face in the door said indignantly. "My brother's dead. It seems...an unwarranted invasion of privacy." He started to close the door but Krull's foot was in the way.

"I assure you, it's not." He adopted a conciliatory tone. "Let me explain, Mr. Butterfield." The watching eyes remained suspicious, hostile.

"Your brother was well-known, respected, then he vanished—inexplicably. Five years later he was found dead. Don't you think it logical we try to establish the facts concerning his whereabouts during the years he was lost to sight?"

"Who are you?" Butterfield's face took on a look of resentment. Krull displayed his credentials. The little man's mouth fell open and he managed to say:

"Won't you come in, Mr. Krull?" He stepped to one side and the agent entered, trying to conceal a faint smile. His host's awe was quite a contrast to Hardface's reactions when confronted with the same credentials. Butterfield retreated and indicated a soft chair in one corner of the room, then sat facing him. He fussed at getting comfortable before he managed to say:

"It must be quite important if the Prime Thinker is concerned."

"Very important," Krull said gravely. "Now Mr. Butterfield..."

Butterfield talked, talked in a barely audible voice with Krull occasionally interrupting with a question. He continually shifted his eyes and his fingers intertwined nervously. He told of his brother's boyhood, school life, friends (he had few)—his love of math, electronics, physics, his flights into fantasy and his dreams, little odds and ends concerning his likes and dislikes. Despite his nervousness and low-pitched voice he made his brother live again, until Krull felt almost it personal relationship with the mysterious professor who had, somehow, tampered with the atom—and died.

George Henry Butterfield narrated his brother's life up to the moment he had accepted the position on the faculty of the University of

Palmerston North—and abruptly stopped. Krull waited for him to continue. Butterfield flicked his eyes nervously around the room, averting the agent's face. Nervous, Krull thought. Unduly nervous—like a man sitting on a bomb. He encouraged:

"What then?"

"Nothing."

"Nothing?"

"I didn't hear from him again."

"Not at all—ever?"

"After he disappeared there were a few inquiries from the police. That's all." Butterfield sucked his lip.

"But nothing from your brother?"

"Nothing." He looked a trifle defiant. "The only thing I heard was…about his death. They informed me, just a few days ago."

Krull nodded sympathetically and asked more questions. He drew blanks. As far as his brother was concerned, William Bixby Butterfield had been born in Benbow Deeps, educated, had shunned girls, loved the physical sciences, had taken a job in New Zealand—had vanished. Krull tried a new line of questioning with the same result. No go.

"It's no use," Butterfield finally said. "I guess I just can't help you, Mr. Krull. I wouldn't keep any secrets—not from the Prime Thinker. I wouldn't do that." He spoke the denial in a burst, twisting his fingers furiously. Deciding there was nothing more to be gained, Krull rose, thanked him, and started toward the door; the engineer followed him. As he started to leave Butterfield blurted:

"This must be awfully important."

"It is." A note of regret seeped into Krull's voice.

"The Prime Thinker really sent you?"

"That's right, Mr. Butterfield, and I'm afraid he'll be terribly disappointed."

"Oh…" The little man hesitated as if torn with indecision, then drew his shoulders up sharply and looked at the agent with brave resolution. "Mr. Krull. there is one other thing."

"Yes…?" Krull felt an odd surge of hope.

"William had a secret…"

"Go on," Krull prompted.

"He…he was a hidden esper."

BEFORE he'd taken a dozen steps from Butterfield's door, Krull knew he'd had it. The little man's words had given the investigation an ominous twist.

Espers!

He momentarily clutched at the hope that William Bixby Butterfield only incidentally was an esper that no real relationship existed between that fact and his toying with the atom. But he knew better—knew it absolutely. He cursed softly. He couldn't enter their lonely world without revealing his own talents. The first telepath he encountered would read the secret in his mind or sense his mind shield—catastrophe.

He took the tube to Tonga and made connections with the Sydney carrier, glad of the few solitary hours the trip afforded. He had to think. Plan. Anticipate the contingencies which might arise when he moved into the shadow land of the espers, for he had no doubt that was exactly where he was headed. He shuddered at the thought of the first contact. Should he reveal his kinship and hope they would keep his secret? Or should he erect mind shields and say to hell with them? He decided on one thing: he'd be prepared. He'd read the esper tapes, the psychmaster studies, learn their organizations—determine his own powers. Up till now he'd hidden his talents, avoided using them. Okay, he'd test them, develop them, and the hell with consequences.

He reached Sydney and strolled toward the hotel with a pleased feeling. The decision to draw out his talent—use it—was almost a physical release, a sense of power. He peeped several passing pedestrians, catching odd fragments of thought; none were very clear and he wondered if it were because they had been picked out of context. Well, he would learn. If only he didn't encounter an esper in the process!

He entered the lobby of the hotel, absently peeping, and was startled by a thought of such vivid clarity that he stopped abruptly, staring at a young woman entering the lobby. She clutched the arm of a middle-aged man whose clothing proclaimed him a MIQ. He peeped again, fascinated, then withdrew from her mind and saw her clearly for the first time. She had a serene open face with candid blue eyes, which could be termed either vacuous or innocent. She appeared over-dressed in a pale blue semi-transparent tunic, matching sandals, and elaborate freshly lacquered top-knot hairdo. He watched the couple stroll toward the lift and grinned, deciding he had learned two things: one was about innocent faces; the second was the reason espers were shunned and feared.

He had scarcely entered his room when the phone rang—he debated answering it. The ringing persisted. Cranston, he thought. What the hell does he want? After a moment he lifted the receiver.

"Mr. Krull?" He didn't recognize the voice.

"I have a message for you..." The voice paused.

"Well...?"

"Are you interested in knowing the whereabouts of William Bixby Butterfield before he died?"

Krull was startled. "Who is this?"

"Just answer the question."

"I am," he snapped.

"Meet me in front of the Edward Crozener statue in Crozener Park at twelve midnight—tonight. And come alone."

"Who is this?" Krull demanded.

"Remember, come alone—if you want the information." The phone clicked in his ear. He looked thoughtfully at the instrument, glanced at the clock, debating if he should call Cranston. He decided against it.

KRULL reached the park with an hour to spare and strolled around its borders once to get his bearings. Crozener's statue was located in a small plaza boxed in by shrubbery and overhanging trees. He walked to the far end of the park and, certain he wasn't observed, stepped into the shrubbery and backtracked toward the plaza keeping in the shadows of the tree. He halted at the border of the clearing, spread the bushes carefully apart and peered out.

The square was empty.

He looked around until he found a tree that afforded a good view of the clearing and silently climbed it. He looked at his watch, 11:15, and almost immediately heard low voices. A couple strolled into view talking and laughing in intimate tones. He peeped them, got a few details and grinned. There was a long period before the next passerby came, a lone man who paused to light a pipe. His mind was pleasant, mellow. Krull grew uncomfortable. The tree limb pressed sharply against his stomach and his muscles ached from the unaccustomed position. He tried to shift to a more comfortable position. An old couple airing a dog passed him.

Midnight.

He started to shift his body again when he caught movement in the bushes on the opposite side of the square and froze. Illusion? It had been just a flash of black against black. No, there it was again, someone crouching...waiting. He smiled grimly and played it safe by slipping his gun from its holster, holding it in one hand while he steadied himself with the other. He tried to peep the shadow but there was no answering thought, no imagery, and he wondered if telepathy were limited to having the subject in close visual range. He'd have to determine that.

The shadow ceased moving and he decided the watcher had settled down to wait. After a while one leg began to cramp and he cautiously moved it, aware that the pain was spreading up his thigh. Hours seemed to pass. Still he waited, silently moving to ease the muscle. At twelve-thirty the black shadow opposite him moved again; a figure stepped out onto the edge of the square and looked up and down the walk. Krull strained to see, simultaneously trying to peep him—no results. He was trying to ease his cramp when the limb supporting him cracked. The shadow came to life, leaped to one side and three slugs ripped up through the tree. Krull cursed, fired twice, released his hold and dropped to the ground just as another slug whammed past his ear. He fired twice more; his attacker half spun and dropped heavily. There were shouts in the distance. He ran to the side of the fallen man and flipped the body over.

Cranston's dead face stared up at him.

HE released his hold and fled, keeping in the shadows until he was several blocks from the park. Sirens screamed as he neared the hotel and he smiled grimly. Cranston's troubles were over now—the roly-poly little man with the cheerful voice had smiled his last smile. For him the conspiracy was ended; but, he thought, his own troubles had just started. He entered the hotel through the garage and got to his room without being observed, pausing to peep the interior before entering. Not that he expected to read the mind of any chance intruder—he had failed to read the mind of the shadow that had been Cranston—but he did suspect he could discern the presence of another mind, even though it might come through as a patchwork of formless imagery. He locked the door behind him, conscious that he was breathing hard. He studied his hands—they were sweaty, shaking. He half-expected to see blood on them, but there was none. Cranston was the first; something told him he wouldn't be the last. After a while his breathing eased and he debated his next move.

Cranston's attempt to kill him left him standing at the fork of a road. Either Yargo had ordered his murder—or the conspiracy extended into the Prime Thinker's household. Which? He weighed the possibilities. It wasn't logical that Yargo would assign him to the investigation and almost as quickly decide to have him killed. Certainly the world's top leader wouldn't chance implication in the murder of a lowly agent. That was more Hardface's speed. It was more likely Cranston was linked to

Hardface—(What was his name?—Cathecart, that was it)—or Gullfin. Or the Manager. He made his decision.

At one a.m. he picked up the phone and called the Prime Thinker's secret number.

Yargo answered on the second ring. That was suspicious; almost as if he had been waiting for the call. Confirmation from Cranston? But Yargo probably worked three-fourths of the way around the clock. No, it wasn't unreasonable for him to be at his desk. He thought about it while making his request—an immediate audience.

"Is it that important?" There was an edge of doubt in Yargo's voice.

"It is," Krull said firmly.

"Where are you now?"

"My room—at the Edward Crozener."

"There'll be a car to meet you at the garage in fifteen minutes." The phone clicked; he replaced the receiver in the cradle thoughtfully. He didn't particularly like the idea of being whisked away in the dead of night by Yargo's men. It seemed like leaving himself wide open, but it all depended upon whether he had guessed right about Cranston's loyalties. When there were three minutes left to go, he checked his gun and headed for the garage. At exactly one-fifteen a white Capricorn rolled down the ramp and stopped. He approached it from the rear, one hand gripping his gun, and stopped, bewildered. The driver was a woman. For a moment he thought he had made a mistake and started to retreat when she called after him:

MR. KRULL?" He hesitated, cautiously returned to the side of the car. She smiled.

"If you'll get in…"

For an instant he struggled to remember where he had seen her before, but gave up and went around to the opposite side and slipped in beside her. She pushed the car into gear, reached the thoroughfare and turned in the direction of the House of the Prime Thinker. She finally broke the awkward silence:

"You seem surprised."

He grinned sheepishly. "To be frank, I wasn't expecting a woman."

"I was pressed into service. I happened to be with dad when your call came."

"Dad?"

"I'm Jan Yargo."

"Oh, I didn't know." He shifted in his seat until he could see her face in profile. Her eyes were large—blue, he guessed—and her nose was a straight line above a well-formed mouth. Her hair was piled high in the elaborate lacquered hairdo currently the style among HIQs; it dazzled with jewels. She was more than pretty, he decided, and placed her age in the early to middle twenties. The conversation died down. After a while she turned into a lane leading to the House of the Prime Thinker and a sentry waved her through. She parked under a portico and said:

"Please follow me."

She led him upstairs to the library and knocked lightly before entering. Ben Yargo was busy at his desk. He rose and came around to the center of the room, extended his hand and smiled briefly. "Good evening, Krull. Or should I say, good morning?"

"I'll be saying goodnight," Jan said.

Krull turned toward her. "Thank you very much, Miss Yargo."

"I'm glad to have been of help." She smiled at him and withdrew; he turned back to face the Prime Thinker.

"It is late—I'm sorry," Krull said. He saw that Yargo was wearing an open dressing gown thrown over a pair of tropic shorts, and sandals; his face was drawn and tired, all but the eyes. They were bright, alive and disconcertingly penetrating. He released Krull's hand and indicated a chair opposite his desk. Krull sat down and waited until Yargo was settled before he spoke:

"I wouldn't have bothered you at this time if something important hadn't come up."

"I'm sure of that." (A touch of irony?)

"Someone tried to murder me tonight." He paused…waited. The eyes watching him were unmoving.

"Well…?" Yargo uttered the single word. Krull blinked—he had expected amazement, possibly incredulity. The immobile eyes watched him impassively. For an instant he wondered if he dared peep the mind of the man opposite him and as quickly discarded the idea. Too dangerous. Yargo was too sharp, too alert, would sense the act. Instead he said:

"The assassin was your man—Cranston."

Yargo didn't change expression. "What happened?"

"I killed him," Krull said brutally.

"Good, I'm glad you came through all right. Anything else?"

Krull was momentarily shaken. Yargo's calm, in view of the implication, seemed unnatural. He hesitated, groping for words and said:

"Yes, there is." For a few moments the room was so still he could hear the ticking of the clock on the opposite wall. He said audaciously:

"Either Cranston acted under your orders or he was a traitor to your cause."

"I had already considered the implication from your point of view." Yargo leaned forward and rested his arms on the desk. "The conspiracy has reached to high places," he said quietly. "Cranston was a traitor."

HE leaned back and contemplated Krull for a long moment. His face was a mask and when he finally spoke his voice was crisp.

"As an agent of the State I expect you to go on with the investigation. As far as I am concerned, nothing has changed. Agents—by the nature of their work—are expected to face intrigue and death."

Krull flushed at the reprimand and started to protest when Yargo smiled. "So are Prime Thinkers."

"I would like your permission to investigate Cranston's connections."

Yargo shrugged. "If you're convinced it's related to the Butterfield case—yes. I usually don't try to tell an agent how to do his job. To that extent, I won't dictate your actions, as long as you don't deviate from the original intent of the investigation—to determine whether or not there is an atomic conspiracy; and if there is—the persons involved."

"I won't deviate," Krull informed him.

"No, I'm sure you won't." Yargo got up as if to terminate the meeting.

"One other thing…"

Yargo looked expectant.

"William Bixby Butterfield was an esper."

"Oh!" He sat down again.

CHAPTER SIX

THE first mutant telepath (esper), a boy named George Gollar, was discovered in Wellington in 2010 A.D., forty years after the Atomic War. It was disclosed that his grandparents had been among the few survivors of Greater London.

Gollar was declared a freak, a mutant spawned by radiation-altered genes. Soon after, other mutant telepaths were detected. They were few in number, at first. Freaks…mutants…telepaths. Peepers! In time the words took on an ominous note. Whispers grew, were fanned into fears and, in the end, open hostility.

Public demands led to the rigid "Esper Control Laws" of 2036, promulgated by Paul Bertocci (IQ 207), the Eighth Prime Thinker. These required the screening of school children for telepathic taints, the registration of all adult telepaths, and their prohibition from holding any public office. Severe penalties were imposed on "hidden espers," defined as persons not registered under the laws governing mutants and found to have telepathic traits."

Despite public unease, the esper problem did not flare into public prominence until the "Sawbo Fang affair."

The Searchers were established soon after...

Blak Roko's
Post-Atomic Earthman.

* * *

AN alarm bell rang in his brain.

Krull froze by the door of his room with the key half-inserted in the lock, feeling his heart thump against his chest walls while he tried to discern the cause. The warning in his brain had subsided, but he had the distinct feeling of another presence, as if someone were standing next to him. He looked swiftly along the halls. Empty. Someone must be inside. He hesitated, assessing his reaction. No, it hadn't really been a danger signal; it had been more the sensation of a *presence*. An awareness of someone nearby.

He deliberately finished turning the key, stepped aside and pushed the door ajar. A shaft of light came from the room. He caught his breath. There was a moment of stark silence followed by a feminine voice.

"Please come in, Mr. Krull."

He started involuntarily. The voice was low, pleasant. He tried to peep the room. There was no returning thought; neither was there any hint of danger. To the contrary...

He threw caution to the winds and stepped quickly through the door. A young woman was sitting in the room's one soft chair by the lamp watching him with bemused eyes. She was slim, dark, with unlacquered black hair and lashes, and a slightly almond cast to her eyes that reminded him of Rea Jon except for a strange wistfulness of expression. He took in her figure with a swift glance: the soft lavender, semi-transparent dress she wore emphasized the clean lines of her body. Her legs were long, slender and bare, and her simple sandals matched the yellow sash at her waist. He pegged her for a MIQ by her colored dress and simple hairdo.

"Do I meet with your approval, Mr. Krull?"

He reddened and finally found his voice: "Who are you?"

"Anna." The single word was uttered with an almost musical quality.

"Anna who?"

"Just Anna."

"Well, Miss Anna whoever-you-are, you're in the wrong room."

"No…I'm not."

"What do you want?" He said roughly.

"To help you."

He thought of the help Cranston had tried to give and smiled grimly. "No thanks."

The girl arose with a single graceful movement and took a few steps toward him. Her face was appealing, devoid of guile, but the lithe lines of her body, visible through the dress, disconcerted him. He caught the fragrance of a delicate perfume.

"Are you afraid, Mr. Krull?"

His lips pulled into a sardonic smile. "Frankly, yes."

"Of what?"

"Of getting murdered."

"Do I look like a murderer—or should I say murderess?"

"No—but you might lead me to someone who is."

"Oh, no." She appeared aghast at the thought. "I don't represent violence. I'm only here to help you; or, rather, take you to someone who can help you." Again he caught the fragrance of perfume and was stirred by the softness of her voice.

"What kind of help?"

"Information…just information."

"From who?"

"Mr…Mr. Bowman." She seemed to hesitate before uttering the name.

"And who is Bowman?"

"The person who wants to help you."

He couldn't suppress a grin.

"That's a nice round-about explanation. You'll have to do better than that…Anna." He deliberately let her name drop from his lips.

DON'T I look trustworthy, Mr. Krull?" There was reproach in her words, just the right amount, he thought. He tried to peep her again while appearing to think. If he had expected a clear thought pattern he was disappointed. He had the momentary sensation of standing in a light and airy garden, cool with soft breezes, fragrant with the scent of flowers. He half-expected to hear the trill of birds but the garden was silent. The pleasant sensation changed subtly; there was the beginning of imagery, the jelling of color and form into recognizable geometric patterns. A face emerged from the pattern, that of an old, old man, pale and drawn, with live bright eyes set under thinning wisps of snow-white hair. (Pictures instead of pure thought!) He tried to focus on the details and caught the pallor of the skin, thin nets of blue veins traversing the temples, giving the face an almost ethereal quality. There were no discordant lines, no harshness—only complete harmony and tranquility as if the face were the mirror of a saint's soul. He didn't know how long he held the vision before it began to fade, vanishing in a formless pattern of color. The lively brown eyes were the last thing he saw; then he was looking into a gray field. He became aware that he was standing stiff-legged, staring at the lovely face of the girl who called herself Anna. It was expectant.

"Who is Bowman, again?" He asked the question to give himself time to think. He was scarcely aware of her answer, gripped with the elation of having accomplished a successful mind probe.

The second since peeping the girl in the lobby.

But Anna's thoughts had come through so clear and vivid he had been able to discern the most minute details of the face in her mind; he had no doubt it was Bowman. And Bowman didn't look like a murderer. He stalled a moment longer.

"Exactly why does Mr. Bowman want to see me?"

She smiled faintly. "To give you information about atomic research, Mr. Krull."

THE car zoomed west along the freeway leading from South Sydney. It was a small, two-passenger Tropics-6 with a tan finish and bubble-canopy to allow full vision in all directions. The girl drove silently, swiftly, skirting the end of the harbor and heading toward North Sydney, the major residential area of the City where, he knew, large new apartment developments constructed of plastics and lightweight block housed the MIQs, mainly middle class workers. The seat was narrow and Krull occasionally felt the pressure of her thigh but she didn't appear to notice; indeed, she seemed completely oblivious of his presence.

He tried to piece the puzzle together. To the best of his knowledge only Yargo, the members of the Council of Six, the Manager and, yes, the coroner knew the real secret behind William Bixby Butterfield's death. Now, Mr. Bowman and the girl beside him. That made, not counting himself, eleven people who knew that William Butterfield had died tampering with the atom, for it seemed almost certain Anna and the man called Bowman must know the whole story. He wouldn't be a bit surprised, he thought, to read it in the headlines of the Anzaca Press.

The girl turned off the freeway onto a narrow road and began climbing toward the crest of one of the low hills. Off to one side the lights of the city fell away to the bay, a dark expanse broken by the occasional running lights of ships and smaller craft. The new Sydney

Harbor Bridge was a lighted arc against the night, connecting the north and south sides of the harbor. The red and green running lights of cargo copters moved high above the span. He turned in his seat. The multicolored lights and flashing neons of South Sydney had been swallowed in a light haze, leaving only a bright hue in the sky. He made mental note of street names so he could find the place again. The car abruptly slowed, and swung into a driveway in front of one of the newer apartments. The girl turned off the engine and lights.

"We're here."

He followed her to the door of one of the ground-level units. She opened it—the interior was softly lit.

He hesitated before entering. She turned, her face only inches from his. He saw that a slightly uneven front tooth added to her attractiveness.

"Still worried, Mr. Krull?"

"Puzzled." She laughed lightly and entered the room. He grinned sheepishly and followed, closing the door behind him, wondering what would happen if there were no Mr. Bowman. He followed her over to the fireplace, and for the first time saw the frail figure sitting in a deep chair next to the hearth. It was the man he had seen in her mind.

MR. BOWMAN, this is Mr. Krull," Anna said.

"Ah…yes, I know." The old man smiled gently and extended a bloodless hand, cold to Krull's touch. "Anna, get a chair for our guest."

Krull placed the chair so he could see both Bowman and the door.

"I'll be in the next room," Anna said. She smiled and left. Bowman was smiling gently.

"Thank you for coming."

Krull debated. "I have some questions to ask," he said finally.

"Certainly—feel free."

"You appear to have certain knowledge that could get you into serious trouble." He continued briskly, "I should warn you, I'm an Agent of Police."

"Yes, Agent Max Krull, Territory of Waimea-Roa, graduate of the Sydney Branch of the World Police Academy, class of 2446 A.D. with an IQ 113 rating. I know all that, Mr. Krull, and the fact you're conducting the Prime Thinker's investigation into circumstances surrounding William Bixby Butterfield's death as result of radiation burns."

"You know too much, Mr. Bowman. You could be considered dangerous."

"Nonsense, how can a man of eighty-seven be dangerous?"

"The knowledge you have is dangerous," Krull corrected.

"No—I don't believe so," Bowman said gently.

"How do you know of Butterfield's activities."

"That's not important."

"I consider it important," Krull said stiffly. "Are you a member of the conspiracy?"

"Do I look like a conspirator?" Krull detected a note of mockery in his voice.

"Let's start over," he said woodenly. "Why did you bring me here?"

"To ask you not to try and unmask the conspiracy."

"If there is one…and if I find it," Krull said acidly.

"There is one—and you'll find it."

"You sound certain."

"I am certain."

He was momentarily nonplused. The frail man opposite him spoke with absolute conviction. More, he had the audacity to ask him to break his oath. He watched the aged face. "Then you are a conspirator."

"No." It was a gentle denial.

"But you speak in their behalf."

"Yes."

"With their consent?"

"No."

"Then—why?"

"Because the objective of the conspiracy is essential."

"What objective—the destruction of the world?"

"No, Mr. Krull, the conquest of the solar system, then the stars—the fulfillment of human destiny."

"Fantastic…" He snapped the word out and stopped, leaving the sentence unfinished. It struck him that the old man was talking about achievements that would take decades of development, even with atomic power. He momentarily wondered if he were dealing with a madman, a feeling dispelled by Bowman's eyes. They were mild, but sane. "They'll never get the power for that," he finished.

"They have the power," Bowman observed quietly.

"Atomic power?"

"Yes, of course."

"That's where Butterfield got burned."

"It was unfortunate."

"You speak as if the conspirators were already to hop off," Krull said derisively.

"Yes, soon," the old man replied imperturbably, "at least on the first exploratory ventures."

"Fantastic," Krull repeated.

The ancient eyes contemplated him serenely. "Yes, perhaps in this age of denial of reason, of mental and cultural stagnation; but it wasn't fantastic once. Men were poised, on the verge…"

"And almost destroyed the world," Krull interjected.

"Not in trying to get to the stars," Bowman reminded. His eyes seemed to look into vast distances and it was a moment before he resumed: "No, we have denied our heritage through fear. The shadow of the Atomic War has never lifted. Now we live only for today, afraid to plan or think of the morrow…"

"You might explain that," Krull said ruffled. "I don't regard Edward Crozener as stupid, yet you propose violation of his first law—the First Law of Mankind."

"EDWARD CROZENER was a great man," Bowman agreed. "I have studied his life intensively. But he was a man of a certain age, a certain social pattern, dealing with circumstances of his day. I'm sure he didn't intend his law as a perpetual ban, but only as a stopgap precaution until humanity learned to direct its destiny. No, with all due respects to Crozener, I am acting on philosophical motives I am sure he would approve were he here today."

"What philosophical motives?" Krull spoke harshly. He felt the interview was getting into deep water.

"Philosophical and ecological," Bowman corrected. "Philosophical because man would be destitute were his future limited to this…clod. It would be tantamount to racial death, for man can only survive while he can progress. Stop progress and you stop evolution—and all else dies. The spirit can't survive in a stagnant state, Mr. Krull."

"I don't see that."

"You've never really thought about it," Bowman countered, "but the seeds of stagnation have already set in. Look about you: over half the world are the drones we smugly call LIQ's. For them there is no tomorrow. But even the MIQ's and HIQ's are stopped, for there is no progress. We drive virtually the same cars, live in virtually the same houses and pursue the same sort of life as the pre-bomb man. In short time, as race history is charted, man would be at the end of his road. Ecologically, the earth is limited in the size of population it can support."

His eyes fastened on Krull and he said softly: "If the saturation limit were reached, either man would perish in a world battle for individual survival or—worse—he would adapt to his environment, with all the limitations it would impose. That would end his upward climb. He'd be just a bigger ant culture."

"We have the sea-bottoms, surface seas and lands yet untouched," Krull remarked drily.

"True, but I am thinking in terms of...ages."

"People can worry when the time comes."

"No, the time is now. We can't afford more lost centuries. That is important, Mr. Krull. There must be a continuity of knowledge."

"It's illegal."

MR. KRULL, there are people who...at this moment...are preparing for the next step, the stars. The new frontiers are very close. I'm not a conspirator"—he chuckled—"I'm much too old for that, but I do ask your aid in one respect: don't try to unmask those who are."

"I couldn't consent to that."

"I know that."

"You know it?"

"Yes."

"Then why bother to ask—why bring me here?"

"Because that's my role, my minor part in destiny, Mr. Krull. I am...a faint force in the causal chain."

"You believe that?"

"I know it."

"You sound certain."

"I am." The ancient head nodded and the eyes closed, as if he had suddenly fallen asleep. Krull studied the lined features. He hadn't learned a thing. The old man knew...*knew*. He felt the inclination to shake him to life, demand that he speak. All at once a weariness came over him and he got to his feet.

The girl called Anna drove him back to the hotel. It was late and she drove fast, without speaking, but she didn't appear angry. He maintained silence until she reached his destination, then got out and held the door a moment.

"Thanks, Anna." He lingered over the name.

"Thank you, Mr. Krull."

"Sorry I couldn't go along with Bowman."

"He didn't expect you to." Again he caught the suggestion of sorrow in her face.

"So he said." He stepped back almost reluctantly and watched the car thread into the traffic pattern. When its tail lights merged with those of other cars he hailed a cab.

"Anzaca Press," he snapped, getting in.

"Right-o." The cab screeched around a corner, mingled with traffic a few blocks and pulled to the curb in front of a squat, three-storied building topped by a gigantic public news screen. Krull dropped a coin in the driver's hand and entered the lobby. The directory said the news room was on the second floor.

HE reached it and looked around. It was late, close to midnight, but there was still the stir of life amid endless empty desks. On one wall a huge screen flashed news scenes from other parts of the world while beneath it a machine cranked out radio pictures.

He spotted an elderly graying man sitting off to one side with a limp cigar drooping from his lips. His feet were propped on a desk and he was reading a copy of *After Dark*. He didn't bother to look up at Krull's approach.

Krull glanced around, found several pieces of copy paper, and sat at an empty desk and began sketching. Anna's face came to life under his pencil but, several times, he caught himself confusing her features with Rea's. He finished, studied the sketch critically, then slimmed the cheeks slightly and added a touch of shadow to the eyes. Anna's face stared back at him.

Bowman's face was easier to do. The details were vivid in his mind and he translated them to paper easily and quickly. He thinned the eyebrows and added the suggestion of veins to the temples. Satisfied, he approached the elderly man.

"Are you one of the newsmen?"

"You might say so."

"Mind if I trouble you a moment?"

"You already have." The tired eyes looked questioningly at him.

"I'm a stranger in Sydney and there's a couple of people I'm trying to locate." Krull tried a smile. "I've always heard a newspaperman knows everyone, so I thought you might be able to help."

"Maybe." He grunted noncommittedly.

"Ever see that face before?" Krull slid the sketch of Anna across the desk. The tired eyes studied it a moment.

"No, but I can see your interest. She looks pretty smooth."

"Right," Krull rejoined. "How about this fellow?" He dropped the sketch of Bowman on the desk. The man's eyes flicked down, then fastened curiously on him.

"You pick strange friends."

"Oh…" Krull felt elated. "You know him?"

"Who doesn't?"

"Who is he?" Krull asked impatiently.

"I don't know what your interest is but your friend here"—he tapped Bowman's face with a pencil stub—"is Herman Bok."

"Bok…" Krull stood frozen. The world spun and for an instant the room was deathly still.

"Herman Bok," the voice was saying, "President of the World Council of Espers."

CHAPTER SEVEN

KRULL got nabbed that evening.

He had spent the day trying to piece together bits of information about the world esper organization headed by the frail aged man named Herman Bok, who paraded under the pseudonym of "Mr. Bowman," and who seemed to know more about his job than he did himself. Bok's entrance into the case scared him. The king peeper. He had to watch out. Had the old man discovered he was an esper? The thought made him jittery.

He had quickly found himself against a blank wall; Bok seemed shrouded in complete anonymity. He was a name, world known; but he was also a shadow, a man without substance. It was easy to find his name on public records—but few facts. In desperation he turned to Peter Merryweather.

Shevach's assistant turned out to have an office on the top floor of PAB, the Planet Administration Building. It was finished in decorative plastics and adorned with exotic tropic plants and an inch-thick rug. Krull paused to admire a painting on the wall—an original by Surrey depicting the launching of the weather satellite Atea-Rangi—before taking a chair across from Merryweather's expansive desk.

"Like it?" Merryweather inclined his head toward the painting.

"Beautiful," Krull said. "I've never seen a Surrey original before."

"They're not too plentiful," the gaunt man modestly admitted. "Interested in art?"

"I like to sketch."

"I try." Merryweather sighed and leaned back. "Always wanted to be an artist but I can't seem to get past the beginner stage."

He chuckled. "But I don't think you came to talk about that."

"No, I came to talk about…Herman Bok." He watched the thin man carefully as he dropped the name. Merryweather's expression didn't change.

"I take it you can't find out much about him," he said drily.

"Practically nothing," Krull cheerfully admitted.

"That's not surprising. Bok's pretty much of a mystery despite the fact that he's the world's number one esper. However, like I said, I'm here to help."

He flicked a switch and spoke into an intercom: "Chen, get me all the tapes we have on Herman Bok." He cut the connection and looked interestedly at Krull.

"Must be some case you're on," he observed quietly. Krull was glad he didn't press the point. He had the feeling it would be hard to lie to Merryweather, even if he were Shevach's strong right hand.

As it turned out, there wasn't much to go on. The official name of the organization headed by Bok was the World Council of Espers; it seemed to be largely a social group tied together through the exchange of tapes, films and letters. There was a world convention once every five years to elect officers. He didn't think it amounted to much: Bok, alias Mr. Bowman, was serving his eighth consecutive term as president. But he did learn one thing: the king esper had a confidential secretary named Anna Malroon who lived at the address where he had met Bok the previous evening. Bok's official residence was called the House of Espers, a mansion sprawled atop a hill in the HIQ section of northwest Sydney. It was the property of the esper organization but the old man seemed to have made it a monopoly. At least that was Krull's observation. There was a lot more, but nothing that really told anything. Like Merryweather remarked—Bok was a shadow.

HE left the hotel at dusk. The street lights were blinking on, yellow in a light ground haze, and the air was heavy with harbor scents. The raucous horns of tugs and the deeper voice of a freighter spoke from the waterfront. He had scarcely left the hotel before he sensed someone fall into step behind him. His scalp prickled, a warning flashed in his brain and he started to whirl when a harsh voice gritted:

"Keep walking...slow. Don't turn or I'll burn you."

The voice wasn't joking. Krull kept his pace steady, feeling his tensions ebb. This was the kind of action he understood. A man with a gun was real, something that could be tackled—like Cranston. He tried to peep his shadow. No good. He got the impression of savage brutality, hate, but no coherent thought pattern. He grinned wryly. For an esper he was something less than third class. He drew near the end of the block just as a black car slid alongside the curb and stopped.

His shadow said: "Okay, this is it. Get in."

He turned toward the car and someone inside opened the rear door. He tensed, then relaxed, thinking he wouldn't have a chance with the cannon poking his back. He got in and a gun jabbed his ribs.

"Sit back, relax and don't try anything funny."

"Sure, relax," Krull grunted. The man sitting next to him dug the weapon into his ribs and he winced. His captor climbed in next to the driver and the car swung into the stream of traffic. His captor had a bullet-shaped head with close-cropped dark hair and undersized ears pinned close to the skull. He turned and Krull started involuntarily. Gullfin—the Manager's chief of special agents. The flat face with the smashed nose and pig eyes grinned evilly.

"So, Yargo's pet got himself snarled."

"Have a good time while you can," Krull replied complacently. "You'll play hell trying to hold me."

"Think so—killer?" Gullfin spat the word in his face. "Not even Yargo can pull you out of this one."

"That remains to be seen." Krull added: "Who am I supposed to have murdered?"

"Ha, a comedian," Gullfin snarled.

"Comedian?" Krull sounded puzzled. "What was his name?"

Gullfin swore. "You'll remember when I get the rubber hose working."

KRULL didn't reply. He had little doubt the Manager's chief of special agents was right. Gullfin looked like a sadist and a sadist with a rubber hose was an unbeatable combination in the gentle art of persuasion. There was no further conversation until the car turned down a ramp and stopped in an underground garage. Gullfin emerged first. made motions of patting his shoulder holster and rasped:

"Out."

A gun prodded Krull's ribs and he obeyed; his companion in the back seat followed, a short heavy man with odd yellow eyes.

"Take killer boy to the reception room." Gullfin leered at Krull. "Make him comfortable until I get there."

"Right." Yellow Eyes hefted his weapon. "Straight ahead."

Krull sighed and started in the direction indicated, thinking he wasn't going to like the next few hours. He contemplated tackling Yellow Eyes but decided against it when he heard the driver following a few steps behind. He was directed down a flight of stairs to a passage ending at a steel-barred door. The driver waited half a dozen paces behind while Yellow Eyes pushed past Krull and opened it, then stepped aside.

"In," he said briefly.

"Looks comfortable," Krull murmured. He paused on the threshold. "I suppose you know it's illegal to toss a man in the cage without booking him."

"I know," Yellow Eyes said sympathetically. His voice changed to a strident snarl. "Get in there and quit stalling."

Krull shrugged and entered the cell. It contained a single metal cot, a couple of stools and little else. The door clanged shut behind him and footsteps receded down the hall. He made a few experimental peeps and drew blanks, then sat on the cot and tried to figure what next. Yeah, Gullfin—and a rubber hose.

After a while he heard the clatter of feet and the rumble of voices echoing in the stairwell; Gullfin turned into the passageway followed by his companions. True to his word, he carried a short flexible length of hose. He opened the door and entered with Yellow Eyes at his heels while another man remained outside. Gullfin grinned wickedly and slapped the hose against his thigh, nodding to Yellow Eyes.

"Stand up, killer." Krull rose from his cot; Yellow Eyes slipped behind him and applied an armlock. "Don't worry, we're not going to beat a confession out of you." Gullfin's face twisted in a brutal leer.

"We want more than that and we got scientific ways of getting it, huh, Kruper?" So, Yellow Eyes' name was Kruper. Krull tucked it in his mental file without removing his eyes from Gullfin's flat face.

"We're real scientific." The agent's small eyes glittered and Krull peeped him. The imagery came with a smashing shock—a picture of himself reeling under Gullfin's blows. A tremor shook him and he hastily removed the probe.

"All I want is to warm you up first." Gullfin spat out the words; he simultaneously raised his arm and chopped the hose down in a short hard arc that ended against Krull's shoulder.

SICKENING pain shot through his body; he felt nauseated and the sweat began to come.

"Warm-up," Gullfin said. He shifted slightly and whipped half a dozen slashing blows back and forth across Krull's arms and ended with a slashing chop against the cheek. Krull staggered and would have fallen were it not for Kruper's hold. His head was spinning. Gullfin stepped back.

"How did you like that?"

Krull raised his head and cursed him.

Gullfin responded with another series of brutal lashes before stepping back, breathing heavily. He nodded. Kruper released his hold and Krull fell to one knee feeling sick. He managed to get to his feet. His vision swam and his body was a sea of agony. He felt his cheek, dully wondering if it was still there; his hand came away covered with blood. Gullfin laughed harshly, spun around and left the cell with Kruper at his heels. The steel door clanged and their footsteps echoed down the hall.

Krull staggered to the cot. His body was stiff, sore, and his bones felt as if they were on fire; the harsh lights burned his eyeballs. A short time later he heard voices and struggled to a sitting position. Feet clomped on the stairs and Gullfin turned into the passageway with Kruper and several more men. Krull rose, startled. Merryweather! The tall cadaverous man was shambling behind Gullfin wearing a genial smile, as if he were a host come to welcome him. They reached the cell door before he saw Merryweather's companion; the sweat began to come.

Shevach.

Ivan Shevach.

There was no mistaking the pale cruel face. He dropped back to his seat sweaty and jittery and a vein began throbbing at his temple.

"Nothing to worry about," Gullfin taunted. "I forgot the rubber hose." He roared with laughter, slapping his thigh as if it were a huge joke. Krull didn't appreciate the humor.

GULLFIN opened the door and entered with Shevach and the shambling Merryweather following while Kruper stationed himself outside. The Manager's eyes probed Krull curiously. Merryweather smiled pleasantly. The smile told Krull all he needed to know about Shevach's so-called public relations man. He was one of those people who wore a smile for all occasions, a mask he had interposed between himself and the world. It could mean...anything. The Manager's voice broke into his thoughts, a cold, precise voice that set Krull's already ragged nerves on edge.

"You are agent Max Krull, IQ 113, Territory of Waimea-Roa." It was a statement of fact and he didn't bother to answer. Shevach's lids half-closed and his face got a tight look.

"You are IQ 113?"

Krull felt the beginning of panic. Gullfin wore a sneer but Merryweather's expression hadn't changed.

"Silence won't help," Shevach said in a low flat voice. "We have ways of finding what we want to know—for instance, why you murdered Cranston."

Krull watched him, trying to conceal a tremor. Gullfin was brutal but Shevach was deadly, much the more dangerous of the two. He had to be on guard.

"We know you murdered him," Shevach taunted, "but why? Who ordered it? Yargo?" He rapped the questions out with gunfire rapidity, his eyes boring into Krull's skull. He ceased speaking and the cell was absolutely still. Krull fancied he could feel his nerves vibrating. He looked at Merryweather. The smile was there, pleasant and warm, but his eyes were two drills, two slivers of ice stabbing into his brain. The beginning of a thought nibbled at Krull's mind, tantalizingly beyond his reach. It had something to do with the gaunt man. Shevach broke the tableau by stepping back.

"Now we'll get down to business," he said. "First about your supposed IQ..."

Krull never had a chance to discover what he was driving at. There was a commotion in the hall, several loud voices and the Manager turned with a startled look. Yargo pushed his way into the cell followed by a tall square man with silvery hair and a hard face mellowed only slightly by jovial blue eyes. The Prime Thinker glanced at Krull, Merryweather and looked last at Shevach.

"You have booked agent Krull?"

"Not yet." The Manager compressed his lips in a thin slit. "We will."

Yargo turned to his silvery-haired companion. "Grimhorn, this is illegal. Agent Krull hasn't been booked." Krull looked up with sudden interest. Joseph Grimhorn was another of those names very seldom accompanied by a face. He was Chief of World Agents.

"You will bear witness to that fact?"

"I will," Grimhorn replied softly. Krull watched the blue eyes. They were open, candid, with it tinge of laughter, yet hard. He swung his gaze to Gullfin. Shevach's chief of special agents didn't look overly perturbed. Yargo contemplated Shevach's pale features before speaking.

ON what charge did you intend to book agent Krull?"

"Murder," Shevach snapped. "The murder of agent Oliver Cranston."

"Murder?" Yargo seemed astonished. "Since when is an act of self-defense construed as murder?"

"Self-defense?" Shevach smiled thinly. "The court might hold a different view: will, I think."

"There will be no court trial."

"You are setting yourself up as the law?" Shevach spoke defiantly. "The public would be interested to learn that."

Yargo looked musingly at him and finally said: "The matter of agent Krull's guilt will be handled by the Prime Thinker. Release him."

"Not without a trial," Shevach snapped. "I know the law...even if the Prime Thinker doesn't."

"It is within the province of my office to grant pardons," Yargo reminded. He turned to the Chief of World Agents. "Grimhorn, you will bear testimony to the fact that the Prime Thinker has granted an unconditional pardon to agent Max Krull, Territory of Waimea-Roa, effective immediately."

"Certainly," Grimhorn replied. He swung toward Gullfin. "Release him."

Gullfin's flat face was venomous but the Manager had regained his composure. Disregarding Yargo, he turned to Grimhorn, compressed his lips and said softly:

"I don't believe a man can be pardoned prior to a finding of guilt by a legally constituted court. I wouldn't be surprised if Krull were arrested and tried—after the coming election. It also looks as if we might need a new Chief of World Police."

"It's possible," Grimhorn conceded. His voice grew hard. "It's also possible that the Chief of World Police might file charges against the Manager for malfeasance in office. I might remind the Manager that the law prohibits a person found guilty of such a charge from holding government office."

"Malfeasance?" Shevach arched his eyebrows questioningly.

"Yes, malfeasance," Grimhorn said, "subjecting a prisoner to a third degree without booking him. Krull was denied due process of law. That makes it malfeasance."

Shevach's face was a study in anger and frustration. He sucked his underlip, started to speak, then swung around and left the cell with Gullfin at his heels. Yargo looked at Krull's bloodied face.

"FEEL up to leaving?"

"Can't be too soon for me." He grinned. "Personally, I was beginning to get jittery." Grimhorn laughed and Yargo said:

"I can understand that. Let's go." Krull nodded and followed him from the cell with Grimhorn following. They reached the street and stopped.

"Thank you for coming, Chief. You've been a big help," Yargo said.

"Glad to have had the opportunity." Grimhorn pursed his lips thoughtfully. "Sort of a revelation. Maybe my department needs an overhaul."

"The lemons are probably few," Yargo encouraged. They said goodnight and Krull followed the Prime Thinker to his private car. Yargo remained silent until the driver pulled away from the curb.

"I came as soon as I learned what had happened."

Krull was curious. "How did you find out?"

"A call over my private wire: the details of your arrest and the rubber-hose persuasion."

"Even that? I'd like to thank your tipster, whoever he was."

"Oh, he gave a name all right, but I think it was false."

"False?"

"Yes, a Mr. Bowman; just Mr. Bowman. I've heard from him before," he added wryly.

Krull concealed his amazement. The president of the World Council of Espers seemed to possess an omniscience little short of uncanny. And there was his penchant for using false names. He started to blurt Bowman's true identity and stopped. Something told him to keep the information to himself—at least until he learned more about the mysterious old man. Another thought occurred.

"How did Gullfin tie me so definitely to Cranston?"

"Bowman explained that, too," Yargo said grimly. Krull looked expectant. "It was Saxon."

"Saxon—your personal aide."

"Saxon *was* my personal aide," Yargo corrected. He didn't amplify the statement.

CHAPTER EIGHT

YARGO'S visitor came at midnight, a tall, cadaverously thin man, egg-bald, with luminous myopic eyes tucked behind old-fashioned thick-lensed glasses. The agent who met his car had taken extreme precautions to assure his arrival—and departure—went unheralded. Even the customary guard at the entrance had been removed.

The agent led him directly to Yargo's study. The visitor followed, walking with a slight limp and appearing to be trailing his long, high-bridged nose as if it were some kind of direction finder. Despite the severe architecture of his features, he had the strangely whimsical expression of an adult watching the cavorting of playing children. His name was Karl Werner and he was Chief Psychmaster of the world. Yargo rose to meet him, smiling cordially, but waited until the agent discreetly withdrew before speaking.

"Karl, it's good to see you again."

"Good to see you, Ben." The voice was a flat, precise razor. He flicked his eyes professionally over the Prime Thinker's body. "You look good, but tired. You're working too hard."

"It's a salt mine," Yargo agreed, "but come, sit down. Care for a drink?"

"The old standby."

Yargo mixed two drinks at a wall cabinet and handed one to Werner. "Here's to your health, Karl."

"And yours, Ben." They touched glasses and drank, then Yargo sat on the edge of his desk facing the psychmaster. He said solemnly:

"I should apologize for bringing you all the way from Africa, Karl. I hope I didn't disrupt anything too important."

"You did," the psychmaster said succinctly.

"How important?" Yargo was curious.

"More important than anything you have to say."

"I doubt it, but tell me," Yargo said expectantly.

"Last month we got word of a seven-year old boy in Tanganyika who passed the Breck-Munson Intelligence Measure with an IQ 212…"

Yargo whistled softly and looked thoughtful a moment before speaking. "Hidden esper?"

"Right, he was reading the testmaster's mind. But that part's not important."

Yargo became instantly alert.

"Another Sawbo Fang?"

Werner nodded grimly. "I tested him, Ben. He made…pencils…move." He dropped each word, watching the Prime Thinker's face.

"A psychokinetic." Yargo's face showed excitement and anxiety. "Does he realize his talent?"

"No, he's too young. He didn't realize the nature of the tests. I made sure of that."

"But he will know…soon?"

"Very soon. He's just learning to handle the talent…can just manage to jiggle small articles by intense concentration. But give him another few years…" He left the thought unspoken.

"What's the full potential, Karl?" Yargo asked uneasily.

"Frankly, we don't know. But we don't think it's like dynamite."

"What do you mean?"

"The energy released by dynamite is in ratio to the amount used; psychokinesis seems more an all-or-none power. If he could shake a pencil, he could shake a mountain."

"Or the Universe…"

"Perhaps," Werner said grimly.

"That's three counting Sawbo Fang," Yargo mused. He seemed to be looking into a great distance, scrutinizing times and places to come. The psychmaster spoke softly:

"Yes, a pk, like Sawbo. The other, a girl of eight, is a *down-through*... can read the future. And see around corners," he added.

"We're coming to a new era, Karl. *Homo Superior.* The Man of Tomorrow. The new race is coming but the world isn't prepared."

"No, it's not," the psychmaster soberly agreed.

"How about the searchers?"

"They don't know, won't know...can't know. We've got to save them, Ben."

"How are you handling it?"

"Playing safe, we hope. We've isolated them...are going to control every facet of their lives, hypnotically indoctrinate them to high moral standards and raise them to become members of the Psych masters Guild—hope to god they use their talents for the betterment of the race."

"YOU'RE wide open, Karl. The Guild, by its very nature, is always suspect. I happen to know the searchers keep it under eye."

"We know, but we have an ace in the hole. We've placed the children under the wing of a man who isn't a member of the Guild. Isn't even a psychmaster, in fact. But he's got the power to shield them."

"Oh. Is he safe?"

"Absolutely." Werner studied the question in Yargo's eyes. The Prime Thinker waited. "Hans Taussig," he added softly.

"I'll be damned."

"He's their shield against the world and I know we can trust him," Werner said absolutely.

"Yes, you can trust him," Yargo agreed. He thought of the scene in the Council Chamber when Taussig had denied such a talent was possible and smiled wryly. The sociologist was also a consummate actor.

"We can't take chances," Werner observed. Yargo nodded slowly. "But that's not what worries me, Ben."

"No?"

"It's the ones we don't detect. My god, imagine what could happen if just one slipped through and used the power for his own ends. He could control the world. Especially a pk."

"I know." Yargo smiled curiously. "Sometimes you feel inclined to favor the searchers."

"Not that," Werner exclaimed harshly. "You can't deny evolution. *Homo Superior* is around the corner, Ben, and we've got to live with the fact. More, we've got to protect them, nourish them, feed them the reins. They're the only hope of this damned stagnant mudball, the only hope that humanity will rise above the present mediocrity and make itself known in the Universe. If we let the searchers find them we're as guilty as the mob that killed Sawbo Fang."

"I didn't mean that, Karl. I fully realize the world needs new blood. That's why I summoned you." He looked at the psychmaster for a long moment and the room was deathly still.

"Would you jump if I told you that what I have to say is even more important than your new-found pk?"

"You know I certainly would."

YARGO set his glass on the desk and began talking, carefully selecting his words as if he didn't want Werner to miss a single detail. The psychmasters face took on an initial look of astonishment, gradually replaced by absolute absorption, nor did his myopic eyes ever leave the Prime Thinker's face. Yargo finally finished and leaned back, watchful. Waiting. Werner remained silent, thoughtful.

Yargo spoke tersely: "That calls for another drink."

"Yes, I believe it does, in view of the fact you're asking me to become an arch criminal."

"You're already one," Yargo said urbanely, "hiding the new race progeny from the searchers." He kept his stare riveted on the thin man's face. Finally the corners of Werner's eyes crinkled and he chuckled.

"Before I came here I would have considered such a request unthinkable. Now...I'm not so sure."

Yargo slowly exhaled, visibly relieved. He went to the cabinet, speaking while he mixed drinks.

"You've got to admit this is more important than your pk, Karl."

"Yes, but only because of its immediacy. My god, Ben, will the world pull through? The future scares me."

"It scares me, too, but I have faith in the future." He turned with a smile. "That's the good thing about the human race: it always has an ace in the hole."

"It needs a royal flush."

"I've put the cards down. What does it look like?"

"A royal flush," Werner admitted.

"Right. You can see the necessity of what I'm asking?"

"Yes, Ben, I can."

"Needless to say, I've placed myself in your hands." He returned with the drinks and placed one before the psychmaster, and again perched on the edge of the desk. "You're in a position to scuttle me, Karl. I've never trusted anyone that far before."

"I appreciate that." Werner's mouth crinkled. "Of course, if I go along with you, the shoe will be on the other foot."

"It's for humanity."

"I know that."

"I've delayed because of ethical considerations, Karl. Have I allowed enough time?"

"Just…"

After they finished their drinks, Yargo went to a wall safe and returned with a heavy volume, handing it to Werner. The myopic eyes glanced at the title—*Alexander*—before he slipped it into his briefcase.

"Alexander rides again," he quipped.

"I hope so, Karl. I hope so.

KRULL caught the morning carrier to Waimea-Roa. He was stiff and sore and his jaw ached intolerably but his physical discomfiture seemed minor compared with his other problems. The investigation into a possible atomic conspiracy rapidly was becoming a nightmare peopled with sadists, espers and—he thought wryly—power politics. He felt like the proverbial sparrow caught in a badminton game.

He was relieved when Waimea-Roa finally crawled over the horizon and pushed his troubles aside, momentarily excited at the prospect of seeing the atolls again. And Jonquil. Jonquil knew the ropes. The Inspector had not only been around but he was IQ 172, with plenty of extra savvy thrown in. He had no doubt but that Jonquil could tell him plenty about the power politics involved, perhaps help him chart a course through the maze of intrigue in which he was snared. He might even have time to see Paha Jon's granddaughter, swim the green waters of Abiang Lagoon with her and, in the cool of evening, walk to Coral Sands Cove, the secluded beach they had claimed as their own.

There were other things he would like to do, too, such as loafing in the shade of Alba Hoyt's thatch-roofed garden and drinking beer, exploring the barrier reef in search of octopus—or lolling in the sun in Paha Jon's yellow-sailed outrigger while the old man spun tales of his ancestors, the early Polynesians who had sailed their huge twin-hulled log ships across the uncharted wastes of the Pacific centuries before the Atom War, to find and people Waimea-Roa. But, he thought glumly, there would be no time. Not this trip. He'd have to wind the job up first—if someone didn't wind him up in the process. He grinned weakly. Just now he didn't seem to be doing so good.

THE atoll chain came up like a string of green-tinted pearls flung randomly on the sea, the white arcs of its coves gleaming against the pale green water on one side and the darker green interior foliage on the other. The barrier reef joining the two ends of the atoll to create the triangular-shaped Abiang Lagoon appeared like a thin rope awash in the sea. Abiang Village on the central atoll came into view, its coral-pink and emerald-green plastic houses and shops intermixed with thatched native huts, making a neat geometric pattern between ocean and lagoon. Chimney Rock was a black splotch against the sea. The larger plastic-block headquarters of the Agency of Police hove into view, then the plane banked, dropping, and the waters of Abiang Lagoon rushed to meet it.

Krull and another passenger, who looked like a commercial salesman, were put ashore and the plane rose again, climbing into the tropic sky in a northwesterly direction. He paused on the landing to breathe the clean warm air; caught the musky fragrance of the verdure beyond the clearing. It felt good to be back. He walked from the landing to Aula Road, the village's only thoroughfare; his step quickened as he drew near his house. The friendly nods and waves of the villagers—he knew almost all of them—gave him a warm feeling and he wondered why anyone would ever want to live anywhere else.

He stopped at his place long enough to glance around and deposit his bag. Everything looked the same—the untidy bed, dirty breakfast dishes in the sink, a roughed-in sketch of Pahara Rua, one of the village elders. His eyes rested a moment on the sweeps and planes and tilts of Rea Jon's body and face, struck again by her similarity to Anna Malroon. There was one noticeable difference. Rea Jon's face was saucy, provocative, while Anna Malroon's held a note of deep sorrow. He weighed one against the other, decided he liked them both, and went next door to the Agency of Police.

"Hi, Derek."

The wizened desk clerk looked up, startled, and his face wreathed in a smile. "Glad to see you, Krull." His eyes grew curious. "I thought you were transferred?"

"Vacation," Krull said cheerfully. "Jonquil in?"

"Isn't he always?" Derek answered. Krull laughed and knocked on the Inspector's door. He went in at the answering grunt—Jonquil's face lit up with pleased surprise.

"Krull, I'm glad to see you. How come back so soon?"

"You won't be so happy when I give you my load of troubles," Krull said humorously, "but it's good to be home."

"Home is the hunter," Jonquil quoted.

"A nice kettle of fish you stuck me in." Krull grinned. "Now you're going to have to bail me out."

"Rough, eh? I thought it might be." He extended a pack of cigarettes. Krull lit his and inhaled deeply before speaking.

"Advice is what I need—plenty of it." He looked intently at the Inspector. "Are you acquainted with my assignment at all?"

"No—only that they needed a good man."

"Good, hell, they needed a goat."

"I've found that to be one of the prime requirements for the force." Jonquil chuckled. "Don't be bitter."

"Not bitter—just puzzled," Krull confessed. "I've broken every other law so I might as well break another and spill the works."

"LET'S have it." The Inspector leaned back and clasped his hands behind his head as Krull began talking. He started from the first and tried to fill in all the details. He told about his discovery of Butterfield's wild talent, Cranston's attempt to kill him, Yargo's reactions and Herman Bok's strange entry into the picture. Jonquil's expression grew puzzled when he narrated his arrest by Gullfin and the Manager's attempted inquisition, but didn't interrupt. When Krull finished, he remained silent, idly watching his cigarette smoke curl upward. Finally he said:

"You really do have problems."

"Enough to strain my 113 IQ," Krull wryly commented.

The Inspector was thoughtful. "I don't know how much help I can give you," he said finally. "Frankly, I don't understand the implications any better than you do."

"It's not the assignment that has me baffled, it's the people." Krull shrugged helplessly. "I don't know enough about the background politics to make any assessment."

"Perhaps I can help there." He leaned back and puffed on his cigarette a moment before continuing. "You probably don't know that I served with the Agency of Police in Sydney for several years before I was shanghaied." His eyes met Krull's.

"I still have friends there and, of course, have maintained a certain amount of communication. I know a little about the backgrounds of some of the people you've mentioned—a great deal about several of them. I only mention this so you can assess my opinions."

"A run-down on personality profiles is just what I need," Krull affirmed. "Right now I can't pick the villains from the heroes—except in the Manager's setup," he added.

"Okay, let's start there." Jonquil suggested. "I can tell you this much: Ivan Shevach is arrogant, ambitious, ruthless—and brilliant, but his mind has a twist. I think he's capable of anything to achieve his end which, of course, is power. He's power mad. Now, with elections so close, he'll do anything he thinks will help him—or hurt Yargo."

"That's about the way I sized him up."

"He uses people like Gullfin and discards them when their value is lost. His tactics are both intellectual and physical, which makes him doubly dangerous. He's a mean one, Max. Don't underestimate him and try to steer clear of him. That's the best information I can give you."

"It's not a question of steering clear of him, but of eluding him. His men are birddogs."

"That could be a problem. Did anyone get off the plane with you?"

"Some guy that looked like a commercial traveler—a tall, lanky fellow lugging a sample case."

"It's my guess he'll board the plane with you again."

"A shadow?"

"I would guess so," Jonquil commented drily. "I don't think Shevach would let you out of sight a minute after what's happened."

"Okay. I'll watch him."

"Gullfin's probably a bigger danger because he's unpredictable," Jonquil offered. "He's a sadist and a killer and, unlike Shevach, has no mental brakes to control his emotions. Shevach's a logician; because of that there's a certain predictability about his actions. That doesn't hold with Gullfin. He's an out-and-out killer with no thought of consequences." He paused.

"I can't place Kruper or Cathcart, but they're probably late comers, of Gullfin's ilk."

"How about a gent named Peter Merryweather?"

THE Inspector's head jerked up, startled. "Merryweather—is he in it? You didn't mention him before."

Krull nodded. "He didn't seem to be too important." He caught Jonquil's intent look. "Or is he?"

"Tell me about him," he brusquely ordered. Krull related their meeting and the gaunt man's offers of aid. The Inspector smiled faintly when he gave Merryweather's job as public relations for the Manager. He finished and looked inquiringly at Jonquil. The latter's fingers were drumming restlessly against the desk, his eyes were closed, and he seemed lost in thought. Finally he asked:

"Max, you've heard of the searchers?"

Krull was jolted. "But they hunt hidden espers?" He bit off the words, for a moment fearful.

"And pk's and other dangerous mutants," Jonquil finished grimly. Krull squirmed uneasily without taking his eyes from the Inspector's face. His hands had become wet suddenly and he was conscious of a vein throbbing at the base of his neck. He tried to conceal his discomfiture and said:

"Merryweather—a searcher?"

"The Searchmaster," Jonquil corrected. "He heads the thing. His agents are all over the world."

"Oh," Krull said in a small voice. The news shook him. Jonquil's face was perplexed.

"I can't figure out what he's after."

"I'll watch him," Krull supplied quickly. He felt jumpy, uneasy, and wanted to get off the subject. "How about Yargo?"

"You can trust Yargo implicitly," he flatly stated. "He's a rock of integrity."

"I would have guessed so," Krull broke on, "only several things disturbed me."

"Such as...?"

"His apparent disinterest in what I do, almost as if he weren't too concerned about the case...aside from lip service."

"Typical of him," Jonquil interjected. "That's the way he operates—confidence in the man he selects."

"What did he know about me?" Krull challenged.

"Don't make any mistake," Jonquil advised. "He studied your record exhaustively—enough so that he was completely satisfied you were the man he needed."

Krull grinned wryly. "At IQ 113?"

"Intelligence is not the only attribute," Jonquil rebuked. "Perhaps, in this case, he was more interested in loyalty, dependability and courage...as well as mental attributes. Knowing what I do of him I can tell you this: he made his evaluation and is willing to back it by not tying your hands."

"There's one other thing, Cranston was Yargo's man—and he tried to kill me."

"You don't know that he was his man," the Inspector pointed out. "It's more probable he cast his lot with Shevach."

"Why would Shevach want to kill me?"

"Why would Yargo?" Jonquil countered. He leaned back in his chair and gave him a fatherly look. "Max, you've got one strike against you—one thing to learn, which you couldn't be expected to know from atoll duty. A position of power is always a center of intrigue—and the office of the Prime Thinker is the biggest such center in the world. No one knows that better than Yargo, which is probably the reason your revelation didn't shake him. He's dealing with dozens of intrigues, Max, and the Cranston affair was just another twig on the blaze. You can't hold him responsible on that account. My best advice would be—trust him implicitly, but don't always try to understand him. That's just my opinion, but that's the way I'd play it," Jonquil advised.

"WELL, I feel somewhat better," Krull confessed. "Frankly, that was my own opinion, but it's nice to have it confirmed." He paused a moment. "That takes us to Bok."

"Herman Bok, President of the World Council of Espers." Jonquil spoke the words half-aloud, then his voice raised. "That's the man I can tell you most about."

"Glad to hear it—he really has me stumped."

"You and lots of other people." His eyes narrowed slightly and when he spoke his voice was grim. "Herman Bok is an old man with the face of a saint and a voice to match. He leaves the impression of righteousness and dedication to his fellow men—just a shade short of appearing sanctimonious."

"The way he struck me," Krull admitted.

"Don't let it fool you. He's dangerous, cunning, with a lust for power that probably overshadows even Shevach's."

Krull lifted his head, surprised, and found himself echoing Bok's words: "How can a man of eighty-seven be dangerous?"

"What's age got to do with lust?" Jonquil rasped. "He's a master schemer, plotter, but too wily to pin down." He looked inquiringly at Krull. "Doesn't it strike you as strange that he's hung onto the presidency of the espers for eight consecutive terms? That's power, boy, power that's secured by harsh means."

"I did think of that," Krull confessed. For a moment his eyes avoided the Inspector's. "Of course I don't know much about the esper set-up, or about espers."

"The espers are dangerous." Jonquil said point-blank. "They believe they are some kind of super race, destined to rule the world. That's their prime objective. It's not just persecution that has led the Government to keep sharp strings on them. Give 'em half a chance and we'd be under their heel. That's why the searchers."

"I never particularly considered them dangerous, perhaps due to their small numbers." Krull said mildly.

"The ruling class is seldom large," Jonquil pointed out. "History will authenticate that fact. But there's never been a ruling class as potentially dangerous as the espers. Think, Krull, of the power that resides in the ability to read minds and, far more dangerous, mutants like Sawbo Fang." He smiled half-apologetically. "Maybe I'm a crank on the subject but that's the way I feel."

"Guess I'll have to reappraise my thinking…"

"Not on my say," Jonquil interrupted quietly. "I'm just telling you my viewpoint: but I could be wrong." The tone of his voice indicated he didn't think he was.

Krull hesitated as if loath to ask the next question, but finally did: "Do you know anything about his secretary, Ann Malroon?"

"Not a thing," Jonquil replied promptly. "She is, of course, a peeper, but I never heard her name until you mentioned it." He grinned knowingly. "A man could use up a lot of secretaries in eighty-seven years."

"Yeah, I can see that," Krull said drily. They fell into a discussion of the pros and cons of Krull's position and what steps he might take next. Jonquil was of the opinion he should stick to the elusive past of William Butterfield in an effort to reconstruct the conspiracy and, secondly, to keep open the strong possibility that Herman Bok had a long finger in the case. When they finally finished, the Inspector asked:

"When will you be returning?"

"Morning carrier." Krull grinned. "I'm going to make the most of my vacation."

"Do that." Jonquil glanced at his watch. "Let's go eat."

AFTER lunch Krull returned to his quarters debating how to pass the afternoon. Merryweather was a disquieting figure in his mind. The searchmaster! There was something sinister about him. Was he suspected? He tried to think back. No, he hadn't tipped his hand—no one could know he was an esper. He tried to push Merryweather from his mind by thinking of Rea Jon. She lived on Ati-Ronga, the northernmost atoll—he decided to go swimming and see her later.

He stripped, donned a pair of trunks and sandals, got his swim gear and sheath knife and headed for the lagoon. At the beach he adjusted his oxygen equipment, donned his goggles and flippers and tucked his knife in his belt, studying the scene a moment before entering the water. There were several sails in the distance and the hulk of Paha Jon's outrigger. Beyond, Chimney Rock protruded black and shining above the sea; the base must be a fantastic jungle, he thought. If he had a torp like the hermit... He regretfully dismissed the conjecture and entered the water, swimming along the bottom in the direction of the reef.

He paused to explore some coral heads and investigate a niche where a giant crab had scuttled at his approach; he swam leisurely, feeling his tensions gradually melt away. This was a peaceful secure world, with its waving sea fronds and familiar bottom life. He paused occasionally, watching the bubbles from his exhalation valve slide upward through the water like gleaming silver spheres. He came to a coral garden filled with odd toadstool formations, arches, and bizarre limbs reaching crookedly through the deeps, the ghost arms of a stone forest. It was a favorite spot of his, an enchanted fairyland built from the calcareous skeletons of untold eons of marine zoophytes. He knew its every turn and twist and passage from countless hour's of exploration. He dived deeper, made a loop in the water and shot into a narrow tunnel, stroking toward the pale circle of light at the opposite end. As he emerged, he glimpsed movement out of the corner of his eye and automatically spun around and withdrew into the shadows.

Swimmer—another swimmer in the green depths of the lagoon! It wasn't one of the natives—somehow, he knew that with certainty. He was startled momentarily; one didn't expect to encounter anyone in such a spot. The thought flicked through his mind that the unknown swimmer was seeking him—trailing him. Absurd, he told himself, yet he wouldn't have spotted him if he hadn't turned back on his trail in the coral forest. He moved forward to get a better look; the newcomer was swimming with a slow leisurely breast stroke but moved with purpose, turning neither left nor right. Krull saw he would pass just to one side of him. His curiosity was aroused and he moved out from the shadows—the strange swimmer instantly altered his course and came toward him. Krull saw the bubbles rising from his exhalation valve and caught the impression of a long lean body, whiter than that of a native. Suddenly the newcomer stopped, kicked himself into upright position and started to fumble with something in his hands.

Spear gun!

KRULL froze, whirled, dived and began stroking furiously toward the protecting arms of coral. He reached the tunnel and cast a backward glance—the other swimmer had lowered the gun and was moving toward him with a powerful leg kick. Krull swam through the tunnel, emerged on the other side and began threading his way into the network of coral, twisting among the bizarre formations in an effort to shake his pursuer or, at worst, keep him from getting a clean shot. Halfway through the stone jungle he reached a clearing and looked back. The strange swimmer was closer than ever. He struck out again, swimming with near desperation, momentarily expecting to feel the fish spear rip through his body. He reached the end of the stone jungle, hesitated, and headed toward the reef with powerful strokes. Just this side of it was another skeletal forest, where he could twist through to safety. He was almost there when a danger signal flamed in his mind—he automatically veered to one side and dived deeper. He felt the stir of the spear, heard it climp against the coral just inches from his body, and noted it had no line attached—a sign that his pursuer probably had a quiver of the missiles.

He breathed easier as the shadows of the coral outcrops closed around him, and twisted through the labyrinthine formations searching for a spot he knew, a natural cavern with an opening just large enough to accommodate his body. He rounded a familiar formation and saw it, a black hole couched deep in the pinkish-white rock. He cast one hurried backward look before darting into the narrow opening into a world of stygian darkness. He paused, treading water, and drew his knife, moving into a position where he was facing the opening. He waited, aware that his heart was pounding furiously. If he were trapped inside...

The water beyond the entrance seemed peaceful and undisturbed. A school of small fish swam past and disappeared and a large crab scuttled across the floor of the lagoon, moving between waving sea fronds. Still he waited. An odd silvery fish with bright red stripes and a hideous mouth paused to gape in front of him and suddenly darted away. He tensed, bracing his legs against the back of the shallow cave. An instant later his pursuer came into view, swimming cautiously, holding the deadly spear gun ready, peering ahead and to both sides as he kicked his way along.

KRULL drew his body backward, tensed, and propelled himself violently outward just as the other passed the mouth of the cave. He crossed the swimmer's back, reached down and managed to circle his arm around his throat. A strong hand reached up and caught Krull, pulling his head violently down in an effort to break the hold. Krull brought his knife down in a short sweeping arc—once, twice, thrice. His assailant's body contorted and went limp, but he struck twice more before releasing his hold and pushing himself backward. His heart was pounding at a furious rate and he fought to control his breathing.

The pale green waters took on a pinkish tint, and he could see the ugly red against the broken flesh where he had struck. He moved forward again, got hold of an arm and tore the goggles and oxygen mask from the dead face. The sightless eyes of the supposed commercial traveler stared blankly at him.

He shivered. His victim was tall, well-muscled, with a broad flattened nose, high cheek bones and heavy ridged brows over sunken eyes. In life the face might have been classified as tough, he thought—but now, in death, the features were loose, relaxed, giving it a slightly foolish look. He shuddered again and pulled the body through the narrow opening of the cavern, wedging it between two coral outcrops. He pushed back and grimly surveyed his work.

Mr. Mystery Man had found his niche in eternity.

TWO killings in almost as many days. He was beginning to see why Yargo had selected a low IQ agent. He felt like the executioner on a whale farm—except these were humans. Well, he'd better get used to it. He swam thoughtfully back to the beach. His victim had come fully prepared for the death struggle, had known that Krull wouldn't leave the atolls without at least one swim in the lagoon. He had intended that swim to be his last. More important, it meant that his moves were being assessed, predicted—someone was going to a lot of trouble to get him out of the way. Murder was no bar.

He removed his goggles and fins on the beach and started a slow search of the sands. Just yards away from where he had entered the water he found footprints and, in the nearby shrubbery, a sample case. It contained sandals and some clothes. His fingers extracted a wallet from one of the pockets and he flipped it open; there was an ID card and a miniature gold shield pinned to the inside flap. He studied the card curiously; it identified its owner as Winslow J. Earlywine (IQ 121), Agent of Police, Sydney District. He wasn't surprised. He returned the contents to the case, pushed it back into the bushes and started back toward the village.

Crantson.

Earlywine.

Who next?

CHAPTER NINE

ALTHOUGH the Empire of Earth was founded upon Crozerian principles, dissidents appeared from time to time. Some early writers (e.g., Huxtel, 2210, and Brinkton, 2309) saw Crozener as a harsh, unjust, dictator who imposed his philosophy of government upon the planet without the people's consent. Huxtel portrayed civilization as "...a monstrous vegetable, devoid of thought."

Chau, in his *Regression Into Stagnation* (2356), followed Brinkton's earlier thesis that human progress had stopped, the world was static and mankind was living "in an intellectual vacuum, much like a hive of bees."

Kloppert's *Slumbering Race* (2395) argued that humanity had cut itself off from its natural destiny, the conquest of the stars. He referred to space as "the waiting cosmic biosphere" and termed human efforts to develop a far-flung empire of submerged cities as an "escape into a womb" symbol. Wallfort, in his remarkable biography, Edward Crozener. The Saintly Benefactor (2396), argued against Kloppert, stating that only dangerous progress had been stopped (i.e., atomic research). Wallfort noted that Leon Konstantine (IQ 213), the seventh Prime Thinker, had ruled that satellites used as weather stations and communications relays did not violate Crozerian principles, and that such space vehicles had been used for these purposes since Konstantine's time. He saw this as proof that mankind had not abandoned space. Far from being in a state of slumber, as claimed by Kloppert, Wallfort contended that planetary civilization had achieved a serene equilibrium, in which the very predictability of the future was its greatest assurance of security.

In 2410 A.D., Kemal Nazir (IQ 198), the 82nd Prime Thinker, made opposition to Crozerian principles a felony.

Blak Roko's
Post-Atomic Earthman.

* * *

KRULL returned to Sydney with a sense of urgency, a feeling he had to conclude the investigation to Yargo's satisfaction and get back to Waimea-Roa before he was caught in a political explosion. Jonquil had given him a better insight and for the first time he fully appreciated the tremendous undercurrents swirling around Yargo's throne. That was the danger. The election was only days away. If Ivan Shevach won...the prospect wasn't pleasing. The disquieting revelation of Merryweather's true role shook him. Why the searchmaster? He shuddered inwardly. The gaunt man was a chilling specter.

When the carrier landed, he hurriedly disembarked, almost bumping into Hardface Cathecart coming down the ramp. Krull recoiled and managed a grin.

"Nice to see you again."

Cathecart tried to conceal his surprise. He grunted and walked past him, stationing himself on the float. When the last passenger emerged, he turned with a frown. Krull grinned. He wanted to tell him that Earlywine must have missed the plane, but refrained. He returned to his room to formulate a plan of action and the esper seemed his best bet. He discarded the idea of working through Anna Malroon—that would forewarn Bok—and finally settled for a frontal attack.

After dark he took a cab to an address a few blocks from Bok's house. His destination turned out to be an area of rolling tree-shaded hills occupied by spacious mansions that clearly spelled HIQ. He smiled grimly. At least Bok was human enough to enjoy the better things of life. His heart might bleed for the LIQ's, but not to the extent that he lived among them. When the cab's lights receded, he started toward Bok's address.

The House of Espers proved to be a spacious two-story residence of pale green plastiglass and brick with a large pyrmont stone fireplace climbing up one side. It was, he noted, more pretentious than the mansion allotted Yargo. At the moment it seemed dark and lifeless except for a yellow shaft of light from an upper window that made a long rectangle across the ground. He paused a moment before going to the porch. The wind stirred through the trees but the house was still. He reached the door, hesitated, rang the chimes and waited. No answer. He tried again with the same result. He debated a moment and tried the knob. It turned.

HE paused inside to get his bearings, aware that he was perspiring and his nerves were on edge. Because he was going to face the esper? That was silly. Bok was a doddering eighty-seven. There was a flight of stairs that led toward the place he had seen the streamer of light. He reached the top of the stairs and spotted a half-open door leading to the room he sought. He moved quietly, and stopped with his eye against the opening. The opposite wall of the room was lined with books and, lower, the top of a nearly bald head protruded above the top of an easy chair. Beyond was the reflection of flames from an open hearth. He was congratulating himself when an ancient voice wheezed:

"Come in, Mr. Krull. I've been expecting you."

He sheepishly pushed the door open and entered.

"Come, sit by the fire." Krull glanced around. Bok—for it was Bok—was alone. He tried to conceal his discomfiture as he walked over to the hearth and looked down at the esper.

"Old bones like fire," Bok said. "Sit down, Mr. Krull." He motioned toward an easy chair alongside the hearth.

"Thank you, I will." He studied the old man while trying to pull his thoughts together. For the moment, the esper had him off balance. If the ancient man facing him felt the victory, his face didn't show it. Instead, it bore a look of warm welcome, as if a dear friend had come to visit.

"I've always liked an open hearth," Bok continued conversationally, "much better than electrical heat." He chuckled. "A psychmaster would probably say it's related to racial memories, when man had no other form of heat. Or maybe it's because a hearth always seems conducive to dreaming. He smiled gently. "Old men do fall into the habit, you know. In fact, their lives center around their dreams. But I suppose you wouldn't know that—yet."

"We all dream." Krull retorted, trying to figure out the best way to launch his attack.

"Yes, I suppose so, but with a difference."

"What's that?"

"Young people dream of the future—old men of the past. Your dreams, I suppose, are largely hopes. Ours...are regrets. Regrets mixed with pleasant memories; thoughts of what might have been as well as what was." He looked gently at Krull. "But I don't suppose you came here tonight to hear an old man reminisce."

"No, as a matter of fact, I didn't." He tried to introduce a note of harshness into his voice and failed. It was difficult to be harsh with such a saintly-appearing old man even if—as Jonquil claimed—he had the soul of Lucifer. You have information I need, Mr. Bok. Need and intend to get."

"Ah, yes, Mr. Butterfield again."

"And the rest of the facts about the conspiracy."

"I'm not a conspirator," Bok remonstrated gently.

"I won't argue the point," Krull said coldly. "You've already admitted extensive knowledge of the conspiracy. Now I want the rest of it."

Bok smiled. "I'm afraid I can't supply the information you want, Mr. Krull."

"Can't or won't?"

"I'm only interested in guiding you into proper channels of thought. Have you ever considered the satellites, Mr. Krull? Aren't they more to you than mere weather-forecasters—TV relay?"

"I don't know what you're driving at," Krull snapped harshly. "I'm interested in conspirators, not weather stations in space."

"Ah, yes, just weather stations." Bok contemplated the flames. "Yes, they go around and around, unvarying, telling us about such things as monsoons and sunny days. Very practical, Mr. Krull, but consider their history."

"I'm not interested," he answered bluntly.

"THE conspirators are." Bok's pale eyes caught and held his. "The first satellites were put up before the Atom War—
Sputniks, Explorers, Vanguards and dozens more. Mechta still circles the sun; probes lie on the barren deserts of Mars and beneath the mists of Venus. The heavens are not entirely alien to the hand of man. The moon was circled and televised. In time men went up, Mr. Krull, went up and rode the fringes of space in manned orbital vehicles. Do you know why? The future. They were seeking the future. It was the first step into space. All they needed was more power—atomic power. They built the first interplanetary vehicle, were ready to strike out when the Atom War dawned...and darkened the world." Bok's voice dropped.

"Now we use satellites to tell us about winds and rains and we've forgotten our dreams...content ourselves with mediocrity. We send satellites into orbit to use as TV relays. Do you know why, Mr. Krull? To transmit lurid pictures and sensational plays, to keep the populace amused and"—he chuckled whimsically—"to transmit commercials. Oh, yes, now the backward peoples of the world can be apprised of the IQ value of wearing Zarkman clothing. That's what we do with our knowledge, Mr. Krull—prostitute it. But the men you call conspirators remember. They know that man has a destiny far beyond the borders of this speck of dust we seem to prize so highly. Now they have the power..."

"To wreck the world," Krull grimly cut in. "Do you want that to happen?"

"I want to see mankind realize its destiny," the old man said quietly. "Unfortunately, I won't be here when that event actually occurs. But it will occur. I can tell you that much."

"You couldn't know so much without being a member of the conspiracy," Krull accused.

"Wrong," Bok replied, "but my role is more than that of a sympathizer. They haven't asked my aid, but I'm giving it...freely."

"They're undoubtedly appreciative," Krull said drily.

"Yes and no."

"Explain that."

"Only a few of the conspirators are aware of my—shall we say—sympathy toward their cause. None know I hold the key to their success."

Krull was startled. "Key?"

"Yes." Krull felt the ancient eyes, the color of sun struck ice, rest on his face. "You see, the conspirators are working in the blind, lack the knowledge of how to make the final step come true; they know, only, that some miracle will happen to make the dream live. They are working on faith, Mr. Krull."

"And you…?"

"Will help the miracle come true."

"How?"

"You will see, but it's no honor to me. I'm merely a link in the casual chain, a pawn that moves and acts according to destiny. Not that I have any alternative. *'Tis all a chequer-board of nights and days where Destiny with men for pieces plays,'* but perhaps you've never heard of Omar, Mr. Krull." He chuckled softly. Krull suppressed the desire to shake the information from the frail body. Was Bok sane?

"Men…men with dreams. That's all I can tell you. The rest you'll have to find out for yourself."

"I could force it from you," Krull threatened.

"No—no, you couldn't. My frail body couldn't take any force, and you couldn't get information from a corpse. But that's beside the point. You wouldn't use force." He smiled faintly. "It even makes you wince to contemplate it."

HE FELT trapped. No, he couldn't use force, not on such a harmless old man as Herman Bok. Harmless? He remembered Jonquil's words. But even if the Inspector were right he couldn't do it. Bok had him whipped—at least on that score.

Bok said thoughtfully: "My murderer will be a much more brutal man, Mr. Krull."

"Your murderer?"

"Yes, I suppose you would call it murder. Like I said, I'm frail. It would take but slight force."

"No, I don't think anyone would use force on you, Mr. Bok."

"You're wrong—unfortunately."

"You seem to know?"

"I know."

"You're a fatalist."

"With good cause."

"Or, perhaps, I should say a pessimist."

"No, not a pessimist, Mr. Krull. To the contrary, I'm exceedingly optimistic about the future."

"Even if you're going to be murdered?" Krull shrewdly shot.

"My optimism is not for me." Bok chuckled. "A man of eighty-seven would have to be optimistic, indeed, to see a good future in terms of himself. No, I'm optimistic for mankind. I see a glorious future."

"But there's nothing you will tell me?"

"Nothing beyond what I've already said," Bok answered firmly. "Except, when the time comes, you won't disappoint me."

"What do you mean by that?"

"You'll see, you'll see." Bok smiled. "Don't be discouraged, though. You'll find your conspirators. I can promise that."

"Thanks," Krull said drily. He debated his next move. It was clear that questioning Bok would yield nothing. The old man was shrewd, elusive, too wily to pin down. Okay, he'd play it another way. He got up to go.

"Be ready when you leave the house," Bok said.

"Why?"

"There's a man waiting for you."

Krull was startled. "Why?"

"To kill you."

"Is that a joke?"

"Do I look like a joker, Mr. Krull?"

He searched the ancient face. No, he thought, he didn't. The old man who headed the espers might he mad but he wasn't a joker. He momentarily wondered if Bok's telepathic powers were great enough to enable him to peep someone outside and almost as quickly discarded the idea. He would have to know someone was there before he could peep him. How would he know? He looked down at the esper. Mild blue eyes peered back at him. He's peeping me, Krull thought, but he didn't bother to erect a mind shield. Somehow, he felt it wouldn't do much good. He returned his thoughts to the esper's warning.

"How do you know someone's waiting to kill me?"

"I know." The words were uttered with finality.

BOK smiled faintly; his eyes closed and his head nodded as if he were falling asleep. Krull studied the fragile figure; the narrow chin was slumped forward and the hands, blue-veined talons, lay relaxed on the arms of the chair. He turned and stole from the room, pausing at the door for a final backward glance before leaving, then descended the stairs. He hesitated at the front door. Was Bok mad? A dreamer? A senile old man with an overworked imagination? He decided he was none of those and drew his gun, then opened the door a few inches and peered out. The porch and sidewalk seemed clear, but the latter was hedged in with tall shrubbery and overhanging trees. He decided he'd have to chance it and stepped out on the porch, glanced nervously around and started down the walk.

He had taken only a few steps when he sensed rather than saw movement in the bushes beside him, and automatically ducked and whirled just as a hand came through the bushes.

A gun blasted alongside his face.

He brought his weapon up and triggered it three times, leaping backward. A dark form stumbled from the shrubbery, staggered with loud gasping wheezes and slumped to the ground at his feet.

He held his gun ready and bent down, grasping the man's arm and flipping him over. Kruper's face stared vacuously at him. The Manager's man! He dropped the dead arm just as a voice grated in his ear:

"Stand still—don't move."

Krull froze, feeling his heart rise to a hammer in his chest; slowly, deliberately, he turned his head. Gullfin's flat evil face stared at him and his hand gripped an automatic that resembled a field piece.

"Drop the gun!"

Krull straightened his fingers—his weapon clattered on the walk.

"I'm going to kill you," Gullfin taunted. "Rip you open."

"No you won't," Krull countered, trying to sound calm. He heard a thumping and realized it was his heart.

"Why not?" Gullfin sneered.

"Because—if you were going to kill me, you would have done it already."

"Wrong. I want to see you squirm—feel it, taste it, sweat a little, then I'll let you have it right in the middle; scramble up your guts so you'll suffer a while. I don't want it to be easy."

"Lousy rat!" Krull spat the words without losing his watchfulness. When Gullfin's finger started to tighten...

"I know what you're thinking but you won't have time," the burly agent taunted. His eyes became pinpoints, his lips pulled tight against his teeth. The gun moved upward slightly.

The front door opened...a sharp scream...Gullfin whirled with a startled curse and Krull twisted, bringing a smashing right against the stocky agent's jaw. Gullfin staggered backward, and he followed through with hard chopping lefts and rights, dropping him with a hard rabbit punch.

"Quick—inside." Krull whirled toward the porch and saw Anna Malroon standing at the door, beckoning him to hurry. He stooped to retrieve his gun and took the steps four at a time. She stepped back into the house and slammed the door behind him. "Follow me—out the back," she gasped.

SHE turned without waiting for his answer and darted down the hall, Krull at her heels. She fled through the rear door and across the lawn, keeping in the shadows of the trees until she reached the street. There she stopped, motioning him to silence, before starting rapidly down the sidewalk. He reached her side and whispered:

"Where to?"

"Don't try to talk now," she gasped. "My car's parked around the next corner." She walked quickly, her breath coming in short violent pants.

"Take it easy," he counseled. She didn't answer. When they reached the next intersection she motioned to a car parked halfway down the block. When they reached it, he saw it was the same one she had used the first time he'd met her. She had the engine started almost before he got in beside her, and pulled away from the curb. She pushed to a high rate of speed, twisting down the hill to the freeway, turned and reduced her speed until she was moving with the flow of traffic. Krull broke the silence.

"You showed up just in time."

"Yes, I was on schedule." The way she said it caused him to turn toward her; her face, in profile, looked taut and pale.

"Schedule?"

"Mr. Bok's schedule," she explained.

"At least he's Bok instead of Bowman," Krull observed. When she didn't reply, he said: "What does Bok do, schedule things like this for a hobby?"

"He didn't schedule it, really. He just told me of the schedule," she explained. "He was a wonderful man."

"Was?" He questioned, startled.

"Yes, Mr. Bok is dead, now."

"What do you mean dead? I just saw him."

"Gullfin just killed him—a moment ago."

"How do you know that?"

"When Gullfin regained consciousness, he was enraged. He figured Mr. Bok was in league with you and he...handled him roughly. Too roughly."

"How do you know?" Krull repeated. "You weren't there."

"Mr. Bok told me."

"Oh..." He slumped back in the seat and gave up trying to solve the puzzle. Anna was talking riddles. The fact she was an esper didn't answer anything—not the kind of information she fed him. Of course, that had held for Bok, too. The old man—somehow Krull was convinced Anna spoke the truth when she stated he was dead—had been an odd duck. It was hard to fit Jonquil's description of him to his own observations. His saintliness had seemed genuine—as real as his expressed concern for the future of mankind. He had no reason for acting Lucifer's role; not with the knowledge of his own imminent death. He only wished Bok had come through with more information—such as the identity of the people involved in the conspiracy. Conspiracy? Actually, he didn't have a shred of evidence that one really existed, if one discounted William Bixby Butterfield's death—and Bok's admission.

THE car swung off the freeway, climbing along a narrow road, which lead to the brow of a hill. He recalled the route from the first visit; Anna's apartment lay just ahead. She turned into the driveway and parked.

"Wait here," she said hurriedly, and got out of the car without waiting for a reply. He heard her sandals receding down the drive toward the front of the house. A door banged, then there was silence. She returned a short time later.

"I've called a cab."

"Oh...?" He looked inquiringly at her, but she didn't offer any further information. She looked nervously over her shoulder and said: "Let's wait in front."

"Okay." He crawled from the car and walked with her back along the dark driveway to the front of the apartment, halting in the shadows of a lace fern tree. She was visibly nervous and kept scanning the street in both directions. Finally she turned to him.

"Do you have a light, Mr. Krull?"

"Sure, but call me Max." She smiled wanly, fumbled in her purse for a pack of cigarettes, extending it toward him.

"Thanks, Anna." He took one and held a light for her, looking down into her face. He wanted desperately to ask questions but refrained—she seemed to have a course of action in mind. They smoked in silence. After a while a cab cruised up and halted at the curb. Anna flipped the stub of her cigarette into the shrubbery, looked nervously up and down the street and started toward it. Krull followed at a more leisurely rate.

"Emberly Hotel," she told the driver. He nodded and pulled away from the curb, heading back down the hill. Krull watched the flashing colored neons of the town draw near while he tried to fathom his position. The cab pulled up in front of the Emberly; Anna paid the driver and got out before Krull could offer a protest. He followed sheepishly. She waited quietly until the cab pulled back into the stream of traffic before speaking.

"Let's get another one." She looked both ways along the street and started in the direction of another parked taxi. He nodded and followed, getting the idea—she wanted to scramble their trail. They changed cabs several times before they finally reached the center of the LIQ business district.

THE cab passed through a series of narrow streets lined with small plastiglass houses of soiled shades onto an older street dominated by small businesses and somewhat decrepit hotels. The driver stopped at the address Anna had given, and this time Krull was ready with the change. After the cab left, she led him down the street to a shabby building whose flashing red neon proclaimed it the Charles Hotel. She paused and turned toward him, looking up into his face.

"Take my arm," she murmured. "For the time being we are Mr. and Mrs. Bowman...Chester Bowman."

He grinned. "I like the idea, but why Bowman?"

"It's as good a name as any," she parried.

"I suppose Bok dreamed this up."

"As a matter of fact, he did."

"Well, bless him." He took her arm possessively as they entered a dilapidated lobby and approached the desk clerk, an ancient bespectacled man with a tired face. He lowered his girlie magazine and got slowly to his feet. Krull was momentarily alarmed—were they already registered? Anna hadn't mentioned that. She saw his predicament and spoke up:

"Room 211, please."

"Yes, Mrs..." The clerk fumbled for the keys and waited.

"Bowman...Chester Bowman," Anna supplied.

"Yes, Mrs. Bowman." He slid the keys across the counter and returned to his magazine. Krull held Anna's arm up the stairs. She steered him to the right at the second floor and stopped before Room

211. He followed her in and looked around curiously at the large, square somewhat old-fashioned room with its sagging divan, double bed, battered chairs and small wall TV. There were a couple other items of equally dilapidated furniture and, off to one side, a door leading into a bath. At the opposite side of the room was a small pantry-type kitchen from which he could hear the steady drip of a leaking faucet.

"Looks homey," he observed. "Part of the plan?"

"Yes."

He glanced around, then looked at her. "I think I'm going to like it," he said firmly.

"I hope so—Max." She looked wistfully around the room. "It's not the best place in the world but it's...it's anonymous, safe."

"Bok said that?"

"Yes..."

"Then it's safe," Krull decided. Somehow, he had come to have great confidence in the dead esper's predictions."

"Coffee?"

"Ummm, yes, please." He heard the rattle of pots in the kitchen and mused over his situation while waiting for her to return. Mr. and Mrs. Bowman—he liked the idea. Was she merely following Bok's directions? She was a strange girl—beautiful but with an aura of sorrow surrounding her that puzzled him. Her dark eyes were haunted; her olive face was taut, expectant, as if she were awaiting some blow.

"The news should be on," she called. He walked over, pressed a button and the screen came to life. The fat face of a well-known newscaster looked out at him. The lips were moving rapidly but it was a moment before the sound came on. When it did, Krull caught his breath.

"...IQ 113, Agent of police," the voice was saying. He heard Anna's quick footsteps coming from the kitchen. "...Wanted for the brutal double murder of Herman Bok, President of the World Council of Espers, and Joe Kruper, a fellow agent who had been instructed to question Krull on a routine matter..."

"They can't hang Bok's murder on me," Krull said savagely.

"Listen..." Anna beckoned for silence.

"Bok was slain in his quarters in the House of Espers, located in the exclusive HIQ district of northwest Sydney just moments ago." The announcer paused to lick his lips before continuing:

"Krull was believed fleeing the house when he met and killed Agent Kruper, IQ 116. Gordon Gullfin, Chief of Special Agents for the Manager, witnessed the fatal shooting and immediately subdued Krull, but in turn was attacked from behind and slugged unconscious by an accomplice of the slayer. Regaining consciousness, he sought aid at the House of Espers and subsequently discovered the body of the esper leader. Bok was serving his eighth consecutive term as President of the World Council of Espers…"

THIS makes it rough," Krull said. She nodded silently and he saw her eyes were tear-filled. Clenching his teeth, he turned back to the screen.

"…Agents of police believe Krull was engaged in a secret conspiracy with the leader of the espers, who was eighty-seven years old, and killed him following an altercation. All agents of police, troop police and private citizens are warned to watch for the killer and immediately report his presence to the nearest police agency, or directly to Gordon Gullfin, who is spearheading the search. Now…here is what the killer looks like…"

The announcer held up an enlarged photo. Krull was startled, recognizing it as a picture taken in his room at the Edward Crozener. So, they'd had the room tapped. He cursed at his failure to inspect it. The camera swung in for a close-up—a straight-on shot. Krull grimaced—every detail was clear. The announcer lowered the photo. Krull reached over and snapped the set off.

"I won't be able to budge from this trap," he said grimly. Anna watched him quietly. "I can't risk trying to call Yargo from here—they'd nail us in a second."

She looked thoughtful. "The clamor will die down in a day or two, at least as far as the general public is concerned."

"Can we risk it here that long?"

"There's no other choice. I don't feel any sense of immediate danger." She went to the kitchen and he heard some cups rattle before the significance of what she had said struck him. She returned with their coffee and he thoughtfully said:

"I forgot you were an esper. Can you really sense danger—at a distance?"

"It depends…" She set the cups on the table. "It's related to, well, the intensity of the thought. A hateful, violent mind like Gullfin's is like a broadcasting station." She looked quizzically at him. "You should know that." Of course, she would know he thought.

"I don't really know if I am an esper," he replied truthfully. "I seem to draw mostly blanks."

"Of course, it takes practice, like learning anything else. It's not much use in the latent state." Her lips pursed speculatively. "You've spent your life hiding your talent, submerging it, denying it was there. That was a mistake, Max. There's nothing wrong with being an esper…"

"Except that it gives you an advantage over other people that they resent," he cut in.

"So does a high IQ."

"I don't have that trouble." He grinned. "I'm 113."

"Part of your hiding role," she said softly.

"Besides, a high IQ doesn't bear the same connotation. There's no invasion of privacy involved. That's the difference: the LIQ's and MIQ's and HIQ's aren't peeping one another."

"Good espers don't invade the privacy of others either," she said defensively. "Telepathy is just another form of communication—another sense receptor put to use."

"But you peep non-telepaths?"

"Occasionally," she said calmly," but only as a means of self-preservation.

Krull grunted. "Bok must have done it on a mass scale."

"Oh no," she denied. "Mr. Bok never peeped people."

"Never? Come now, that's a big statement in view of what he seemed to know."

"Never," she repeated stoutly. "You see, Mr. Bok wasn't a telepath."

"Not…a telepath?" Krull uttered the words slowly, with disbelief. There was a span of silence before he continued. "But he was an esper—President of the World Council of Espers."

"The greatest esper," she affirmed. Her eyes shone as if she were looking into some corner of hallowed ground. He pulled his thoughts together with effort and said harshly:

"How can an esper not be an esper? Tell me that."

"I didn't say Mr. Bok wasn't an esper. I distinctly said he was the greatest esper."

"You said he wasn't a telepath," he accused. She faced him, a look of understanding growing in her face, and she quietly replied:

"All the known adult espers—all members of the World Council of Espers, as far back as we know—have been telepaths. All but Mr. Bok—that's what made him the greatest. He was a *down through*. He saw down through time. We regarded him as a further step in evolution. Even to us he was a kind of superman—a wonderful kind of superman."

"Impossible," Krull snapped.

"Down through is a case of special clairvoyance." She looked speculatively at him. "You've heard of clairvoyance?"

"Certainly," he said ruffled, "the theoretical ability to see objects or events not present to the known senses, but it's strictly a psychmaster's dream."

HAVE you heard of precognition?"

"A fancy word for prophecy—also a theoretical possibility."

"Mr. Bok combined them," she said simply. "He saw...future events."

He started to protest and abruptly closed his mouth. He recalled the incident when he had come up behind the old man unawares, or so he had thought. Bok had said:

Come in, Mr. Krull. I have been expecting you.

Bok had seen him entering before, perhaps, he had left the hotel. It also explained his knowledge that Kruper would try to murder him. A telepath might have detected Kruper's presence, but Bok had known his physical location; had also stated that Krull would uncover the conspiracy—stated it with undeniable certainty. A sudden humility gripped him. It must have shone on his face for Anna said:

"Now you believe..."

"Yes, I believe." He was silent a moment, absorbing the drama in the life of the fragile old man who had so calmly planned Krull's deliverance in the face of his own imminent death. Jonquil had been wrong. But, of course, he couldn't have suspected the esper's special talent. He had forgotten the presence of Anna until she spoke:

"I'll be going now."

"Going?" He asked, startled.

"We're hiding out—remember?" She flung a cape over her shoulders and drew it together at the neck. "My name's Ruth Bowman, IQ 90, and I'm a poor working girl."

"Is this a joke?"

"Not at all. It's part of the camouflage."

"What kind of work—where?"

"The Cassowary Cabaret, up on the next block. I got the job last week when...when..."

"When Bok told you to?"

"No, when Mr. Bok told me I was going to," she corrected. There's a difference." Her eyes were grave. "If I acted on Mr. Bok's orders, he would be influencing the future, but when he tells me what is going to happen, he is merely reporting the future."

"Supposing you don't do something he says you're going to do; that is, you know what's ahead and deliberately take another route, so to speak. Then the future would be different."

"No, that's not possible," she contradicted. "When Mr. Bok reported what he saw in the future, that meant it would actually happen. But if the causal chain which led to the event were changed—which isn't possible—he could not have seen the event but, rather, the event which would have occurred in its place. Can't you see that?"

"It's not crystal clear," he confessed, grinning.

"I'd better hurry. I'm going to be late as it is."

He looked ruefully around the room. "I thought we were supposed to be married," he complained. She laughed and went to the door, then turned and gave him an impish look.

"Not that married."

CHAPTER TEN

KRULL slept. He kicked off his sandals and flopped on the divan the moment the door closed behind Anna's slim figure and was asleep almost immediately. It was a deep, undisturbed sleep, without dream or awareness; when he woke the pale dawn light was filtering through the smudged lace curtains of the room's single window. He raised to his elbow and looked around—Anna had returned sometime during the small hours of the morning and was asleep on the bed. Her bosom rose and fell gently under the thin covers and her face, in repose, had lost its haunted look. It seemed peaceful, yet somehow pale despite the normally dark texture of her skin, and he noticed for the first time the extremely long curved sweep of her eye lashes and that her lips were a trifle too full to support her small jaw. Yet, he thought, it was a beautiful face, more beautiful since the haunted look had gone.

He swung off the divan, slipped on his sandals and left the room without disturbing her. He passed through the deserted hotel lobby—the clerk was nodding behind the counter—and paused when he reached the sidewalk. The street was just awakening to the day's activity. A few cars and trucks were on the move and farther down the block a couple of pedestrians were ogling a drunk passed out on the sidewalk. The air held the tang of the harbor, the industrial odors of smoke, coal tars and fish scents from nearby canneries.

An elderly couple pushed a handcart laden with junk toward some unknown destination, their heads bent into the morning chill. Krull listened to the rattle of the wheels over the uneven pavement and wondered if this was what Bok had meant when he referred to the people for whom there was no tomorrow. But there had to be workers—society couldn't be blamed for the vagaries of genetics. Still, the sight disturbed him. He watched the couple until they disappeared around a corner, then walked down the block until he found a place where he could buy a morning paper and breakfast.

A tired, middle-aged waitress with shadowed eyes looked up at his approach, closed the magazine she was reading and smiled artificially. He nodded, glancing around, disturbed to find he was the only customer; it would make him more conspicuous. Sighing, he sat down and gave his order. As the waitress shambled toward the kitchen he opened the paper. A picture of himself leaped to meet him. He quickly scanned the accompanying story, conscious of mounting tension, then looked at the headlines again:

BOK'S KILLER LINKED TO ATOMIC CONSPIRACY.

The picture was the same one shown on the screen. He read the story again, this time more slowly. According to the paper, "...A high government official who refused to allow his name to be used last night disclosed that the renegade agent, Max Krull, sought for the murders of Herman Bok, President of the World Council of Espers, and Agent Joe Kruper, was believed implicated in a secret atomic conspiracy that had seizure of world power as its goal."

KRULL whistled softly. The story named him as a special agent assigned to the Prime Thinker's personal staff. Further down it stated Yargo had secured his release from police a few days before, following his cold-blooded slaying of Oliver Cranston, another agent assigned to investigate his alleged role in atomic activities. The story obliquely inferred his activities had Ben Yargo's sanction.

Shevach—It's Shevach, Krull thought. The Manager was using him to undermine Yargo. The article was calculated to arouse public anger on one issue that was practically a world phobia—atomic research. Was there some other motive? More important, could Yargo ride it out? The waitress slid the coffee and hot rolls in front of him.

"Anything else?"

"No thanks." He glanced up—her face held a coquettish look.

"It's awful about that killer, isn't it?"

"Pretty bad." He stirred his coffee, keeping his face averted.

"Imagine, a man wanting to blow up the world."

"What?" he asked, startled.

"That's what it says—he's making atomic bombs, just like the kind that wrecked the world before."

"Hadn't read that part," he admitted. The waitress got an interested look.

"With a killer like that around, I'm almost afraid to go to my room...alone." Her eyes flicked to the clock. "I'm off in half an hour. I feel afraid living alone."

"You don't have to be," he consoled.

"Why not?" Her face perked up.

"He only kills agents—not pretty girls."

"Oh..." She looked pleased until he returned to the paper. When she saw he had no intention of following her lead, she sauntered disconsolately back to her magazine. Finished with his coffee and roll, he tucked the paper under his arm, left some change on the counter, and returned to the hotel. Anna was in the kitchen making coffee.

"A working girl needs more sleep than that," he reprimanded.

"I'll nap in the afternoon," she promised. She saw the worried expression on his face and came out to meet him.

"Trouble?"

"A storm brewing." He forced a smile and indicated the paper. "Now I'm a member of the atomic conspiracy—along with the late Mr. Bok." He heard the sharp intake of her breath and handed her the paper, pouring himself a cup of coffee while she read it. She finished and looked up at him with fear in her eyes.

"You didn't expect that?" he asked.

"No, of course not."

"I thought you knew the future?"

"Only milestones along the way." Her eyes met his. "It would be terrible to know every moment of the future. There would be nothing to live for—no anticipation or expectation because the end would already be known. Mr. Bok knew that. That's why he only told me certain things— and even his telling was part of the causal chain in events to come. No, I couldn't stand to know the future in its entirety."

"Bok did."

"That was his tragedy. He even knew...his murder."

"Yet he didn't try to change things," Krull mused.

"He couldn't. I've explained that before. He was only seeing what was to happen...just as a historian sees what has happened. But neither has the power to change what he sees."

"No, I suppose not."

SHE glanced toward the TV; he nodded and turned it on, discovering he had become a world villain overnight. The announcers had tried and convicted him of triple murder, violation of the First Law of Mankind; he was pictured manufacturing atom bombs in a secret laboratory, plotting to destroy the world. Anna got more coffee.

"Good for the nerves." She set a cup in front of him and sat down, smiling faintly. The commercials were followed by a geography professor who used a large globe to show how radiation from the Atomic War had blanketed all but a few areas of the world.

"But we could not expect to be so fortunate next time," he concluded. He smirked at the audience and withdrew, making way for the commercial. Krull flipped the switch.

He looked at Anna. "What now?"

"Wait. We'll have to wait."

"Wait and get trapped. I think we ought to be getting out of here."

"Where to?"

"I'll have to figure that out."

"We'll be safe...for a while." Her eyes were pleading.

"I won't do anything rash," he promised.

"You did this morning."

"I didn't think it was rash, then."

"But you won't leave again? Everyone will be watching for you."

"Not until I can figure a plan of action," he promised, "a safe way of getting in touch with Yargo."

"That might be the answer," she mused. They fell silent for a while, then she began talking about telepathy. He got the idea she didn't think he was much of an esper. She switched to Bok and her face became almost reverent. Unaccountably, he felt angry.

"I'm glad I'm not like Bok," he brutally cut in.

"No, you're not like Mr. Bok," she said quietly. Her eyes got a strange look. "Max..."

"What's the matter, Anna?"

"Nothing."

"You were going to say something."

Her eyes brimmed with sudden tears. "Max, I'm frightened for you."

"Why?" he demanded.

"Mr. Bok's burden was easy in comparison." She rose suddenly and left the room; he heard her heels echoing through the hall. Now what in hell, he thought savagely.

HE STAYED close to the room the rest of the day, occasionally turning on the TV to catch the news. The story had blown big and before evening dominated the world news. According to the announcers, Yargo had declined to give an official press release; the Manager smugly confirmed that Krull had been assigned to the Prime Thinker's staff "…in a secret capacity that Ben Yargo declined to reveal to the public."

Rumors cropped up in legion. Krull variously was reported spotted in Wellington. Melbourne, the floating city of Kulahai and as far away as Leningrad and Capetown. A man answering his description had been arrested boarding the Hawaii carrier at Honolulu, and agents of police had picked up a number of suspects, including a wino, an IQ 50 farmhand with a record of window peeping, and an IQ 90 laborer who had just been released from the Dreamland Mental Hospital as a cured manic de-pressive. All espers suspected of political activities or who had majored in physical sciences at a post-graduate level had been rounded up for questioning by the searchers. Anna returned in time to hear the last bit of news.

"Regular witch-hunt," Krull growled.

"Dangerous," she said soberly. "Everyone will be watching for you."

"Maybe not so dangerous," he reflected aloud.

"How do you mean?"

"By now I've been reported seen all over the globe. Everyone will think I'm somewhere else."

"I know." She was quiet a moment. "I worry, even though I know you'll…come through all right." She went to the kitchen leaving him to puzzle her meaning. After supper they talked until it was time for her to go to work. She made him promise he would remain in the room.

"Cross my heart," he told her.

"I'd be afraid if you went out." Her eyes were soft; she turned suddenly and departed. After a while he kicked off his sandals and lay on the divan.

Sleep came slowly.

"Max …" He woke with a start, pushing himself to his elbow.

"Max…" He saw her or, rather, her shadowy form.

"What is it?" he asked guardedly.

"Max, there's not much time left." Her voice was low, husky, intense.

"Not much time…" His vision cleared and he cut the words off abruptly, catching the reflection of dim light through the window on the dusky skin of her body.

He got up, slowly, and moved toward her, realizing that, somehow, time was running out—for Anna Malroon. Time was running out and she wanted something to take with her. She moved to meet him and he saw that her breasts in the dim light were paler than the rest of her body.

THEY were subdued during breakfast but Anna looked happy, contented and, for the first time during wakefulness, had lost the haunted look. She hummed softly while she returned to the kitchen for more coffee. It was good to see her so cheerful, yet he was uneasy. He had the feeling she had come to a crisis, had met it in her own way, now was waiting for some predetermined destiny to come to pass. Foolish, of course, but that's the way it seemed.

How much had Bok told her?

Did she know, like the esper had known, the coming shadows?

They spent the day as they had the previous one—listening to news broadcasts; but, unlike the day before, she avoided any talk of the future. She knows, he thought. Bok has told her. When night came, she prepared for work, only this time she didn't caution him against leaving the room. She merely said:

"Goodnight, darling." Her eyes flooded with tears. She closed the door and rushed down the hall before he could stop her. He waited, half expecting her to return—knowing she wouldn't. Later he turned off the lights and went to sleep.

He was awakened by a sensation almost as sharp as an electric shock. He sat upright on the divan, feeling his heartbeat rise to a fast hammering, conscious of a warning signal flashing in his brain like a signal light blinking on a dark sea.

Danger! Danger!

The warning screamed in his brain. He leaped from the couch, shoved his feet into his sandals and stole to the door. The faint sound of music came from somewhere down the hall; the warning came again, sharp as a rapier—the slow shuffling of feet in the hall came to a halt at his door.

"Here."

He heard the low single word and backed quickly into the room, peeping the hall. He got the vague impression of several forms, a towering figure, a mixed jumble of thought. He grabbed his gun and moved to the single window which overlooked a dark alley—closed his eyes and concentrated. The sense of danger diminished; he deliberately concentrated on the hall again—the warning rose to a high jangle in his brain.

Danger...

Run! Run!

He raised the window without hesitation, slipped through feet first and hung from the sill while trying to see the ground below. No use, it was lost in shadows. The door splintered inward and he released his hold, flexing his legs to absorb the impact. He struck hard—involuntarily winced—and fled down the alley toward the nearest corner, slowing his pace when he reached it. A few pedestrians were abroad and several small groups of loafers stood before a bar on the opposite side of the street. The garish reds and greens of neons gave the scene an odd pattern of shifting light and movement. A few cars and trucks were parked at the curbs but moving traffic was light—nothing resembled a police car.

The flick of danger came again, this time from the alley at his rear; he started hurriedly down the street. He reached the next corner, glancing over his shoulder in time to see several figures emerge from the alley and start in his direction. He turned the corner and increased his pace, conscious that his shadows were closing in.

Faster…Faster!

HE WAS halfway down the block when a police car rounded the corner, a spotlight combing the street. He cursed and ducked into a dark doorway, hugging the wall. He sensed his pursuers—how many?—drawing near. The danger signal rose to a discordant howl and he tried to peep the source. A now familial mental pattern filled his mind, movements in various shades of gray; it sharpened and the imagery of a face took form.

A face…

His face!

He was startled until he remembered. Of course, they were concentrating on him; he was picking his picture from their minds. Hunters—he was the hunted. The police car swept its torch across his hiding place and moved on. He exhaled slowly and fled down the street. He spotted a pub garishly lit by green and red neons and filled with the sound of raucous music. It would be jammed, noisy, filled with people.

A place to hide!

He slowed down and pushed through the door. It was crowded. Most had their backs toward him—they were watching a tall blonde perform a strip tease. Her arms moved languorously in rhythm with her hips, her skin was golden. She was down to the last garment and the crowd was tense. He elbowed his way to the rear and, as he hoped, found an exit. He turned the knob and looked out; it opened onto a dark alley.

The jangle rose in his brain again and he quickly looked back. The strip teaser was whirling naked; the crowd was hanging on, whistling and making guttural cries. The dark lantern-shaped face of Henry Cathecart was framed in the door. Another figure loomed behind him, thin, gaunt, tall...Merryweather...

The searchmaster!

A lean arm swept up and pointed in his direction: Krull flung the door open and fled into the night, his mind a jumble of thoughts. He heard feet pound the pavement behind him and gave an extra burst of speed, rounding the corner onto the street without slacking his pace. Several startled pedestrians stepped aside without trying to stop him. Run. Run.

HE REACHED the next corner, fled halfway down the block and ducked into a recessed doorway to get his bearings. His heart pounded and sweat dripped from his body and stung his eyes. He gripped his gun and peered back down the street. Empty. He was starting to breathe easier when three figures rounded the corner. One of them crossed the street—all three moved in his direction. Merryweather was tall, thin, an ominous skeleton towering above his companions. Krull cursed savagely, debating whether to try and ambush them. He watched, gripping his gun, feeling his heart thump against the rib case. Suddenly they stopped and the bony hand came up again, pointing toward his hiding place. He broke and ran, trying to fathom Merryweather's uncanny ability to detect him. Run, dodge, hide... He twisted through the dark narrow streets of the LIQ section, frantically trying to elude his pursuers—trying to shake the gaunt lean figure of Merryweather.

He ducked through several groups of bystanders and rounded corners at top speed, fearful he would encounter a police car. He was halfway down another block when the alarm sounded in his brain. He stopped abruptly. It was ahead of him... No, behind him. He turned bewildered. Boxed in! Trapped! He spotted an alley almost across from him and fled toward it. If he could reach it, reach the shadows...

"Stop that man!"

The cry was harsh in his ears and it took him a second to realize it was a human voice and not a telepathic warning. Several men standing in front of a bar ran to intercept him—he tried to dodge them. A hand caught him and he slugged out, feeling the crunch of bone beneath his fist followed by a sharp cry of pain. Before he could twist free someone struck him a glancing blow on the jaw. His head reeled and he staggered, his gun clattering against the pavement as he broke free and darted into the black mouth of the alley. Shouts... the sound of running feet...the raucous jangle of danger...darkness...the thump of his heart.

Wham! Wham! Something stung his shoulder. Wham! A bullet whizzed past his ear and he broke into a frenzied burst of speed. A whistle shattered the air—the raucous behind him grew until he couldn't separate the jangle in his brain from reality. Hide. He had to hide! He raced into the alley. There were more shouts, another whistle, this time ahead of him. He stopped abruptly, breathing heavily, conscious of a dull burning ache at the top of his shoulder.

Boxed in—done for...

He hurriedly studied the sides of the alley and tried to allay his panic. His breath was a hoarse rasp in his throat. He saw the dim outlines of a door and twisted the knob. Surprisingly, it was unlocked. He leaped in, closed it behind him. His hand located a small bar lock and slipped it in place—he leaned against the door trying to control the harsh sound of his breathing. Feet pounded up the alley; they stopped—silence—followed by a faint shuffling.

"Here," a monotone voice said, "he's inside."

Krull recoiled, feeling a stab of fear. Merryweather! Only Merryweather wasn't the genial man he had met. This Merryweather was a bloodhound. He heard the boom of his heart and wondered if it carried outside.

"Krull—give yourself up or we'll kill you."

HE FROZE, immobile. They were bluffing—they hadn't seen him enter, couldn't know. Couldn't? It struck him then. Merryweather—an esper! That accounted for his role of searcher. He was a renegade, hunting his kind. A telepathic killer! He had been trailing him by thought pattern—that was the only explanation. Suddenly he saw the whole picture. His first encounter with Merryweather hadn't been happenstance. No, the gaunt man had met him for the sole purpose of peeping him. He was Shevach's eyes and ears, Shevach's hidden power, the lever he used to propel himself into high places. He knew it—knew it beyond the shadow of a doubt. Then Shevach knew he was an esper, knew it and feared him. That explained the attempts on his life.

"Krull—we're coming in!"

He turned, moved deeper into the cellar, feeling his way and trying to find an exit.

"Krull ..." The voice was soft, almost at his side. He recoiled instinctively. "Follow me—I'm a friend."

"Who?" He whispered harshly, girding himself to either fight or run.

"There's no time to explain. Follow me." The voice was soft, yet imperative, and all at once he saw the outlines of a man's body. A small man. "This way!"

The figure started to retreat and he followed carefully, watchful, certain it was a trap. If he had a gun... Behind him the door splintered inward and a beam of light caught him in full circle. He whirled toward it and froze, half-blinded, conscious that his breathing was harsh in his ears. He tensed his body to spring.

"Don't try it," a voice grated. A figure moved into the circle of light and Krull struggled to clear his vision. Hardface! Hardface Cathecart, holding a gun.

"Not so damned mighty this time, are you?"

Krull spat an oath and moved his eyes sideways from the center of the light, trying to see the man holding the beam.

"You've come to the end of the rope—Killer." Cathecart's eyes swung around the cellar as he reached over and took the flashlight from his companion:

"Leave us alone, Peter. I'll handle it from here." Krull heard a merry chuckle; the door opened outlining a tall gaunt figure for a moment before it closed behind him. He was alone with Cathecart—except for the mysterious man hiding somewhere in the shadows behind him.

Cathecart glanced around the cellar. "Nice execution chamber you've selected."

Krull cursed him calmly. The hard faced agent's eyes glittered, and the hand holding the gun moved up; he found himself looking down its barrel. Cathecart sneered.

"You've murdered a couple friends of mine. Seeing as we're alone, and you're attempting to escape..."

HIS finger tightened on the trigger. "It's not going to be easy...I'm putting 'em where it'll hurt!" He held the muzzle steady.

"Go on, sweat," he taunted. "Beg for mercy—and I might allow you another minute. Go on—plead."

Krull tensed his body and told him what he could do with his gun. Cathecart's voice dropped to a toneless grate:

"So long—killer!"

Krull dropped to a crouch and sprang sideways at the same time. Wham! Wham!—flame laced past his ear. He sprawled off balance, hearing the sound of bullets thudding into flesh. Cathecart staggered and grunted. Wham! The flame laced out again and this time he saw it came from his rear. Cathecart swayed, tried to raise his gun, half-spun on buckling legs, gasped, and slumped to the floor.

"Let's get the hell out of here," the voice behind Krull growled. "My car's around the corner." The shadow broke into a blur of movement and Krull scrambled after him. His companion broke into a sprint when they reached the street, but Krull noted that his unknown benefactor was short, slender. They reached the corner—there was a small black car parked against the curb. The man pulled open the door and leaped in; Krull followed. The engine roared to life.

He pulled the car away from the curb, rounded the first corner too fast for comfort, zigzagged for several blocks and finally turned onto a freeway. Krull studied his profile; it was familiar, a face he knew and couldn't place. He remembered the voice...it was familiar also. A name was surging at the back of his mind and he fought to recover it, a tantalizing moment. An overhead street beam lighted the man's features, jolting Krull upright in his seat. The man beside him was...

"Butterfield!" The little public works engineer from Benbow Deeps. Butterfield turned and looked at him full-faced.

"Butterfield." He repeated the name, stupidly, then a wave of anger struck him. Butterfield, the meek little engineer who had been awed by his credentials, had fearfully confessed his brother was an esper, was a phony. He finally managed words.

"Just who the hell are you?" he rasped.

"Oh, I guess you could call me the head of Yargo's special agents. Sort of an honorary title," he admitted reticently.

KRULL was jolted. Butterfield, the timid engineer, wasn't an engineer. Furthermore, he wasn't timid. Not by a damned sight. Not the way he had coolly blasted Cathecart to death. Krull's anger turned to Yargo. The Prime Thinker had suckered him, played him for a clay pigeon. Why? He savagely promised himself he'd find out. Butterfield spoke:

"Looks like I got to that cellar just in time."

"Yeah...you did." Krull uttered the words thoughtfully, then swung toward him curiously. "How did you know? I picked that particular spot on the spur of a moment."

"Damned strange." The engineer's lips pursed thoughtfully—

"How did you know that I'd be there...at that particular spot, at that moment?" Krull demanded.

"Like I said—damned strange. All I know is that Yargo got a letter saying you'd be there...and under what circumstances. So he sent me."

"Who was the letter from?" Krull asked harshly.

"Bowman. Some guy named Bowman, but I can't get a line on who he is."

"Was..." Krull corrected automatically.

"Was?"

"Listen," he interjected angrily, "you've got some questions to answer."

"Not me," Butterfield said, his voice cold and hard. "Ask Yargo."

"Damned tootin' I'll ask him."

"You might ask him about Bowman, too," Butterfield said hopefully. "That one's got me baffled."

"No problem there," Krull answered maliciously. The engineer turned toward him inquiringly, but he remained silent. If Butterfield wouldn't talk, neither would he.

CHAPTER ELEVEN

KRULL idly watched the lights of oncoming cars sweep past while he tried to untangle the latest twist in the complicated plot in which he seemed to be the main character Herman Bok knew the end of the story; otherwise he wouldn't have bothered to post the letter that had brought Butterfield to his rescue after his own death. And Anna Malroon had known what was going to happen. Why hadn't she warned him? Had she known he would be saved by Bok's intervention? It was all a weird tangle—one which, for the moment, he despaired of solving.

His companion swung the car into the lane leading to the House of the Prime Thinker and Krull's interests perked up. How would Ben Yargo explain Butterfield—the use of Butterfield to decoy him to Benbow Deep? And why the decoy? Yargo had better start talking, he moodily told himself. He didn't like the idea of being a clay pigeon. They passed the sentry box and the house came into view, a black square against the sky with only a single lighted window at the upper story. The car rolled to a stop under the portico and Butterfield got out.

"Wait here," he ordered softly. He walked toward the porch; a shadowy figure emerged to meet him. They huddled a moment before he returned and beckoned Krull.

"Follow me." He led the way into the house, went upstairs in the dark and opened a door at the end of a second floor corridor, stepping aside to let Krull enter. He closed the door behind them and switched on the lights.

"Part of the family quarters," he explained. "You're to stay here until Yargo decides what to do with you. Don't leave—and keep out of sight."

"How about seeing Yargo?"

"In the morning."

"Is he up now?" Krull asked doggedly.

"I wouldn't know."

"Listen…" he started to protest. Butterfield opened the door and cut in decisively:

"It'll keep."

Krull watched the door close behind him and fumed inwardly. He didn't like being pushed around, and Yargo was pushing. Butterfield's words implied he had become some kind of liability to the Prime Thinker, a millstone around his neck—someone to hide in corners until he could be gotten rid of. He was a prisoner. He cursed softly. He didn't need Yargo or anyone else to pull him out of the hole—all he wanted was free rope, and the Manager's killers kept off his neck. Then he might get somewhere. But he'd never crack it at the present rate. A thought buried in the back of his mind plagued him: he wasn't so certain any more that the power politics in which he was snared and the conspiracy were two separate things. Something told him they were linked, that both Yargo and the Manager knew a lot more than he had been told. Maybe Yargo himself was involved? Okay, if that was it, he'd have it out with him in the morning.

HE LOOKED around; the room was large, comfortably furnished and possessed a wall TV and—yes—a phone. He listened—the house was quiet. He crossed to the phone, looked up a number and dialed, waiting impatiently while the phone at the other end rang. It occurred to him that the room was probably bugged, but he didn't care. Someone answered:

"Cassowary Cafe."

"I'd like to speak to one of your employees—Ruth Bowman."

"The cigarette girl…she's not here."

"Where is she?" he asked.

"Can't say. She didn't show tonight…left us shorthanded."

"Thanks." He hung up thoughtfully. Sure, she had known what was coming—had taken off. Yet, there had been something more in her voice than just the end of their short masquerade when she had said:

There's not much time left, not much time…

She had sounded more as if she had been referring to herself—and time was short. That tied in with her one brief pre-dawn search for happiness, a frantic quest to cram a lifetime into moments.

He moodily undressed for bed when he saw blood on the shoulder of his shirt, and remembered the stinging bite of the bullet that had struck him in the cellar. He went to the bathroom and examined it—the wound was superficial, creasing the top of the shoulder. He found a tube of antibiotic salve in the medicine cabinet, rubbed some into the wound and dropped into bed. He was just getting to sleep when a light knock at his door jolted him to sudden wakefulness. Instantly alert, he shoved his hand to the gun under his pillow.

"Come in," he called softly.

The door opened, framing a slender figure against the rectangle of dim light; it closed and he caught a whiff of fragrance.

"Mr. Krull." The voice was soft, husky and definitely feminine, but he wasn't about to be caught off guard. He kept his fingers curled around the gun and replied:

"What do you want?"

"To talk with you." The voice was faintly familiar, but he couldn't place it.

"At this time of night?" he asked sarcastically.

"Yes, at this time of night," she answered calmly, adding, "I'm Jan Yargo."

"Oh..." Sure, he placed the voice now. He snapped on the bedside lamp, at the same time relinquishing his grasp of the gun. The girl watching him from the foot of the bed was Yargo's daughter, all right. Her blue eyes held a bemused look. She wore a light house cape over a negligee—more revealing than concealing, he thought—and she hadn't forgotten to make up her face. He was pondering the proper etiquette of his next move when she solved the problem for him by coming around to the side of the bed and sitting on it. He felt a sudden unease. He didn't mind pretty girls popping into his room in the dead of night but she was, after all, daughter of the most powerful figure on the planet.

"What now?" he asked.

"Please don't be rude."

"Excuse me," he said stiffly, "but I didn't expect the Prime Thinker's daughter after midnight—in my bedroom."

She smiled unexpectedly. "You sound like a stuffed shirt."

"Don't make that mistake," he advised softly.

Her smile sobered. "I won't."

"How did you know I was here?"

"Butterfield told me." He weighed her a moment, started to ask a question, let it pass. Instead he said:

"I suppose I'm a prisoner."

"No—not that." She looked levelly at him. "But it wouldn't be safe to leave."

HE deliberately moved his eyes the length of her body, taking in the curving lines beneath her thin attire and ending at her face. She didn't alter expression and he said:

"At least I've got a lovely jailer."

"Not a jailer, Mr. Krull."

"Call me Max."

She laughed softly. "And I'm Jan."

"Okay, Jan, now that we're on first-name terms, why did you really come here?"

"Because...well, for my father."

He asked shrewdly; "Does he know you're here?"

"No," she confessed, looking suddenly defiant. "You represent a danger to my father."

"I didn't ask for the job." He suppressed the desire to peep her.

"No, I suppose not," she said finally.

"If your father's on the level, why the run-around?" he shot.

"Run-around?" She looked puzzled.

"The agent," he said softly, watching her face. "He's no more Butterfield's brother than I am."

She regarded him calmly. "No, his name's Foxhill...Raymond Foxhill."

"Why did Foxhill—if that's his real name—tip me about Butterfield being an esper? Was that hokum, too—a red herring?"

"No, it was true..."

Another thought occurred to him. "If Butterfield had just been dead a few days, how did your father know he was an esper?" He watched her, sharp-eyed.

"He was informed of it," she said simply.

"By who?"

Her face clouded. "A Mr. Bowman, but I'm not quite sure who he is. Dad didn't explain."

He dropped the subject of Bowman.

"Why the wild goose chase in the first place?" he pursued. "Why did he have Foxhill pose as Butterfield's brother?"

She deliberated a long moment, watching him enigmatically, and he saw her bosom rise and fall with suppressed emotion. Finally she said:

"He had to be sure of you—he needed time."

"Benbow Deep was just a stall?"

"Yes."

"But why the tip about Butterfield?"

"He wanted to know your reaction."

"Why?" he asked curiously.

"He wasn't sure of you."

"If he wasn't sure of me, why did he summon me in the first place? It doesn't make sense."

"No, I suppose not." She bit her lip. "It was because of some developments that came up after he talked with you," she explained finally.

"What developments?" he challenged. She hesitated, obviously nervous, and he repeated the question without taking his eyes from hers.

"You...you weren't truthful about your past and...he found out."

Krull was startled. "Not truthful?"

"You didn't tell him you were an...esper."

"What!" He stared incredulously at her, and broke into a mirthless laugh. She waited, her face expressionless.

He asked tersely, "who told Yargo that—Mr. Bowman?"

"No."

"Who, then?" he persisted.

"Can I trust you to keep it in confidence?"

He looked curiously at her. "Yes, certainly."

She hesitated before answering. "I did."

"You?" he blurted.

"Yes."

He didn't bother to deny the accusation. The certainty of her words told him she knew it was true, knew it beyond any shadow of doubt. His eyes searched her critically. She was an overly-tall, slender girl with evenly-chiseled features, disarming blue eyes, a mass of red curls piled high and just now—dressed in disturbingly scanty attire. She was, he thought, every bit as lovely and desirable as Anna Malroon, but with a difference. The girl sitting on his bed didn't possess the dark girl's haunted look. Her face was calm, certain, and it was evident she knew exactly what she was saying. He measured her again before speaking.

"Who told you that?"

She pursed her lips, abruptly got up and moved toward the door. When she reached it she turned, with one hand on the knob, and looked at him over the span of long seconds.

"No one told me," she said quietly. She watched him again, watched and weighed and her words, when she spoke again, were so low he scarcely heard them.

"Because I'm like you, Max." She was gone—the door closed silently behind her. He was falling asleep when the real reason for her nocturnal visit came to him. She had peeped him! All the time they had talked she was searching his mind, finding out exactly how trustworthy he was. Why had she revealed herself an esper? He'd have to ask her that. One last thought occurred to him before sleep came. He wondered what she thought of his first reaction to her presence. Well, at least he had given her something to think about.

THE sunlight filtering through the window from a position high in the sky awoke Krull. He had slept long and, for the first time in days, felt completely rested, as if a burden had been lifted from his shoulders. His secret was out—his days of hiding over. For better or worse he was no longer a hidden esper. Jan knew and Ben Yargo knew, and how many others?

Merryweather.

Shevach.

Esper—that's right, Jan was an esper too—a hidden one. Or had been. He wondered if she felt the same relief he did at having disclosed her secret. He hoped so, hoped she wouldn't regret it. He took her confession as an indication of trust in him and, he hoped, a reflection of Yargo's as well. Now he could face the Prime Thinker on even terms, and to hell with the mind shields. Not that they had worked.

He slowly showered, shaved and dressed, luxuriating in the knowledge that for the time being he faced nothing worse than a pleasant confinement, cared for by a quite lovely jailer. He finished and turned on the TV.

Another murder had been pinned on him—this time the killing of Agent Henry Cathecart, IQ 115. The announcer named Cathecart a representative of Gordon Gullfin, Chief of Special Agents for the Manager. According to the broadcast, he had shot the agent to death in the deserted cellar of a furniture warehouse after Cathecart had recognized him and pursued him into the dark building. The searchmaster wasn't mentioned. The announcer pictured him as a maniacal murderer rumored to be allied with a secret group plotting to build atomic weapons; also recalled that Krull was the handpicked choice of Prime Thinker Ben Yargo, Yargo seemed the prime target; he was merely an instrument for his destruction. Shevach—for he was sure it was Shevach—was using him to undermine public confidence in their leader. What could he gain by the attack? Nothing, he thought, unless Shevach hoped to depose Yargo on a charge of malfeasance in office if he lost the election. Or, if he won, it might enable him to order Yargo's arrest the moment he assumed the reins of government.

Why? Could Yargo possess some knowledge Shevach wanted—or knowledge he didn't want Yargo to use if he lost the election? His thoughts were interrupted by a knock at the door. It was Jan with a tray of food.

TOO LATE for breakfast and too early for lunch," she greeted. "I brought along a bite to tide you over." They regarded each other gravely across the short span of feet and Krull said:

"Hello, fellow esper."

"Hello." Her eyes held his and she whispered softly: "I've never known anyone like myself, before. I'm glad, Max...glad." She turned quickly and left. He started to call after her, but desisted. She had told him all he wanted to know. She had been lonely, lonely and hidden, and he had come to free her. Yet, he knew, it gave him a powerful hold over the Prime Thinker's daughter—and the Prime Thinker—and a great responsibility, he mentally added.

Yargo stopped by in the early afternoon, looking calm and at ease. He greeted Krull cordially—nothing in his demeanor suggested he owed him any apologies. The agent marveled at his composure, thinking an outsider would never guess that the square, graying figure was the focal point of a vicious intrigue and, within hours, would be battling for the highest office on earth at what promised to be a bitterly-contested election. Yargo went through the pleasantries of a good host, before plunging briskly into the real reason for his visit.

"It's going to be necessary for you to remain here until after the elections."

"Butterfield told me that," Krull replied drily. He scanned the Prime Thinker's face as he deliberately used the man's false name, but detected no reaction. Yargo said:

"He also indicated you weren't pleased with the idea—that you might have thoughts of leaving." Yargo looked sharply at him. "That would be unwise."

He wanted to reply that it wasn't true, as long as Jan was his keeper, but didn't. Instead he said: "There's no worry on that score. I'll stay."

"Good," Yargo said, pleased. "As soon as the elections are over we'll get this little matter cleared up and you can get back on the job."

"Shevach won't let it die so easily."

"To hell with Shevach," Yargo replied amiably. "The computers indicate I'll have a more favorable crew next term. With a unanimous Council behind me I can remove him from office." He paused and eyed the agent keenly. Krull wondered if he would try to explain his duplicity in sending him on the wild goose chase to Benbow Deep—or his espership. He didn't. He made light conversation for a moment longer, repeated his advice to stay close and departed abruptly.

KRULL passed the remainder of the day alternately reading and watching TV. The announcers were whooping it up and he was, he thought, becoming more of a menace by the moment. Not that he gave a damn. He had all his chips in the pot and there was only one way to win—break the conspiracy. Do that and he'd be god, and not even Shevach could tumble him. In the meantime, it didn't matter what people thought. Except Jan. And Anna, he added as an afterthought. Wherever she was, he hoped she was safe. Later that evening an announcement sobered him a little:

The miners of Melville Deep had gone on strike, demanding that the government do something about the atomic conspiracy. The something they demanded was vague, but the main fact was they had struck, had quit work. He tried to recall when he had last heard of a strike against the government and couldn't. It was a bad omen.

A computer extrapolation of preliminary returns of the latest UPOP results showed Yargo's popularity taking a sharp dip. Seventy-three percent of the people polled expressed the belief Yargo knew where Krull was hiding. Sure, Yargo knew—and so did Shevach and Merryweather, he thought grimly.

Jan brought his supper that evening but, to his disappointment, lingered only a moment. She appeared disturbed. He watched the door close behind her. Well, tomorrow was it. Election day—and Yargo's fate literally hung on the vagaries of the computers. Yeah, Yargo's fate. And his. He went to bed hoping the computers were in fine fettle.

CHAPTER TWELVE

HE awakened to the high clear sound of a trumpet, opening his eyes with a start, and remembering. Election day. The trumpet heralded the formal ceremonies to come. He grimaced, thinking his fate hung on the outcome. If Ben Yargo won, he'd have a breathing spell; Shevach would be off his neck. If he lost...

He hurriedly shaved and showered. It would be a day of rigidly prescribed formalities until the new Prime Thinker and Council of Six were elected. A world-wide celebration would follow; all laws except those governing felonies would be suspended. Festivities, carnivals, brawls—the world would go wild. Social and intellectual barriers would be brushed aside, the rich and poor would mingle and hilarity would be king. Until dawn. To some it would be a time of debauchery, to some a time of prayer.

He finished dressing and went to the window overlooking an open square alongside the house. It was already thronged with uniformed police, black-caped agents, dignitaries of government; a portable platform had been erected and the drive was filled with gleaming open-topped limousines flying purple streamers. Below him a TV crew was positioning cameras.

The crowd stirred as a portly little man wearing a voluminous white cape fringed with red braid started up the platform. His face brimmed with importance. He reached the top and faced the house. The cape denoted his position as Caller of the Bureau of Elections, an honorary position highly sought for its prestige.

Krull idly scanned the crowd. A figure caught his eye and he stepped back, startled, then moved to one side where he could peer out without being seen. Yes, he was right—Merryweather. The Searchmaster stood at the rear of the square. He could see him plainly—a head taller than those around him, a thin face with high cheekbones, eyes deep-sunk in the caves of his face. He studied him with growing apprehension.

The Searchmaster's head was pivoting like, he thought, a radar scan. Suddenly the face stopped, turned toward the window. He knows. Krull was completely dismayed. He felt the tension building up and momentarily tried to squelch it. Merryweather was there but for one purpose. Krull's apprehension was replaced by a feeling of defiance. *To hell with him*, he told himself, and deliberately stepped into full view, disregarding the gaunt man. From time to time the Caller glanced at his watch, finally motioned toward the TV crew and lifted a mike to his lips. A hush fell over the square.

"Hear ye, hear ye, hear ye…"

His voice twanged from the speaker with a nervous tremor. He paused, took a deep breath and continued:

"Now the person of Ben Yargo, having been found qualified on appropriate tests, and having been adjudged IQ 219 by the World Board of Psychmasters, is hereby invited…invited…"—he glanced desperately at his notes—"by the people of the world to participate in election for the office of Prime Thinker."

He paused, a trumpet sounded followed by the low roll of drums, then silence. The Caller threw back his shoulders and boomed:

"If you accept, come forth and so state."

DRUMS rolled, trumpets blared, the crowd milled expectantly and here and there a voice cried: "Come forth." The call became a chant; the Caller threw up his hands for silence. The noise died away, quiet except for the restless shuffling of feet. A moment passed.

Ben Yargo strode purposefully from the house, his formal tri-corned hat and purple garb designating his candidacy for office. The crowd parted before him. He reached a point a dozen yards from the base of the platform and halted, looking up at the Caller. There was an awed silence before he spoke:

"I accept."

A cheer swept the square and trumpets and drums added to the din. He stood with face turned upward until the roar died away: then, to the measured roll of drums, marched to the official limousine which would bear him to the Hall of Elections. Engines roared to life and the cavalcade started slowly down the drive. It was a scene enacted in four parts of the city simultaneously—the official invitation to each of the candidates for earth's highest office.

Krull tried to spot Merryweather but he had disappeared. Within minutes the House of the Prime Thinker was shrouded in silence. Alone and forgotten, his brief moment of glory past, the Caller descended from the platform and walked slowly across the deserted grounds.

There was a knock at Krull's door. It was Jan with coffee. She greeted him with a nervous smile.

"Mind if I share your screen?"

"Not a bit," he promptly declared. He didn't worry her about Merryweather. He turned on the TV while she poured the coffee. Yargo's cavalcade was winding through streets lined with cheering, flower-bedecked crowds, whose dress proclaimed a mixture of IQ's. A close-up of the lead car revealed him smiling, waving, being pelted with flowers. Signs proclaiming *We want Yargo* and large photos of him were hoisted in front of the camera. Krull caught a glimpse of a sign reading, *Down with the atom men* before the camera hurriedly swung away. The cavalcade was met by three similar ones, each bearing an official candidate, and the entire procession moved on to the Hall of Elections. It halted in front of the building, where cordons of police held back the crowds until the candidates descended, bombarded by flowers and shimmery streamers of colored tape.

The camera moved in on Yargo's face: it was square, hard, but a crinkling around the lips gave him a slightly paternal expression. He nodded. The camera swung toward Shevach; his face was lean, saturnine, pale, with the broad high forehead somehow oddly out of proportion with the delicate bone structure beneath.

THE lens moved again. Sherif was a squat dark Asian with bushy brows and piercing eyes set deep in a confident face. He was, Krull knew, a controversial figure. His chief platform was based on what he termed *the equality of man*. He was outspoken in his opposition to castes founded upon IQ, which made him the darling of a large segment of the LIQ's. Watching him now, Krull had the feeling he was sincere; there was a quality about the dark eyes that suggested compassion. Only William Harshberg, scholarly and pale, with a narrow intelligent face and watery eyes, was visibly nervous. The camera recorded the slight quivering of his lips. The candidates met at the bottom of the steps, formally shook hands, and marched into the building flanked by a guard of special agents in spit-and-polish splendor.

"I'm glad this only happens once every five years," Jan said nervously.

"Don't worry, he'll come through."

"Sometimes I wish he hadn't tried again. Two terms are enough to give." He sensed the bitterness in her voice.

"It's for the world."

"I know, he had to run. There was no other alternative," she replied enigmatically, turning back to the screen.

The candidates were entering the main auditorium. One end contained a large stage holding the election booths and computers. A podium in the center was occupied by a florid-faced man whose ceremonial dress identified him as the official Host; behind him sat Karl Werner, Psychmaster of the World, and Marvin Chadwick, the Archon, who headed the World Court. Eight subarchons dressed in formal scarlet top hats and matching capes sat behind them. The Host, whose name was Clender, pompously held up a hand for attention; the auditorium grew silent and he announced:

"Elections are in order. The Right Honorable Archon, Marvin Chadwick, will attest to the procedures." He turned and bowed as Chadwick came to the mike.

"Ladies and gentlemen of the world—Archon Chadwick."

The Archon nodded, adjusted the mike and looked solemnly at the row of scarlet-clad official judges. He was a tall, lantern-faced man with sharp brown eyes and brisk movements.

He announced that a Prime Thinker and six members to the World Council of Six would be elected, in that order. He spoke slowly, measuredly, conscious that his audience was the world. He explained that election to the office of Prime Thinker would be by test. Each candidate would take three tests—the same three—and the person having the highest total score would be adjudged winner. The tests would be machine-scored with the results automatically translated into IQ values. He paused occasionally while the official judges nodded agreement.

KRULL listened interestedly. There were an even twelve thousand tests, of which three would be selected on the basis of random numbers. The scoring and converting to IQ values would be recorded by cameras so the citizens of the world could judge the fairness of the procedures.

He finished. The subarchons nodded and Clender resumed his place at the microphone and announced he would introduce the candidates with precedence based on present IQ rating. He turned toward the entrance and nodded. Ben Yargo rustled forward, his face an inscrutable mask.

"Ben Yargo, IQ 219, philosopher-ecologist..." Clender pumped Yargo's hand vigorously, dropped it and signaled the attendant. Yargo smiled faintly and retreated to a row of chairs set in front of the election booths as Ivan Shevach came to the mike. The Manager smiled sardonically when his IQ rating was announced as 217. He turned abruptly from the mike and sat alongside Yargo. Mustapha Sherif (IQ 216) and William Harshberg (IQ 214) followed. Sherif's expression was wooden, all except the dark eyes glowing under bushy brows. Harshberg appeared jittery and had some difficulty controlling a facial twitch. When he was seated, a trumpeter appeared, sounded a silvery blast and disappeared into a wing. The elections had begun.

Clender beamed into the camera. "Citizens of the world, Dr. Karl Werner, Psychmaster, will activate the election computer for selection of test number one. Dr. Werner..."

Werner stared myopically through thick-lensed glasses, nodded briefly and limped toward the election machine. The camera moved in until only his hand was visible, one finger pointing to a red button. The finger moved, pressed the button, and the camera focused on a spinning counter which gradually slowed and finally stopped at number 8250. Another camera cut in with an overview of the chamber.

The Psychmaster announced: "The official number is 8...2...5...0." The Archon rose, repeated the number and the judges nodded confirmation. Werner came into view again with his hand poised above the control panel. He turned a pointer to figure "4" and moved his hand to a selector dial. Again only his finger and the dial face were visible. He slowly dialed the official number. Another camera cut in to show the face of the computer. Lights blinked, the machine hummed and four booklets tumbled into a slot at the base of the console. Werner scooped them up and held them toward the lens to display the number for the world to witness. An overview came on and Clender said:

"The election booths..." An attendant opened the booths to display their interiors. Each was furnished identically—a straightback chair and writing table holding several pencils.

"They keep it honest," Krull observed.

THE Psychmaster placed a booklet on each table and limped to his seat. Clender ordered the candidates to station themselves by their booths and read the instructions. The test would start at the sound of a gong, would last exactly sixty minutes, and would be terminated by a second gong. Any candidate not leaving his booth within ten seconds of the final gong would be automatically disqualified.

The Archon rose. "That is the law and I so testify." The subarchons nodded assent. Silence.

A gong sounded.

Harshberg popped through the door of his booth like a scared rabbit. The others followed more slowly. When the doors were closed, the Psychmaster dropped a note on the podium. Clender examined it and announced:

"Ladies and gentlemen, the first official test is titled, *Test of Motives Behind Historical Political Actions.* Needless to say, this test definitely favors William Harshberg who, as you know, is a political scientist. For example..."

Jan moodily snapped the screen off, turning pensively toward Krull. "I'd forgotten, you haven't had breakfast."

"I'll help," he offered.

"You won't budge from this room," she replied firmly.

"Until after your father gets elected." He smiled crookedly.

"He'd better."

"He will."

"Sure." After she left he turned on the screen. The camera had returned to the outside of the building. The streets were jammed with jostling, singing crowds bearing placards and huge pictures of the candidates. A woman tried to thrust a Yargo poster in front of the camera and was shoved aside by a rough-looking LIQ bearing a Shevach placard. Two men hoisted a thin elderly woman in front of the camera and she shrilled:

"Down with the atom fiends!"

Hands reached up, caught her and she was pulled back into the crowd. The camera rested for an instant on a young blonde with brilliantly painted face. She saw the camera, winked and jerked open her tunic to display her breasts; the camera swung away. Krull thought the celebration was starting early.

HE SNAPPED the scene off when Jan returned. They ate in silence. She didn't turn the set on until the time for the candidates to emerge from the election booths. Yargo and Sherif appeared stolid-faced, unconcerned; Shevach seemed a bit anxious, Harshberg was plainly jittery. The Psychmaster gathered the tests and held them so the audience could see the numbers, then limped to the computer and fed the first one into a slot.

"Test number one...Ben Yargo," he called.

Clender broke in: The test will be scored automatically and translated into IQ points, which will flash on the master screen at the top of the panel." He broke off as a light winked; there was a low hum followed by a number on the screen: 212.

"Two-twelve, pretty good," Krull mused aloud.

"Yes, it's good," Jan agreed.

"Test number two...Ivan Shevach."

They waited, tense. The light blinked again and number 210 appeared on the screen.

"Beat him," Krull said gleefully.

"Of course."

The Manager's face was slightly furrowed. Sherif scored 214; his expression didn't change.

"Test number four...William Harshberg."

There was an agonizing moment. The thin political scientist tensed in his seat and leaned slightly forward, his eyes riveted on the computer. The screen came to life: 223. Jan gasped involuntarily. A smug smile creased Harshberg's face. Shevach looked visibly perturbed. Yargo didn't change expression and the squat Sherif merely glanced at the reading.

"Don't worry," Krull consoled, "the subject matter was in his field. He won't get that break again."

"I hope not." Jan was shaken. The camera flashed to the exterior of the building. The crowds were noisier. *Elect Ben Yargo* and *We want Sherif* banners competed with signs backing Shevach and Harshberg. One sign borne by a grim-faced delegation proclaimed: *Down with the atomic conspirators.* The camera paused at a corner to show several women dancing, cheered on by a ring of festively-clad celebrants; and swung abruptly away when one of the women began peeling off her clothes.

THE second test turned out to be the analogy variety—things that resembled other things in obscure ways. It was strictly a powerhouse affair and, as Clender explained, was more nearly related to pure IQ than the mere possession of factual knowledge.

To Krull's disappointment, Jan left and didn't return until almost time for the tests to be scored.

The scene was a replica of the first, except for the results:

Yargo: 219
Shevach: 220
Sherif: 217
Harshberg : 214

Krull relaxed with a satisfied smile. That put Yargo's total one above Shevach, a tie with Sherif, and only six behind the political scientist. Jan didn't share his enthusiasm.

"It's too close," she murmured.

"He's got it whipped."

"I hope so, I hope so," she said pensively. "If only he can overcome Harshberg's lead."

"That's the least of his worries," Krull said. "It's Shevach I'm worried about."

"Sherif's strong, too."

"Yes…" They turned back to the screen, Yargo and Sherif remained impassive, Shevach was sucking his long underlip nervously and Harshberg seemed vacillating between elation and despair. If the next test were favorable, he could easily become the 91st Prime Thinker.

The Psychmaster pushed the button to activate the random number dial for test number three. The dial was a blur of movement, gradually slowing, stopping on number 7777. He read the official number and the Archon testified to its correctness. When the doors closed behind the candidates, Clender announced:

"Test number 7…7…7…7, selected at random, is entitled *Alexander the Great*—simply *Alexander the Great*. Ladies and gentlemen, this test is unusual in that it takes us into ancient history…"

Jan snapped the set off.

"That's strange."

"Yeah," Krull said thoughtfully. She started to say something and abruptly stopped. He looked puzzled. The test struck an odd chord but, somehow, he couldn't put a finger on the disturbing thought. He voiced what he was thinking.

"Everyone's heard the name *Alexander,*" Jan replied evenly. All at once she seemed anxious to drop the subject. She smiled and grasped his hand. "But I feel better. Shevach was the only one Dad was afraid of and he's beating him. I'm glad." Krull looked into her eyes and she dropped his hand and retreated toward the door.

"I'll get some more coffee."

"No—stay."

She smiled demurely. "No." She whirled and disappeared through the door and he heard her laugh echoing in the hall. He looked at his hand. The spot she had touched felt warmer than the rest of his body. Strange, she was no more beautiful than either Rea Jon or Anna, but she was more exciting. Rea had been provocative, willing; Anna's forte had been the sorrow mirrored in her eyes that had made his love more an act of compassion. Jan was different. She was alive, vital—whetting him for the chase. But she would be fleet and not easily overtaken; she knew exactly how far and how fast to run. He savored that.

HE browsed restlessly around the room but she didn't return until time for the test scores to be read. He turned to the set while she poured the coffee, impatiently watching the returns.

The camera closed in on the candidates. Yargo was grim. Shevach's face glistened with perspiration; he was sucking his lower lip and his eyes seemed to have become small gimlets. Sherif remained imperturbable; Harshberg's face muscles were twitching and his jaw hung slack. The camera swung back to the Psychmaster.

"Test number one…Ben Yargo." Werner inserted the test into a slot; a light came on accompanied by a hum which ended suddenly as a number flashed on the screen: 229.

"Wonderful." Jan's face was jubilant. An awed sigh rose from the auditorium. Werner inserted another paper.

"Test number two—Ivan Shevach."

The lights and humming came and died, and both Krull and Jan leaned involuntarily toward the screen. The number was 227.

"He's won, he's won," Jan whispered.

"Wait," he cautioned.

Sherif scored 220. There was a moment of anxious waiting while Harshberg's test was fed into the machine. He scored 211.

"He's won," Jan exclaimed. She impulsively flung her arms around Krull's neck and suddenly drew back, as if appalled at her action.

"I don't mind," he said, grinning. He was elated. Now, maybe, his troubles were over. Perhaps Yargo could get Shevach appointed inspector of oyster beds off Easter Island. He turned back to the screen.

The Archon was giving Yargo's official—and winning—IQ as 220, one higher than Shevach and three above Sherif, who led Harshberg by one point. Krull started to snap the set off, then froze. The door of the chamber burst open and a squad of armed agents marched in.

"What's happening!" Jan worriedly asked.

"I don't know."

The agents halted. A stalwart, familiar-appearing gray-haired man strode to the center of the room. Krull was startled. It was Joseph Grimhorn, Chief of World Agents.

"What's the meaning of this?" The Archon asked Grimhorn.

"Your honor, I am sorry but a felony charge has been placed against two persons present."

"Is there a court order?"

"There is, your Honor, initiated earlier. My office just received it a few moments ago."

"And the nature of the complaint?"

"Fraud—fraud involving the operation of the computer."

"What!" The Archon was startled. "Sworn out against whom?"

"Karl Werner, the Psychmaster, and"—Grimhorn's face became sad—"Ben Yargo, the Prime Thinker."

"And the complainant?"

Grimhorn swung angrily on his heels and leveled a long finger. "Ivan Shevach."

Pandemonium reigned in the auditorium.

CHAPTER THIRTEEN

BEN YARGO came home that evening—came without trumpet or drum or waving banner, came without the cheering throngs and honor guard that had escorted him to the Hall of Elections. He was still Prime Thinker, still free, but only because of the privilege of immunity accorded his office. He returned to a house that lay on the hill like a shadow-box, brooding and silent, seemingly deserted—an oasis unmindful of the raging political fires.

Krull sat alone, watching the screen, half his mind occupied by the sudden change in Yargo's fortunes. Jan had fled precipitously following Grimhorn's dramatic charge, nor had he seen her since. Once he had heard her footsteps echoing in the lower hall as she rushed to greet her father.

The stillness had come again. Psychmaster Werner had been booked and released on his own recognizance without making a statement; a team of engineers were methodically examining the election computer under the watchful eyes of Grimhorn's chief deputy and a squad of agents. The Archon had suspended elections of the Council of Six on the legal requirement they follow the declaration of election of a prime thinker—an act which hadn't come off. The old council remained, sadly divided between an outraged Kingman and a calm Eve Mallon.

The scene in the Hall of Elections had immediate worldwide repercussions. Supporters carrying Yargo banners were mobbed, their signs shredded. There were riots in New Berlin, Greater London, Rio de Janeiro; California mobs stormed government offices and Shanghai was in the throes of looting. The Capetown Royal HIQ Society ("All members above IQ 160") demanded immediate self-rule; the Turkish Council of Mayors called for recognition of Sherif as Prime Thinker. New Delhi was in flames. But the public would not be robbed of its holiday; along with the riots there were wild celebrations.

The Archon immediately called a special session of the World Court to decide what action should be taken if election fraud were determined. Yargo's current term expired in ten days. Who would succeed him if the election were found invalid? It was a situation that never before had occurred, one that threatened to split the government right down the middle.

Harshberg demanded the court void the entire election and set an immediate date for a new one. Mustapha Sherif told a TV audience: "I have faith in Ben Yargo's integrity. Let's wait and see." He was stoned leaving the station. Shevach was vociferous. He demanded Yargo's test scores be voided and the office conferred on the highest scoring candidate of the remaining three—which happened to be himself.

Eve Mallon told a press conference that Shevach's charge of fraud had been made prior to the election, thus his participation in an election believed by him to be fraudulent made him a party to the fraud. Shevach vehemently denied the charge. He claimed he had acted in the interests of good government on the basis of anonymous information; he had merely held off having the warrant served until the selection of the test verified the charge. No, he was not guilty. Rather he was the victim of a plot to rob him—and the people—of their just victory.

EVE MALLON countered by producing evidence that Shevach's secretary had withdrawn all books and tapes on Alexander the Great from the public library long before the election. Shevach couldn't explain that. Grimhorn promptly charged the Manager with "participation in a felonious act," which, if proven, would bar him from public office. Shevach responded by attempting to have Grimhorn removed from his post; he suggested Gordon Gullfin as interim Chief of World Agents. Eve Mallon hurriedly formed a council bloc consisting of herself, George Lincoln, Kim Lee Wong and Hans Taussig that effectively stymied the move despite Kingman's angry opposition. UPOP rushed out a spot survey which showed sixty-seven percent of the people believed Yargo guilty, twenty percent thought him innocent and thirteen percent gave no opinion. Broken down by IQ, most of the twenty percent supporting Yargo were HIQ's.

The fast-breaking news answered the question perturbing Krull. Alexander the Great—he remembered now—he had seen the book on Yargo's desk. It could be a coincidence, of course, but it looked bad. Yargo—he couldn't believe it. He stayed riveted to the screen, trying to assess his own moves. The news took an ominous twist.

Shevach stated Yargo was harboring the fugitive killer, Max Krull, and demanded his immediate arrest. The words had scarcely ended before there was a sharp rap on the door, followed by an imperative exclamation.

"Krull!" He opened it and faced Yargo's chief of special agent's.

"Hello...Foxhill." There was no reaction to the name.

"Let's get the hell out of here," he barked.

"Why?"

"Mob coming."

Sure, there would be a mob. Shevach would see to that. Gullfin and the searchmaster were probably behind it stirring it to a frenzy. But what of Jan? The agent saw the question in his eyes and said:

"The Prime Thinker and his daughter have gone; they're safe."

"Where to?"

"I wouldn't know," Foxhill snapped, "but you'd better step on it if you want to beat your admirers."

"Okay," Krull said shortly. "I'm ready. Where to?"

"Wherever you want. You're on your own now," the agent responded grimly. "I'll drive you to any place of your choosing."

"Why?"

"Yargo's orders." Krull tried to assimilate the information. Yargo's sole motive was to get him out of his hair. That made sense. But it would leave him an outlaw, exposed to every hand. If he could crack the conspiracy he could still vindicate himself. He followed Foxhill out the back of the house to his car. They got in and the agent started the engine.

"Where to?"

KRULL hesitated—one place was as good or bad as another. He decided on the LIQ district, thinking the crowd would be a good mask until he could formulate a plan of action. He spoke briefly, the agent nodded and started down the drive. They had scarcely reached the main thoroughfare before they passed a cavalcade speeding in the opposite direction, horns blaring. Krull looked back; the procession turned into Yargo's drive.

"Just beat 'em," Foxhill muttered. Krull nodded grimly. It had been close. The crowds thickened as they drew closer to the heart of the city. People were dancing, shouting, hoisting bottles and waving banners bearing Shevach's name and picture; here and there large photos of him were plastered on buildings. Krull smiled sourly. It was too neat; it smacked of long planning. The crowd grew thicker and Foxhill was forced to stop.

"You'll have to take it from here," he said. Krull nodded and jumped out, then looked back. "So long, and thanks."

"Don't mention it."

He moved away, threading through the crowd without any particular destination. He needed a place to hide…a place to think. But where? He couldn't risk a hotel, not even a rat-ridden hole in the LIQ district. Gullfin's agents would be making the rounds.

And the searchmaster!

He damned the gaunt man mentally, pushing through the mob. He was jostled and hemmed in until his progress practically came to a standstill. A drunk in a LIQ tunic wearing an expensive pink HIQ cape waved a bottle in his face and shouted:

"We want Shevach…We want Shevach…"

A hand reached out and snatched the bottle—and the drunk turned, cursing. A bloated-faced woman naked to the waist grabbed Krull's arm.

"Everybody celebrate, honey." He pushed the hand off and forced his way next to the buildings. People shouting, pushing, singing, dancing—people and banners and laughter and screams. People…Dusk. The shadows came, reached out. He reached a corner and found himself staring into a public screen diagonally across the intersection. Suddenly it was filled with a face—his face! A voice from the speaker rose harshly above the noise.

Watch for killer Krull...

Watch for killer Krull...

He stared, fascinated, waiting for the picture to change. It didn't.

Watch for killer Krull...

He turned his head down and pushed away from the intersection, threading deeper toward the heart of the LIQ quarters. Damn, Shevach wasn't missing a bet. They'd keep his picture on the screens, keep shouting his name. If someone saw him, gave the alarm... The crowd would kill him—tear him to pieces. That's what Shevach wanted. He stepped into a doorway, hurriedly retreating when he found it occupied by lovers.

Shevach... Shevach...Shevach...

SOMEONE started the refrain, it caught on—everyone was shouting the name. After a while it died out. Night came on and the faces under the yellow street lights looked like those of animals; faces and half-naked bodies and the smell of liquor and tobacco smoke. Bedlam. A light haze was coming in, the lights took on a yellowish hue. More screens, each with the image of Krull staring out over the crowd.

Watch for killer Krull...

He hastily retreated. Hide. Hide where? He gave thanks for the crowd; it had forgotten the screens, forgotten Krull, forgotten everything but the revelry at hand. Several times he caught sight of black capes and stopped, watching until they melted away. Agents, there must be a hundred of them watching for him, combing the LIQ quarters. Maybe he'd picked the wrong place. Next time he looked up he was diagonally across from the Edward Crozener Hotel. A screen above street level was filled with his image. He started to turn a corner and stopped abruptly. A gaunt figure stood by the corner of the hotel, towering above the revelers.

The searchmaster!

Krull's blood ran cold but he remained watching. Merryweather was pivoting his head from side to side, covering the intersection. His face looked like a mask under the garish yellow light and where his eyes should be were two black holes. He looked as if he were sniffing the wind. He thought again that the gaunt man was a bloodhound, a shadow he couldn't shake. A peeper who could peep crowds! He felt a tinge of panic, abruptly turned and pushed deeper into the crowd. Merryweather—he had to shake him—put distance between them. His presence there meant he knew Krull was in the LIQ quarters. How? He felt baffled and cursed savagely. Once the searchmaster detected him he would cling to his mind like a leech…trail him through the thickest crowds. Nail him. The festivities and sounds of occasional brawls grew louder. He liked that…something comforting in the din, the press of bodies, the sweat and the odor. Even Merryweather couldn't pick a single mind from a throng like this. The crowd was an animal, a vast protoplasmic mask hiding him from the Manager.

From the searchmaster.

But when the crowd thinned? He'd have to hide, have to hide, hide…hide…hide. The word was a refrain in his mind. Run, hide…run, hide, find a room, a black cellar, anything.

A black cellar?

He remembered.

THE cellar where Foxhill had killed Cathecart. It was the perfect spot, the last place they'd look. It would give him time to think, to plan, time to tie the threads together. He traversed several blocks trying to recall its location. After a while he spotted the pub where he'd taken refuge and remembered. Keeping his face turned down he pushed through the crowd. Capes. Black capes. The agents seemed all around. Another scream, another image, a jumble of milling, sweating, smelling bodies blocking his path, a voice calling his name. He held his head low and hurried.

Noise…

Screams…

Wild laughter

A young LIQ with purpled lips and hair lacquered in a spiral cone stopped his progress, swaying in front of him supported by the arms of the escorts who, he thought, resembled stevedores. She swayed and looked blurry-eyed at him.

"Come along. honey, join the party."

"Get along," one of the drunks growled, looking meanly at Krull. He pushed around them, followed by her shrill laughter. It took him a while to find the alley. It was a black maw opening into the street. Its entrance was blocked by the mob-cursing, shouting, laughing humanity, bottle wavers and half-naked celebrants, some still carrying Shevach banners. He managed to gain the entrance and slip into the shadows.

He probed his way by memory, occasionally circling to avoid a whispering voice or the dim outlines of swaying bodies. The din gradually receded and, as his eyes became dark-adapted, the outlines of buildings took form.

He finally located the door he was seeking, more by feel than by sight. He twisted the knob and it opened. He waited, trying to discern thought in the blackness of the cellar, and failed. After a moment he stepped into the blackness, conscious that he was sweating and breathing heavily. He stood for a while, hearing his heart thud against his ribs. Nothing happened. Strange, he had half-expected Peter Merryweather. He hesitated. Distant cries and laughter came from the street but the cellar was a tomb. He saw nothing, heard nothing, nor did his mind register any cause for alarm. After a moment he breathed easier and felt his way toward one wall where he remembered seeing a jumble of old furniture.

Safe. He was safe.

He found a pile of battered chairs, desks, tables and odds and ends of junk. Some of the better pieces were covered against dust with plastic tarp. He rummaged around until he found a comfortable place to lay; in moments he was asleep. Once he woke to the sound of shrill voices and screams, revelry from the streets. His muscles ached from the hard floor, he shifted position and drifted off to sleep again.

NEXT time he woke it was early morning. Pale light filtered in through cracks above the door and half-covered window. He felt a sudden fear. Perhaps the cellar wasn't abandoned…maybe it was worked in during the day. He rose and peered cautiously around; no sign it had been used recently but he'd have to be careful of watchmen. He debated sneaking out for something to eat and discarded the idea. He'd be too conspicuous on the almost deserted streets. Well, he'd found himself a hideout, all right. Now the trick would be to get out of it. He grinned ruefully and settled back to wait it out, thinking that night was a long time off. During the day he heard activity in the building above him; once someone entered the far end of the cellar and rummaged around a pile of boxes. Krull hid under the plastic tarp until he left.

He passed the hours debating his course of action. He wasn't getting any place this way—he'd have to make a break. How? Bok—but Bok was dead. But the esper would have a successor. It seemed logical that he would have been a party to Bok's activities. Well, this time he wouldn't be so soft. He'd go to the House of Espers and force the information. He felt better at the decision. At least it was a course of action.

The day seemed eternal, but finally the half-light of the cellar darkened and the shadows around him jelled into a solid black. He waited a while longer, planning his exact moves as carefully as he could, knowing that success or failure perhaps depended upon the next few hours. Finally he emerged from hiding and started toward the door.

"Max…"

He froze and his heart suddenly sped up again, booming inside him.

"Max…" It was a soft voice, husky and low. He turned slowly.

"It's…Anna."

"Anna." He repeated the name huskily, without believing; saw the shadow of her body moving toward him.

"How did you know I'd be here?" He asked harshly, conscious that his anger was unreasonable. She didn't answer and he said, slowly, "Herman Bok?"

"Yes," she admitted. She was next to him. "Oh, Max…"

"What else did he tell you?"

"Nothing."

His eyes were becoming dark-adapted and he saw the paleness of her face; even in the darkness he knew it was wistful, filled with sorrow. He spoke more gently.

"Nothing at all, Anna?"

She hesitated. "Nothing, Max, but he gave me some orders." Her voice trailed away.

"Go on," he ordered.

"I'm to take you to the conspirators."

"What?"

She repeated the statement, and added, "But, please, follow me. There's a schedule, Max."

As she started to withdraw, he caught her hand and pulled, gently. She came back, looked into his face a moment, and flung herself in his arms. He felt her body trembling, heard her sob. He lifted her chin and kissed her. Her lips were cold. She broke away again.

"Please, we have to hurry."

SHE led him through the same passage Butterfield had taken. They reached the alley and walked toward the corner. He heard the voices ahead and hesitated.

"Please don't worry, Max. I'll get you there safely," she said, as if reading his thoughts.

"Did Bok tell you that, too?"

"Yes," she said simply.

"Okay." All at once he felt better. This was the break he'd been waiting for. He had everything cinched and no worries—Bok guaranteed that. He followed her to the mouth of the alley, took her arm and walked by her side until they reached her car. She pulled into the stream of traffic and headed toward the bay.

"Where to'?" Krull asked curiously.

"The seaplane ramp."

"The police will be there."

"Yes, but they won't stop us."

"If Bok was right."

"He was right," she said simply.

"Okay, I'll take a chance." After a moment another thought struck him.

"Who are the conspirators?"

"That I can't, say," she answered simply.

"Can't or won't'!"

"Max...please, I've told you everything I can."

"Except the destination."

She turned and looked soberly into my face.

"Well?" he demanded impatiently.

"Waimea-Roa," she said simply. She turned back to the traffic, leaving him for the minute speechless. Finally he slumped back against the seat and murmured:

"I'll be damned."

Anna reached the seaplane ramp and headed directly toward the ticket booth. Krull nervously followed—Shevach wouldn't leave any of the transportation routes unattended. There, ahead, just as he feared he saw a bulky man lounging across from the ticket window watching the crowd. AGENT was stamped across his features. Krull tugged Anna's arm.

"It's watched."

"Bok said we would be safe."

He hesitated, shrugged and followed, covertly watching the man. Krull studied him out of the corner of his eye, prepared to either fight or flee, trying to play it by ear. To his amazement, the watcher didn't seem to notice them. They turned down the ramp, and Krull could almost feel the cold eyes follow them. They reached the bottom.

Anna excused herself a moment.

Krull fretted nervously until she reappeared. Just in time. Five minutes later the seaplane engines roared to life; it taxied into the stream and started its sluggish take-off. Minutes later Sydney was a sea of lights rapidly falling astern.

THE floating City of Kulahai fled past; there was only a vast expanse of stars and black sea beneath until the scattered lights of Abiang Atoll rushed toward them from the heart of Waimea-Roa. The plane dropped lower, banked, let down to a smooth landing on the surface of the lagoon and taxied toward the ramp.

"Okay," Krull said harshly, "now what?"

"Wait…until we're alone."

"That'll be a couple of minutes," he promised grimly.

They were the only passengers to disembark, he noted. At least Shevach didn't have a shadow on his heels yet. He steered Anna to the top of the ramp, halted and faced her.

"Let's have it," he said quietly. "I know every person on the atolls. Start spilling names."

"But I don't know them," she protested. "All I know is the place…"

"Where?"

"Chimney Rock."

"What?" He spat the word incredulously, then laughed mirthlessly. She watched him puzzled. "Bok's been taking us in," he said finally. "Chimney Rock is just a pillar, a massive black chunk jutting up from the sea. Even birds have a tough time getting a toehold," he added grimly.

"Not on the rock—under the rock," she said quietly.

"Under…"

"A cavern, a huge grotto. There's a laboratory, factory, places to live…"

"You've seen that?"

"Bok told me," she said simply.

"Impossible. It couldn't go undetected."

"It's been built over the years…decades."

"I don't believe it."

"I do."

"Then why are you leading me there?" he challenged. "Why would Bok undue the work he says he believes in. No, it doesn't make sense."

"Because you're not going as an agent, Max."

"I'm not?" He smiled sardonically.

"No—Mr. Bok says you're necessary to…to it's completion."

"No," he said stonily. Another thought struck him. "How do we get there?"

"There's a way. I can't tell you yet. I'll have to…"

"Yeah, there's a way," he cut in. "Follow me."

"Max…"

FOLLOW me," he repeated roughly. He started down the main street of Abiang Village and, after a moment, heard her footsteps behind him. To hell with Bok, he thought. He'd break the causal chain. From here on out he didn't need her. Or Bok either. He knew where the conspirators were; he also knew exactly how he'd round them up. He'd smash them and vindicate himself, and not even Shevach could touch him, even if he were declared Prime Thinker. He reached the small pastel house that had been his home since coming to the atolls, unlocked the door and beckoned her to precede him. She walked past him tight-lipped.

"Make yourself at home," he mocked. "I'll be back."

She turned and her voice was a plea: "Max…"

He had one hand on the door when she screamed, "Max—you've got to listen."

He spun back. "Okay, make it short." He held the door ajar and waited. Her voice was subdued, almost toneless.

"Herman Bok was a great man," she said, "great because he was different…because he had a talent no one else in the whole world had. He was a *down through*, Max, could see the future."

"I know that," he cut in.

"Yes, but you don't know what it does to a man…the damnation of being able to see every moment of every day ahead of time; being able to see your own personal failures and disaster, your own death, not being able to change things…"

"So…?"

"Why do you think Herman Bok considered it so important that you find the conspirators?" she blazed. He looked soberly at her.

"I don't know."

"Mr. Bok said you would save the conspiracy. Do you hear that, Max? You're going to save it." She laughed hysterically and he felt a desire to take her in his arms and soothe her. She was wrought up, half out of her mind. He took a step toward her. She halted her laughter and said:

"No, I'm not crazy, if that's what you think."

"All right, you're not crazy," he said quietly, "but Bok was, at least with regard to me."

"He wasn't," she whimpered. "You don't know…"

"No…?" He leaned against the door and contemplated her bemusedly. "Look, Anna, I'm supposed to be an esper. Well, I've tried it. I can get vague impressions from people's minds, but I really can't read them. Once in a while I get sharp images but not often. As an esper, I'm a dud, and I know it…"

"You don't know…"

"I can't see into the future," he said bluntly, "so don't try and give me that." There was a tinge of regret in his voice. "I'm just an agent—a plain agent. But right now I'm going to make the damnedest haul…"

HE yanked the door open and stepped into the night, gritting his teeth savagely. Damn, all his life he'd hated the knowledge he was an esper. Now, when he wanted to be an esper, he wasn't; all Bok's ravings couldn't alter that. He stomped into the station, surprised to find Derek behind the desk. The wizened clerk gasped a flustered welcome.

"What are you doing here at this time of night?" Krull asked.

Derek nodded toward the door. "The Old Man's in. There's something hot."

"You can say that again," Krull snapped. He walked past the clerk and entered the Inspector's office without knocking. Jonquil looked up in surprise and his face wreathed into a smile.

"Welcome home, Max. I wasn't expecting you but I'm sure glad to see you."

"I'm glad, too," Krull said fervently. He plopped into a chair opposite the littered desk. "The chips are down and we're going to work."

Jonquil abruptly rose, motioning him to silence, and drew him to the corner of the room.

"You've located the conspiracy?"

Krull nodded.

"That ties in. I've got orders to marshal my agents and stand by."

"Then why the need for secrecy."

Jonquil looked grim. "The orders were from the Manager. He's coming personally—due to land shortly."

Krull digested the information.

"I also got an order from Yargo not to assist Shevach—I'm in the middle."

"Don't help him," Krull urged.

"We've got to plan but I think we'd better get out of here," Jonquil murmured. "Right now I don't even trust Derek."

"Listen, I've got to break that conspiracy myself," Krull said desperately. "It's the only chance I've got for vindication. Besides, if Shevach beats me, he's got the world in his hand."

"I know. So does Yargo. But he won't beat you. Go over to Dying Girl Point—I'll meet you there in a few moments. Maybe there's a way but we'll have to work fast."

Krull nodded assent and began talking in normal tones for the benefit of any possible electronic listener: "I'll see you in the morning. Right now I'm going to turn in and get a good night's sleep."

Jonquil winked. "Good night, Max," he replied conversationally.

KRULL left the station, hesitated, then popped his head in the door of his house. Anna was studying the sketch of Rea Jon; she turned at the sound of the door.

"Wait, I'll be hack," he snapped.

"Max. Her eyes were pools of sorrow again. "I have something to say."

"Say it," he spat. "I've got work to do."

"Next time you see me, read my mind."

"Why?" He was startled.

"I can't say…now. Just read my mind!"

Mystery. Hell, couldn't she ever come out and say what she thought? He yanked the door shut without giving her time to protest and struck off toward Dying Girl Point. The night was cool in his face and his clothes were damp on his body. He walked swiftly to the promontory which jutted into the sea, picking his way more cautiously until he reached its end. The point was a favorite spot, filled with fond memories. He and Jonquil had set their canvases there, had fished from its heights with both line and speargun. On nights like this he had come here with Rea Jon. He looked upward. Stars—millions of stars pinned against the sky all the way down to where it merged with the blackness of the Pacific.

Stars.

Espers.

Atoms. The world was all fouled up.

He heard footsteps and turned; Jonquil came out of the night, a lean silhouette. Krull moved to meet him and they stopped, facing each other across the span of feet. He saw that the Inspector was disturbed. There was a heavy silence before Jonquil spoke:

"Max, you are my friend."

"And you are mine."

"You've been like a son to me." The anguish in his voice startled Krull. He's worried, he thought. I'm putting a load on his shoulders, asking him to share my job. He felt guilty.

"I didn't mean to burden you, Martin, but I need help. You're the only one I can trust."

"Don't say that," Jonquil replied sorrowfully.

"Why not?" Krull asked. "It's true." He looked at the Inspector's face. Even in the dim light he could see it was a mask of sorrow. A gaunt hand came out from under the cape holding a snub-nosed automatic.

"Because I have to kill you."

CHAPTER FOURTEEN

KRULL stepped back, startled, and fought to relax, conscious that his life span had become measured in moments. He kept his eyes riveted on the Inspector's face.

"Why?" he asked simply.

"I love you," Jonquil said. "You've been like a son to me—the son I never had. But this is bigger than us. I've been asking myself if I could really do this—kill you. Now I know I can—must. But it'll be like killing myself, Max. Worse, for you have been dearer to me than life.

"Then, why?" Krull asked, conscious of a deep inner sorrow, not for himself but for the man standing in front of him, a man going through hell. Jonquil didn't answer. Krull turned and took a few slow steps toward the cliff, speaking as he did.

"You are my friend, Jonquil, more than a friend. We have lived and played and dreamed together—swum these waters…"

"Stop," Jonquil rasped harshly.

"I don't know what terrible thing drives you," Krull continued, trying to keep his voice free of the touch of panic he felt, "but I do know it can't be bad enough to demand such a price."

"Stop—don't move another step," the Inspector warned. Krull hesitated, deliberately took the last step which separated him from the edge of the cliff, momentarily expecting a burst of slugs to rip his body. He turned slowly. Jonquil's eyes in the night were brooding pools, dark and deep, and his skin was pallid in the starlight. Krull flexed his body slightly and dug his toes under the sand without moving his eyes. For a long moment they regarded each other. He saw the muzzle of Jonquil's gun move slowly upward and said:

"You are one of the conspirators."

Jonquil stopped the weapon in midair, hesitating as if to voice a denial.

Krull did something he had never done before—did it feeling as if he had violated a sacred trust. He peeped his friend; he closed his mind to everything except the Inspector's face and concentrated on his mind. In the first seconds it was like looking into a whirlpool, a maelstrom of flurried thoughts, resolution and decision surcharged with pain. The jumbled thoughts focused and became imagery; but it was the imagery of a bizarre montage in which he simultaneously glimpsed a series of pictures, one merging into another. There were faces, an odd-fantastic structure that appeared like a rocket, a grotto bustling with men and machines, filled with a blue dancing light resembling the harsh brittle glare of an arc welding torch—a hand holding a spitting automatic. The imagery suddenly vanished, replaced by a formless gray mosaic, an unbroken pattern of nothingness. He came back to reality with a start.

"You are one of the conspirators," he repeated.

"I am...if you call us that," Jonquil replied woodenly. A touch of pity came into his eyes. "You wouldn't understand, Max."

"What wouldn't I understand?" he asked curiously.

"Why I have to kill you." Jonquil's voice was toneless. "This conspiracy, as you call it, is the work of decades, Max. Untold men have sown seeds that their brothers might reach the stars; the harvest is here and no single man can stand in the way..."

"Harvest of death," Krull broke in bitterly. "You've sold yourself a bill of goods and turned against the law, the First Law of Mankind. Turn back, Martin. Turn back now and no one need ever know," he pleaded.

"No," Jonquil said harshly. His body stiffened.

"Jonquil—wait..." He suddenly knew only split seconds of life remained.

Jonquil's hand was moving up.

KRULL brought his foot up through the sand, kicking it into the agent's face; at the same instant he spun around and leaped from the cliff, hearing the staccato bark of the automatic behind him. He straightened his body in midair and struck the water at a steep angle...swam along the bottom with powerful breast strokes. Have to get out of range, he thought desperately. Jonquil would be waiting for him to come up. He finally broke water long enough to catch a breath and throw a fast backward look. Jonquil's body was silhouetted against the sky. When he came up again, the Inspector was gone.

He debated, then swam toward the beach. Jonquil or no Jonquil, he would smash the conspiracy. There was a conspiracy and it was in the grotto; he knew that from the Inspector's mind. Anna had been right on that score. He smiled grimly. From here on out it was going to be rough.

He clambered up on to the beach and stood for a moment breathing heavily, looking upward into the night. The star's glittered in savage splendor, magically mirrored again in the black water at his feet. Strange, he had never particularly thought of the stars before. He had read some, of course—remembered a description of space that had likened it to a vast box without sides or top or bottom. To the mind of man space is infinite. Logic and reason proclaim the fact; yet the word vast itself implied a finite quality that puzzled him. He knew about the solar system, galaxies, inter-galactic space; but it struck him forcibly that man—here and now—could envision it in terms of conquest.

What power moved men like Jonquil that they were willing to forsake the laws of their kind? His eyes fastened on a brilliant red star and he watched it, fascinated. There was a hypnotic quality about the baleful eye and he reluctantly looked away. Was that it? Did men look at the stars and lose their reason? He wondered. He had always considered the sky an artistic creation; but it was more, far more, to Bok...Jonquil—how many others? It wasn't the beauty of the Universe that caught them. They didn't see it as artistic, not as an awesome and God-formed cosmos, but as something to be conquered. Power—it was the symbol of power. Men looked skyward and became power-mad. Even Jonquil. He returned his thoughts to his predicament.

TRAITORS, conspirators, the Manager's killers—he was besieged on every side. But he knew the secret, knew it beyond the shadow of a doubt. Incredible as it seemed, the conspiracy was centered under black forbidding Chimney Rock. Okay, he'd dig it out, single-handed if need be. Do that and no man could touch him. Not even Shevach if he became Prime Thinker. But he needed help.

Who could he trust?

The agents of police were out. Wait—Grimhorn, he was the man. The Chief of World Agents was a man of integrity. But at the moment he couldn't wait. Jonquil couldn't afford disclosure. Even now he'd be organizing a net to snare him. Kill him. Alba. The innkeeper was a good friend. Alba would hide him, handle the message to Grimhorn.

He abruptly turned and plunged into the shadows of the trees, cutting across the atoll. If Jonquil were right, Shevach knew the secret of the Rock, was rushing to break the conspiracy and grab the glory. Damn, he thought frantically, there wouldn't be time to wait for Grimhorn. He cursed without slowing his pace.

He broke out on the opposite shore and halted, momentarily puzzled. The seaplane ramp was flooded with light, light and movement and sound. He heard the creak of winches and voices borne on the night breeze, caught sight of a moored seaplane carrier. He moved closer, keeping in the shadow of the foliage until he reached the edge of the circle of light.

Shevach! There was no mistaking the Manager's slim figure; the burly Gullfin and cadaverous Merryweather loomed beside him. He cursed savagely at sight of the Searchmaster, stopping as he spotted Jonquil and Anna. They were cagey, he thought. The conspiracy was collapsing like a house of cards and they were joining the winners. Merryweather began pivoting his head with his chin tilted up as if he were sniffing the wind, Krull stepped back in alarm. The man was a bloodhound. Inhuman.

The creak of a winch caught his attention. Torps! They were moving torps from the seaplane carrier. Police torps with weapon compartments in the hull. The conspirators wouldn't have a chance. That explained Anna's presence. She was their guide.

A traitor!

HE wheeled around and raced back along the beach. Damn Shevach! Damn the traitor Jonquil! They couldn't rob him now. He'd beat 'em, beat 'em. The words became a refrain in his mind and he forced his body to greater effort. At the end of the atoll he splashed across the partially submerged bar to Te-Tai and forced his tired legs to a dead run. He was gasping, his lungs burned and sweat stung his eyes. He saw lights on the headland and began shouting while still a hundred yards away.

"Cominger! Cominger!" The name came with a wheeze from his tortured lungs. He had almost reached the porch when a door swung open, framing the hermit's lean figure in a shaft of light. Krull pulled to a stop, breathing harshly, trying to get his voice.

Cominger looked worriedly at him. "What is it?"

"Your torp," he gasped. Cominger took a backward step and eyed him owlishly.

"What about it?"

"I need it."

"Why'!" The hermit seemed to compose himself with effort.

"Chimney Rock—I've got to get to the rock…"

Cominger's body stiffened. "No."

"I'm ordering you as an agent of police."

"No," Cominger repeated.

"Give it to me or I'll take it."

"Why?" the hermit parried, his voice suddenly curious. "What's the emergency?"

"Damn you, Cominger, there's trouble at the rock. The police—Ivan Shevach—are unloading torps at the ramp. They're heading there but it's my baby. I cracked it and I'm going to get there first."

"Shevach!" The name dropped from the hermit's lips in disbelief. Suddenly he drew himself up. "Listen, you don't know the area. You'd wreck the torp, kill yourself. But I know it. I'll take you."

"Then let's get going."

"Follow me." Cominger raced to the far end of the porch with Krull at his heels.

"Grab some gear." He dived into a pile of underwater equipment and Krull sprang to help him. They quickly stripped to their shorts and strapped on compressed air tanks and breathing masks.

"One second." Cominger dashed into the house and returned with a small rubber sack that he hooked to his gear. Gun, Krull thought, he's afraid of me. He made a mental note of it. At least he knew where a gun was when the time came.

The torp was a long cylindrical affair just now above the tide line. The hermit rolled the vehicle into the water and tugged it into position. Suddenly he straightened and raised a hand for silence.

"Listen!"

Krull tilted his head, straining to hear. The sound of a muted roar over-riding the night breeze came to his ears; it grew louder, the noise of spitting motors, and he realized he was listening to the voices of torps boring along the surface of the lagoon. He swung in the direction of the sound in a futile effort to see, then whirled toward the hermit.

"Hurry."

"They're nearer to the reef than we are." They hurriedly positioned and checked their masks and Cominger said: "We'll ride the surface to the reef, then we'll have to go under. It'll be slower but you couldn't hang on in the waves."

KRULL nodded, anxious to get started. He had hoped they could ride the surface all the way out but the hermit was right; the waves would rip him loose. Cominger positioned the torp and kicked the starter. The engine barked to life and spat angrily for a moment before settling into a steady roar. He laid his body lengthwise on the sleek hull, grasped the steering bar and hooked his feet through the end stirrups, then motioned Krull to hang on. The agent checked his face mask, slanted his body down and hooked his arms and legs around the hermit's, hoping the swirl of water wouldn't tear him loose.

Cominger gave a hand signal, cut in the drive lever and the torp moved sluggishly into the lagoon and began picking up speed. Water sloshed against Krull's body and the stars became blurry lights swimming across his faceplate. He tried to catch a sign of Shevach's torps but they were lost, the sounds of their motors masked by the roar of the powerful engine under him. They cut across the lagoon at an angle toward the break in the reef, picking up speed in the smooth water despite the double load.

Shevach would beat him.

No, he couldn't! But he would. Okay, he'd take it from there. Just let him get to the rock.

They passed Paha Jon's yellow-sailed outrigger and the torp began pitching in the swells rolling in through the narrow mouth of the reef. Krull clung to the hermit desperately. Water smashed against his faceplate and his body yawed from side to side. The break in the reef rushed toward them, then fell off on either side as they breached the open sea. A wall of water smashed against him and the blurry stars vanished; Cominger had dived the torp beneath the surface.

They rushed through the black night of the subsea with water tearing at their bodies. Krull's arm and leg muscles ached from his right hold and he shivered in the colder ocean water. A leg muscle began to cramp. He flexed it but the muscle gripped spasmodically, becoming a hot pain. The noise of the engine and the swirling waters drummed against his ears with a tickling sensation. He strained to see ahead, fearful his companion would smash into a submerged rock. But—no!—Cominger was too certain; he drove the torp through the ebony depths at full speed with the certainty of a pilot bringing a ship to safe anchorage. He neither slowed nor deviated; clearly he knew every inch of the sea as well by night as by day.

Knew every inch?

It struck him then that Cominger hadn't bothered to ask questions. He had merely said:

I'll take you.

SURE, he knew the entrance to the grotto! He knew exactly where he was going…could pick the door of the grotto out of the maw of the sea with a certainty born of experience. Yes, he knew where he was going!

And why!

Suddenly Krull knew.

Trapped!

The hermit was delivering him into the hands of the outlaws. Cominger, the hermit—the man with the torp. Only it was Cominger, the contact man for the conspirators. He clung to his back and debated. He could kick free and swim to the reef but he'd be no better off than before; Shevach would still grab the glory and he'd be branded a public enemy. No, let Cominger deliver him; he'd pull the net closed and snare him with the rest of them. Just now he hadn't the slightest idea how he'd go about it but, once in the grotto, he'd figure a way, he savagely promised himself.

The torp slanted downward and the pressure on his ears increased. A beam shot out from the torp, licked across the looming faces of ocean-bottom rocks and waving fronds and blacked out again. The hermit moved the speed lever and the torp slowed, began swinging in a wide half-circle, dropping lower in the velvet water. He periodically flicked the beam on and off, steering through a stone jungle. Krull felt the torp losing speed, swinging; the beam came on again and it seemed as if they must surely ram the base of an undersea cliff. At the last instant the hermit dived it toward the base of the rock bastions; they shot into a narrow tunnel whose walls glowed iridescent under the glow of the beam. The tunnel slanted upward; the hermit gave the torp a burst of power, climbed, leveled off and cut the engine.

Krull felt his body emerge from the water. The torp jarred against sand and he struggled to his feet, staring into the muzzle of a submachine gun. Gordon Gullfin's flat face leered at him from the other end.

"Well, look who's here, just in time for the party."

KRULL froze at the tableau that met his eyes. He was standing knee-deep in water in a black chamber illuminated by a bluish light emanating from some unseen source. The floor was a smooth rocky shelf which retreated and became lost in shadow. The stone walls, floor and ceiling formed a fantastic stage peopled by immobile manikins, garish in the blue light.

Yargo! The identity of the actors struck him with full force. Ben Yargo, Jan, and the short slim Foxhill were huddled in a group off to one side, with a woman whose face was familiar despite her swim attire. Eve Mallon! He was startled until he remembered the rumor she was Yargo's mistress. Now they stood, dripping in swim gear, frozen into momentary immobility.

Ivan Shevach, flanked by two swarthy men armed to the hilt stood a few yards beyond Gullfin's shoulder; behind them towered the lean skeleton of Merryweather, the Searchmaster.

A few yards beyond Martin Jonquil stood alone.

Off to one side, Anna Malroon—thin and wet and shaking with cold—watched him with tragic eyes. He captured the scene in a flash. Gullfin's voice boomed again.

The tableau was magically broken.

"Over there," he waved the gun menacingly, "both of you—over by Yargo."

Krull stood his ground. "I'm an agent of police. I'm here to enforce the law."

"I'm the law," Gullfin snarled. "Get moving—both of you."

"Max Krull is not one of us," a voice said. Krull looked up. The speaker was Yargo. So, the Prime Thinker was one of the conspirators; and Jan, Foxhill, and Eve Mallon of the Council of Six. He wasn't surprised.

"He dies anyway," Shevach cut in icily. He smiled balefully at Krull. "You won't get out of this one so easily...esper!"

"Sentence without due process of law? I'm shocked," Yargo mocked. Shevach regarded him scornfully.

"You talk about law—you, who rigged the election with that phony Alexander test?" Yargo didn't flinch. He stared at the Manager for a long minute before answering:

"True, but I didn't do it for my own self-gain."

"No?" It was Shevach's turn to mock.

"No, I did it for this." His hand swept toward the rear of the grotto. I had to ensure the work would be finished. Fortunately, it has been."

If Krull were startled, he hid it. Shevach merely arched his brow.

"Finished?"

"You might kill us, here, but you can't stop what's beyond this grotto, Shevach."

"I didn't intend to stop your work, Yargo." The Manager smiled thinly. "I merely intend to take it over, and will, thanks to the young lady who tipped us in Sydney, then met us at Abiang and led us here." He nodded toward Anna. Krull was startled but didn't bother to deny the charge; the girl's face gave him the truth. She, like Jonquil, had played both ends. Why?

"She betrayed you, too," Shevach added, looking vindictively at Yargo, "including the fact that your mistress had fled here with you."

YARGO returned his look calmly, without answering. Jan's face was white, frightened, but Eve Mallon stood straight, a whimsical smile on her lips.

"She must have been a member of the conspiracy to have known so much," Shevach resumed, "therefore she dies."

"No," Krull exploded loudly.

"Ah, the lover," Shevach sneered disdainfully.

"You're wrong, Shevach." The soft voice of Martin Jonquil was a velvet note tinged with death. "You've miscalculated." Krull stared at him in surprise. A moment before the Inspector apparently had been unarmed; now he held a wicked looking automatic with its black muzzle centered on the Manager's breast.

"I came to save the conspiracy."

The Manager's face turned white with fear and he nervously bit his thin lip and tried to form words. None came. The silence was heavy.

Krull heard the bullets thud into the Inspector's body; he staggered, dropped to one knee, slipped backward to the floor, his dead eyes staring terribly toward the blue-black ceiling.

Peter Merryweather grinned amiably, bringing the concealed gun into view. A wisp of smoke curled upward from the barrel.

"Read it in his mind," he said pleasantly. He smiled at the dead agent's body. "Fool."

"No matter, he would have died anyway." Shevach's voice rose to a hard rasp. "I almost wish you could live, Yargo. You'd see how a real ruler operates."

"You didn't intend to smash the conspiracy. You merely intended to use the power for your own means," Yargo accused quietly.

"Certainly," Shevach snapped, "do you take me for a fool? I agree with you, we need atomic power, Yargo, and now—thanks to your blundering conspiracy—I have it. But not for the stars. That's for fools and dreamers…"

"You would enslave the earth?" Krull cut in.

"I'll rule the earth, if that's what you mean." His eyes gleamed triumphantly. "I'll rule it for my lifetime, an emperor…pass it to my heirs. I'll make the miserable LIQ's and MIQ's…" He cut off whatever he was going to say and stepped back, breathing heavily. His lips compressed tightly and he snarled, "Kill these scum!"

"MAX!"—Anna's scream rang terribly in the grotto, reverberating from wall to wall—"remember what I told you."

Gullfin snapped the submachine gun up, grinning viciously and his finger came back on the trigger.

"Hold it!" Shevach snapped. Gullfin stopped, bewildered, glancing from Krull to his chief. Shevach disregarded him and turned to the shaking girl. "Maybe it's something I should know. What did you tell Krull that's so important?"

Anna didn't reply. She looked at Krull. Her wan face was filled with anguish, and her eyes were enormous limpid pools.

He peeped her.

A thought screamed in her mind.

Screamed, jolted him, numbed him with its force.

"What did you tell Krull?" The Manager's words jerked him back to reality.

Anna pulled herself together with difficulty, staring at the Manager with large tragic eyes. When she spoke, her voice was so soft Krull could scarcely hear her.

"You're right," she said, "I am one of the conspirators." She half-turned and smiled apologetically at Yargo, then turned back to the Manager. "Only they didn't know."

"Didn't know?" Shevach sneered.

"No, I was working for a man who wasn't a conspirator, but was guiding it. I was his messenger."

"Who?" Shevach snarled.

She looked at him, silently. Shevach lifted his face, arrogantly. "Keep the name," he rasped. "It doesn't make any difference. Die with it." He started to motion to Gullfin.

"But it does," Anna said softly.

"Oh...?" Shevach observed sardonically.

"I didn't betray the conspiracy by bringing you here. I did it because it was part of my job—to make sure no one remained alive who might stop us..."

"Explain that," Shevach rasped, visibly disturbed at her words.

"I was ordered to bring you here for your own execution, even though I would die first."

"Whoever gave that order was a fool." Shevach's voice dropped to a hiss: "Who was it?"

"Got it." Merryweather's voice cut through the grotto like a sliver of ice. His bony face was searching the girl's—he stepped back, white and shaken.

"Bok," he whispered. "Herman Bok..."

ANNA pulled herself erect and looked defiantly at him. "Mr. Bok," she said calmly, "and he was no fool."

"Herman Bok..." Shevach spoke the name wonderingly, then snapped it out like an epithet: "Herman Bok! Doddering esper!" He spun toward Gullfin.

"Kill them."

"Max..." Anna shrieked.

Gullfin's gun came up...swung toward him. Krull looked desperately at him, trying to control and shape his mind to do what he had never done.

What Anna said he could do!

Pk, pk, pk—a pk could control matter. That was why Bok had guided him to the cavern; he was a latent pk. The submachine gun centered on him; Gullfin's face was a grinning evil mask and his body was tensed for the recoil of the weapon.

Shevach...Shevach...Kill Shevach and his men.

The thought streamed from Krull's mind; he tried to focus it, point it at the evil visage behind the weapon. A gun crashed and his concentration was broken. Gullfin turned, startled, for a moment lowering the weapon.

Anna was swaying, blood welling from her breast. The Searchmaster stood frozen...smoke curled from his gun...his eyes were frightened.

Krull pushed Anna from his mind and forced himself to concentrate.

Kill Shevach...Kill Shevach...

Gullfin swung back, bringing the submachine gun to bear.

Kill Shevach...kill Shevach...

The gun barrel wavered and he concentrated on the thought, oblivious to everything except Gullfin's hideous face which, now seemed to fill the cavern.

Kill Shevach...Kill Shevach...

The face grew larger in his eyes until nothing seemed to remain but a single gigantic baleful eye; he sped into the eye, along the optic nerve and stared at the greasy gray coils and crevices of Gullfin's brain.

Kill Shevach, he screamed at the brain, *kill, kill, kill...*

ABRUPTLY Gordon Gullfin stiffened. He spun around. Shevach screamed incoherently, a high falsetto scream like a wounded cat. Merryweather's gun came up. Bullets thudded into Gullfin's body. The burly agent staggered backward, yanked back on the trigger and staccato blasts ripped the cavern. Acrid fumes stung Krull's eyes bringing him back to reality. Shevach was screaming horribly, bending forward with pieces of flesh jumping from the side of his head; he collapsed, gurgling, atop the bodies of the two agents flanking him. Merryweather stood straight and tall, swaying, his eyes rolling wildly; blood gushed from his middle and he slowly bent forward, toppling down across the bodies of Shevach and his men.

The chattering of the gun abruptly stopped. Gullfin stepped back with a bewildered look; his eyes went to Shevach, to Krull, back to Shevach again. The machine gun slipped from his fingers and clattered to the floor. He moved a hand up and rubbed his chest, looked blankly at the blood on his fingers. Krull hesitated, and sprang to Anna's side. He bent down and lifted her head.

"Max...behind, look out!"

He twisted his head in alarm. Gullfin, breathing heavily had yanked an automatic from his belt and was aiming it pointblank at him. He felt death coming and tried to twist aside. Another roar shattered the grotto and Gullfin stumbled, holding the weapon numbly. He tottered, swayed, a glazed expression clouded his eyes and he fell, slowly, across the body of Peter Merryweather. August Cominger stared at the weapon in his hands, let it clatter to the floor.

"I never killed a man before," he said quietly.

Krull stared thankfully at him, and turned back to Anna. Blood was welling from her breast and her eyes were closed— he knew she had already fled the dark cavern. He held her head in his lap and looked up, filled with sorrow, remembering the sadness in her eyes. She had known, had known...

He looked at the body of Jonquil, who had hated espers and, unknowingly, had served one faithfully. Martin had been faithful to the conspiracy. Faith...faith in man's future.

"The story is written," Ben Yargo said gently. "The story of man on earth lies behind—ahead is the story of the stars. If we conspired, Krull, it was for the future." He came forward and rested his hand on his shoulder. "We hope that you will join us."

Krull looked somberly at him; he turned toward Jan. Her lips were parted, expectantly, waiting his answer. There was nothing left on earth for him—not anymore.

"I will," he said steadily. He laid Anna gently on the floor of the grotto and rose, looking down at Martin Jonquil's body. Martin, you were right, he thought.

"Look," Ben Yargo said. He took his arm and walked with him into the deep shadows of the grotto. They came to the end and a door opened; beyond he saw a vast cavern flooded with brilliant blue light, heard the whisper of machines, saw the distant figures of men and women working around the base of a tremendous rocket that reached almost to the ceiling of the cavern. It was thick of girth, monstrous, nestled in a crosspatch of framework set on tracks.

But they can't get it out.

"We can get it out," Jan whispered, reading his mind. She had come up behind him and slipped her hand in his. "Don't you see, dad had to remain in office long enough to protect the ship. That's what he didn't know: how or when it could be gotten out. All he knew was that it would happen someday."

"How...?"

"You found out tonight—in Anna's mind..."

"I don't understand…"

"Psychokinesis."

HE stepped back, awe-struck. Suddenly he felt very humble. This great ship…the labor of decades…the dreams of men had awaited his coming. He, alone of men, had the fantastic power to move the mountain shielding the rocket from the stars. A lonely feeling swept over him. In that moment he knew how the leader of espers had felt. He looked into the cavern, then he saw them.

Children.

He looked questioningly at Jan.

"The children of tomorrow. Children, with great talents. We have to save them from the searchers. They will be the new beginning, Max— they and the children of the pioneers."

He felt a sense of wonder. Thank God there had been dreamers— and men of action. He lifted his eyes. Across the nose of the rocket he saw its name.

* * *

The first spaceship, the *Herman Bok*, lifted from Earth early in January, 2450 A.D., following inauguration of Mustapha Sherif as 91st Prime Thinker of the Empire of Earth…

Blak Roko's
Post-Atomic Earthman
Venusian Press, 2672 A.D.

THE END